I0824553

Good News

Good News

A novel

Alexa Yasemin Brahme

ALGONQUIN BOOKS OF CHAPEL HILL
LITTLE, BROWN AND COMPANY

Algonquin Books of Chapel Hill / Little, Brown and Company
Hachette Book Group
1290 Avenue of the Americas, New York, NY 10104
algonquinbooks.com

First Edition: May 2026

Algonquin Books of Chapel Hill is an imprint of Little, Brown and Company, a division of Hachette Book Group, Inc. The Algonquin Books name and logo are trademarks of Hachette Book Group, Inc.

ISBN 9781643757421

LCCN 2025948401

Printing 1, 2026

LSC-C

Printed in the United States of America

For my canım—my mother, Sevil
Also for her sister, Ayda, and their mother, Sevda

My memory of men is never lit up and illuminated like my memory of women.

—MARGUERITE DURAS

Good News

I

IT WAS STRANGE to see John in the studio, completely at a loss as to how to move his body, unsure of how to orient himself toward art. Maggie guided him to the back of the room, the only place where they could stand and properly see her entire painting at once. They stood side by side with their backs skimming the wall, staring forward in silence. Seven women huddled in the center of the canvas, barely clinging to life. Maggie waited for John to say something.

"It's big," he said finally.

They continued staring at the unfinished painting, which Maggie had not wanted to show John in the first place. He was supposed to wait for her downstairs, like every other time he'd ever swung by the studio. But it was cold tonight, and before Maggie could come down John was already coming up.

"It's very big," John said again, this time nodding.

Maggie tried to weather his response without crumbling. She knew he didn't mean anything by it, that he was just trying to be "right," or at least avoid being "wrong." And he was right. The painting was enormous. It nearly took up the entire west wall of the studio and dwarfed everyone who stood before it. Stretching the canvas had been Olympic, but Maggie had managed to do it with five other students. It was amazing how no one had complained. How they'd all been happy to complete this task together. There must have been some neural reward for teamwork that Maggie didn't know the name of, but they'd all felt the same bright rush of it when the last staple went in.

Maggie glanced back at John, who was craning his neck up and down, side to side, to show her that he'd been intently studying her piece. She decided not to hold his silence against him. She figured only women would like the painting, that only women would know what it meant to be both dead and alive.

MAGGIE HURRIED THEM out of the studio before John could say anything more about the painting or its size. There was a certain relief in his blunt, unobservant nature, since it meant that he likely wouldn't mention the painting to their mother. Maggie could only imagine that phone call. How the painting would inevitably introduce a new torrent of worry that Maggie was on the brink of disaster or, worse, that these half-dead women meant she was suicidal. Luckily, it seemed like John had hardly registered the contents of the painting. Oblivious to the idea that Maggie's work could offer any insight into her inner state.

Once they were outside, John slipped easily into a conversation about his coworkers. He talked about a new intern, who was so consistently tragic in his performance that people had begun placing bets on how long he'd last in the rotation. John thought he'd last another week, but, given a recent win with a tricky IV insertion, he was now kicking himself for putting one hundred dollars behind the idea. Two to three weeks now seemed more than likely, and John felt betrayed by the intern's improvements.

This incompetent person would probably become a doctor, Maggie realized with mild horror. Just like her stupid brother, who was placing bets on potentially life-threatening ineptitude.

"What?" John said, like he was accusing her of something.

"Nothing," Maggie said.

"Just say it," John said. "It was a stupid bet. It's not like I don't already know that."

"That's not what I was thinking," Maggie said. "But, yes, it *is* stupid."

"What is it, then?"

The wind whipped Maggie's hair into her face, and she pulled at the strands that clung to her mouth.

"Do you think Mom and Dad are secretly still waiting for me to become a doctor?"

"I don't think it's a secret."

Maggie swung a limp fist at John.

"Do you think Sofia is going to be a doctor?"

"Yeah." John shrugged. "Just a PhD, though."

Whatever groan she had been on the brink of emitting involuntarily turned to laughter. What failures, her brother and sister. Doctor and doctor.

"You know they don't really care, right?" John looked over at Maggie, his voice normal but his eyes intense. "They just want you to be okay."

Maggie could tell from the concern calcified across John's face that he really believed this. As if he had never seen their mother thrash around the house in fury and disappointment that Maggie was "throwing her life away."

John had been there for the main fight. The one when they'd all come home in December and Maggie had announced she was getting an MFA in studio art. The one where Sofia hid in her room and their mother broke dishes and their father threw his hands up and drove away—to where, he never revealed. Even John had retreated somewhere. None of them able to witness what Maggie and her mother were capable of.

It had been nearly three years since, and while they had technically recovered from the moaning and screaming ("You said *graduate* school!"), the bottom line of every phone call thereafter was: What are you *really* going to do? And John had been spared this part, their mother's fear that Maggie's life wouldn't turn out. But it was palpable in every conversation. Even if it went unmentioned, which it didn't, Maggie was constantly contending with the feeling that it was all going to hell.

"Right," Maggie said, dumbfounded by how her brother could be so dense.

THEY WERE LATE to John's girlfriend's art show, though apparently his girlfriend didn't believe in time and claimed she didn't know what *late* really meant. According to her, everything was unfolding in its "divine timing." John's girlfriend was tedious and infuriating, in ways both like and unlike John, but Maggie had yet to find the parts that were supposed to be endearing. She tried her best to be nice, however, because John thought his girlfriend was "something else."

And she *was* something else. She had renounced her name seven years ago and allowed people only to refer to her as the Artist. The woman didn't have a name, she didn't believe in time, and for someone with impeccable style and a penchant for high fashion, she didn't believe in clothes. Maggie didn't know clothes were something you could believe in. She wondered how John had ever successfully explained any of this to their parents.

Of course, in addition to being perfect by becoming a doctor, John had selected, despite her eccentricities, the perfect mate in their parents' eyes. John's girlfriend was independently wealthy—her father had essentially invented oil, as Maggie understood it—she was American, and she was kind to John and Maggie's parents, always bringing them gifts and writing them handwritten cards.

Beyond that criteria, Maggie's parents didn't care that John's girlfriend's job was insane and ridiculous. She was allowed to be an artist because she was an American with money to burn.

Maggie's one success, according to her parents was that she, too, had selected an excellent mate: Rob was rich (just regular rich, not oil rich), American, and dependable. He had a strong body, which would pull the plow, so to speak, though he mostly sat at a desk and typed. And if Maggie had any sense, she would marry him already.

John didn't have to get married yet, even though he was older. He *should* get married now, if the metric was time having been together, but he didn't have to. He had no biological clock and could pick someone else if he wanted. He was also a doctor. Had that been mentioned? John was doing everything right.

John jerked Maggie back by the elbow and stopped her from stepping into the street. He pointed to the red crosswalk symbol.

"You don't have to be a doctor," he said, "but you can't step into oncoming traffic."

Maggie gave a limp smile, the best she could muster, and they waited for the light to turn.

"What is the show about again?"

"The spectacle of pregnancy." John spoke as if he were reciting something.

"Like women only get pregnant to be a spectacle?"

"No, like once you're seen as pregnant, it can't be unseen, and you *become* a spectacle."

Maggie could get behind this idea. She thought of her own, never-had-been-pregnant-body, and how it had been primed as a spectacle already.

"But I don't really know, I guess," John said, quick to amend himself. "You'd have to ask the Artist."

"Ah, yes," Maggie said. "The Artist."

IT WAS OBVIOUS where the show was, because of the crowd foaming at the entrance. Maggie and John joined the unusually eager attendees and stood at the end of a long, snaking line that brought them to the edge of Tenth Avenue. A woman in front of them was on the phone bemoaning her inability to get reservations for bar seats at a chic restaurant nearby. "Bar seats!" she kept exclaiming. What was next? Reservations to use the *bathroom*? She flipped her hair and tapped her toe in outrage.

It wasn't long before the line charged forward, and they were all allowed into the gallery. The woman in front of them hung up the phone and rushed past the small plaque near the entrance, but Maggie insisted to John that they stop to read.

John wasn't entirely wrong in his summation of the show. The plaque explained that the exhibit was about the spectacle of pregnancy, and how when people know you're pregnant they look at you differently. They look at you as a belly to place a hand upon, as a vulnerable little thing who needs to put her feet up, but also as a mother. One who takes care of things. How you lose all defining features and become life itself. The description went even further, saying that pregnancy is also perverse and grotesque. Egocentric. A power trip. What began as an eloquent paragraph dissolved into a rant, but Maggie thought it had good bones. She wondered if the Artist was also a writer. She could be so many things, it seemed, because she didn't have a name.

The show felt alive, inhaling and exhaling guests in a natural rhythm. Maggie and John were swept in with the next inhale, and they waded into the spacious white room as the Artist was sliding a long slice of papaya into her vagina. Being pregnant was Maggie's worst nightmare, and the Artist's piece did nothing to alleviate her apprehension.

"She's really doing it," Maggie said to the room, both concerned and impressed. *Those seeds!* she thought.

The Artist was mimicking the the-size-of-your-baby-is-the-size-of-this-fruit comparison, which seemed to have been popular for all of time. Expecting mothers loved to cradle their barely protruding stomachs and coo, "The baby's the size of a peach." How darling. Well, now an artist was shoving each type of fruit into her vagina to prove a point. The baby is the size of a slice of papaya.

The Artist had to take some liberties with each fruit. The first trimester, which John and Maggie had missed entirely, mostly consisted of small fruits—a blueberry, a raspberry, a plum. Plopped in and pulled right out. But how was she supposed to fit a grapefruit or a papaya without causing any serious damage? In slices. Maggie was glad to have missed the grapefruit slices. Just imagining the flesh of any citrus coming in contact with her genitals made her body tingle and turned her mouth sour.

"Well..." John said, staring straight ahead and not looking at Maggie.

"Yeah..."

Maggie was relieved for the Artist's sake that a baby is never the size of a jalapeño.

"Did you know—?"

"Nope." John began drifting toward the exhibit.

"Will you grab us some wine?" he asked. "I'm going to go to the other side."

Maggie spotted a table with a cheap black tablecloth stretched over it in the corner of the gallery. A single bartender stood behind the waist-high bar, shaking well drinks and pouring one of two wines. Maggie waited in line to order and watched her brother orbit his girlfriend like he was her moon. She was beautiful; Maggie doubted John was the first man to orbit her. Her brown hair was long and had two distinct creases making it wavy. She had parted it in the middle for the show and let it hang down her bare back. Maggie thought she looked like Eve must have looked in the Garden of Eden. The Artist had a crisp, natural look about her. Like she had just stepped out of a painting and was encountering the physical world for the first time. Maggie felt the urge to reach out and touch her. She got the sense that if she did, she'd leave an ashy handprint on the Artist's otherwise perfect body.

John looked more at ease in the gallery than he had at Maggie's studio. Here, his muscles didn't tense, his weight swayed naturally, as if he somehow understood this work on a base, animal level. Was it because he already knew how to orient his body around hers? Was this the result of the connection they'd built as partners, or was it the medicinal nature of the evening? His girlfriend in stirrups, her assistant slicing the fruit with a scalpel instead of a chef's knife.

"Something to drink, miss?"

Maggie looked into the expectant eyes of the bartender. *Isn't this bizarre?* she wanted to say. *That's my brother's girlfriend. I never thought I'd see her birth a fruit before I saw her birthing their babies.*

She didn't even think she'd see the Artist birth babies, Maggie realized, shocking herself a little. She figured if there ever were babies, she'd be waiting for them in the waiting room.

The bartender blinked.

"Two white wines, please," she said.

He gave a terse nod and began pouring the wine. When he'd released the glasses into her hands, he pointed to his right with two fingers, like a flight attendant.

"Complimentary fruit salad over there," he said, and moved on to the next person in line.

Maggie looked over to where he'd gestured, and, sure enough, there was a bowl of fruit glistening with sugar syrup. Some of the syrup, stained red, had collected on the crystal-looking forceps beside the bowl.

"Clever," Maggie said, letting herself be impressed.

With the wine cool and heavy in her hands, Maggie searched for her brother. He had migrated to the Artist's feet. The block she sat on brought her to about chest level of the average viewer, putting John in the perfect position to watch the crowning of the next fruit. Maggie looked to the left of the platform where the Artist's assistant sat at a small table, each remaining fruit sweating on a silver supply tray before her. Wearing blue latex gloves, she pared each slice down to a manageable size before handing it to the Artist. Up next was pineapple, its spikes thoughtfully sheared smooth and cut into spears. How this was considered a legitimate way to spend an evening was becoming more and more preposterous to Maggie.

All around her, open-mouthed viewers turned to face the Artist. Everyone had their eyes fixed on her body, watching as she braced herself and held her breath. Maggie saw couples pointing, whispering hushed opinions to each other. John had drifted north and was staring at the "piece." Maggie noticed that he managed to avoid the Artist's face, his eyes steady on her body. Next to John, a redheaded woman was eating grapes two at a time. Maggie had officially seen the whole world.

She moseyed over to John, who was transfixed as the Artist slid a butternut squash—halved longways, twice—into her vagina.

Maggie nudged him. "Your girlfriend is funny."

"I don't think her art is supposed to be funny, but I'm glad you're enjoying yourself, I guess."

"No, I mean it," she said, pointing at the fruit salad.

John shook his head, his eyes still on the Artist.

"Whatever."

Maggie didn't bother explaining herself. She watched on as the assistant prepped the next fruit, and the next one, and the next one, until Maggie was sure they were going to have to take the Artist to the hospital. Maggie felt removed from her, though she hadn't looked away. She shut her eyes tight and blinked to bring the Artist into focus and tried to connect with the piece.

It was then that Maggie noticed the Artist was shaking. Maggie could see how the soles of her feet strained against the stirrups, her pale fists grinding into the platform, knuckles first and elbows quivering. Goose bumps covered the entire surface of her skin.

Maggie looked around at the audience. No one with a knotted brow. No one concerned that this woman was clearly writhing in pain. She saw a man toast his glass to another shorter, squatter man. What could they possibly be celebrating?

The exhibit was winding down, and Maggie thanked God under her breath, because she could hardly bear to watch the Artist's clenched fists redden with each passing fruit. Last and longest endured was the watermelon. Maggie hoped it was cold. She imagined the icy fruit crumbling against her skin and thought it might feel kind of nice. But after forty weeks' worth of fruit, Maggie was sure nothing felt nice and nothing would feel nice for at least a little while.

2

MAGGIE'S CANVAS THREATENED her with how empty it was. At the semester's start, she had plotted the whole thing with her advisor. Twenty women crammed from edge to edge, the painting filled with that particular feminine suffering. The suffering of sacrificing your life for the other. The excavation of the bottomless well within which self is stored. Men seemed to have self all over their bodies. They were almost unwieldy with self. It crusted under their fingernails and swung from their hair. Every eyelash that dropped was self. Women's self, on the other hand, seemed like something they had to scavenge, nearly tearing their bodies apart in the process. Their self was stored deep in that well, drowning in the dark.

As it stood, there were seven selves on the canvas and thirteen selves missing, and Maggie's self noticeably absent from them all. She feared that her personal trials would taint the work. That no one would want to look at her small, pathetic pains. Or, rather, that her pain was ridiculous compared to everything she saw around her. Women had lost their children—in childbirth, war, horrible accidents of fate or God. Women had moved to lands with no money, where they knew no one. Women had been raped, mutilated, unspeakably violated and demeaned.

These women felt both near and far to Maggie. She herself had been spared this kind of tragedy, of course, but there was her grandmother's sister, who had died at the hand of her jealous and paranoid husband. To a less tragic degree, there was Maggie's grandmother, who'd raised her two precious children only for her daughter, Maggie's mother, to flee to a country whose language she did not speak, a place she would never visit. There were all the lives not lived, careers not chased, children had or denied or lost. The calculus of their lives felt so profoundly unfair, and, for whatever reason, Maggie could feel it.

Not as if it were her own. She'd never draw such a comparison. It was just that she *saw* it. She saw all that these women had lost as their lives unfolded. The thought that someone could see them in this painting, and yet only see its size, felt like an act of violence against them all. John hadn't meant this, of course, but somehow that made it worse.

The size was obviously not an accident. The clobbering overwhelm of a piece that was nearly twelve feet wide and eight feet tall could never have been unintentional. Though it was incredibly convenient for Maggie when talking to her parents, who dutifully asked about her work in most of their phone calls. Maggie could linger in her painting's bigness. "It's huge," she would say, and they would let that be enough. Occasionally, her mother would probe further: *How* big? How long had she been working on it? Could Maggie send a picture? "When it's finished," Maggie would say. And she dreaded that day. The day she'd have to reveal herself to her parents.

"What's it called?" her mother, now on the phone, wanted to know.

"I'm still working on that," Maggie said.

"I understand," her mother said gravely. "It's like naming a baby. For Sofia, I didn't know until she was in my arms."

She didn't have to say this. Maggie already knew how it had gone for all of them. John's real name—Can—had come first, and easily, like breath. "Life," it meant in Turkish. "Soul." *Can* was the start of everything.

"It wasn't hard when you named me," Maggie said, her voice almost pleading. She hoped her mother would imbue her with some kind of care and softness.

"No, canım," she said lovingly. "You were easy. When I knew you were a girl, I knew."

Müjde, they'd named her. It meant "good news," and their mother liked to credit this as the sole reason they chose the name. They'd been glowing at how it was such good news to be living in America now. At how it was even better news that they were having a girl. But there was a second, secret, reason, which was that Müjde was also the name of their mother's favorite singer, whose every song was an elaborate missive about longing. Their mother would play her music and sway dramatically from side to side, sometimes singing along, and almost always dissolving into tears.

Little Sofia had come six years after Maggie, their life in the United States already in full bloom. Because of her struggles in school, Müjde had become Maggie. Can had seamlessly transitioned to John, a name that lapped effortlessly between their two cultures. Sofia had been born into a life of ease. No mispronunciation, spelling errors, fetishization, or ostracism. The name Sofia worked everywhere, making her a chameleon, a trait her family could have never known she would grow to resent.

"Okay, canım, you go." Her mother was always shooing Maggie off their calls.

"I love you," they both said, and Maggie was left with her painting. Staring down the barrel of all that was left to render.

Unable to face the task of making more women—there was something perverse about generating so much suffering on a Friday night—Maggie decided to devote herself to her tiles, all seven hundred of them. Seven hundred brown outlines, each one precise and equal, that she'd drawn to cover what was becoming the incredibly intricate ceiling of wherever they were.

The top of her painting featured smooth, beige-ish domes with small concentric tiles looping into their centers. Maggie hoped this suggested that the women were in a common place, like a train station or an indoor market. Though their pain was extraordinary, it felt important to Maggie that the women themselves were not. They were ordinary women you'd find anywhere, in any country. They could be your mother or your sister or your daughter. Therefore, the domes were important, Maggie had told herself when she first began shading them. They rooted the women in the world.

Maggie ascended a ladder to bring herself eye level with her tiles. Her work felt completely unimpressive as she thought of the Renaissance masters craning their necks to paint their frescoed ceilings for days on end. Nothing she would ever make could be so beautiful, so why even bother? She had to rid the thought from her mind before it could take hold and invade her completely. Her tiles—that was all there was room for.

Maggie had measured and drawn the tiles in pencil, so they were each careful and even. She imagined someone flippant looking at them from the ground, dismissing them as negligible. But they could be negligible from down there, Maggie thought, because up here, face-to-face, they were geometrically exact. So perfect that any viewer could gloss over them. Maggie could rescue their minds from having to interpret each tile so they could focus on the more important matter—who they saw beneath them.

As she began the work on her tiles, Maggie fantasized about the panel of professors who would evaluate her painting. She pictured them in suits and glasses, ogling at the level of detail. *The commitment to excellence and symmetry,* they'd whisper. *The persistence of the artist.*

ANY THOUGHT THAT Maggie had prior to holding a paintbrush escaped her entirely. She had become automated in the hours she spent with her tiles, using an impossibly thin brush to complete each line with a single stroke. Her mind emptied of any concern she had previously carried into the studio, and all Maggie could sense was her tongue pressed hard against the roof of her mouth as she focused on curving the pattern just so. Working, she was nothing but a body, free and easy, and estranged from the terror of her mind.

She finished a single dome's worth of tiles before losing the last shred of sunlight. Maggie padded down each wrung of the ladder, her arches sore from standing on tiptoe—something she did involuntarily when focused. Hitting the linoleum floor felt like returning from outer space. Like Maggie had been elsewhere, floating for twenty years, and now she was back. Not ready to make contact with anyone, or to speak or breathe. She needed to ease back into things. She needed to blink again. She needed a glass of water.

Slowly, she made her way to the sink. As she began to wash the delicate strands of her paintbrush, Maggie felt a pair of arms snake their way around her torso. She let out a high-pitched yelp before realizing it was just Rob. Maggie leaned back against him and closed her eyes.

"Thank god," she murmured.

"Sorry, baby," Rob said, petting the top of her head. "I didn't mean to scare you."

He unwound his arms to release her, but she grabbed a forearm.

"Stay," she said, and Rob indulged her for a moment longer.

If an evening up on her ladder was like being in space, being pressed against Rob was confirmation of gravity. She pulled him closer. He was warm and sturdy. Maggie always said Rob was made of marble. Everlasting, rooted, firm. Something that would be around for hundreds of years. She couldn't believe a person like that even existed, but here was Rob. A body that would last.

Rob released her, and Maggie turned to face him as he sank into one hip and tucked his hands into the pockets of his coat. A low-frequency good mood hummed from him. Inexplicably, he kept calling her *baby*.

Maggie laid the paintbrush next to the sink.

"I just have to finish a few things," she said. "I'll be ready in a second."

"Sure," he said. "Take your time."

Rob gave Maggie space while she made her way around the room, screwing caps on paint, folding up the ladder. He leaned against one of the tables that cluttered the studio and scrolled through his phone until Maggie moved the ladder from the front of her painting.

"It's really coming together," he said, sounding impressed.

He pushed himself from the edge of the table and approached the canvas, craning his neck up and down just as her brother had, looking at every inch of the painting.

"I didn't get as much done as I would have hoped," Maggie said, waiting for the real meat of his evaluation.

Rob stood with his arms crossed for a long time before speaking. Maggie watched the words form in his mind.

"It's bigger than I remember it being."

Maggie swallowed, trying to move saliva through whatever knots had formed inside her throat. A headache was beginning to throb behind her left eye.

"We're going to be late," she said, rubbing her temple.

Rob stayed planted in front of the women, despite undoubtedly having heard her. She looked down at her phone.

"We should go," Maggie insisted. "John called me a million times."

With her phone pressed to her ear, she told Rob to hurry.

"Did you get ice?" she asked, listening to one of her brother's voicemails.

Rob gave the painting a final nod, at which point Maggie had to turn her back to him. She couldn't watch something so wrong and upsetting. She heard him strolling toward her and felt his arm appear around her waist.

"Yes, baby," he said, easing them forward without urgency. "I got ice."

3

JOHN AND THE Artist lived in one of the new, gauche high-rises that pimpled the southeast edge of the Hudson River. Her father had been an investor in one of the developments and owned three units in the largest building. One he gifted to his daughter, and therefore John, another he kept for himself and his wife, and the third he rented out to make millions off someone who was inevitably making millions off someone else. As an architect, Rob agreed that the buildings were hideous eyesores, and Maggie loved him and his allegiance in this. But she also knew that a hidden part of Rob wished he and Maggie could occupy the third unit. They were so close, related to the owners by proxy, but related to the wrong one in the pair. They were linked to John, and he was just a doctor.

Maggie waited at the curb for Rob to pull the car around to the studio. They had a nice life, too, didn't they? Thanks to Rob's ever-rising stardom at work, they lived in a fancy, soulless building in Brooklyn, with a parking garage and a doorman. They had a car that had been manufactured in the past five years. They shopped at the luxury grocery store on their block instead of one of the average grocery chains. Though Maggie shopped at the chains when Rob wasn't with her. He never knew the difference by the time the food was all cooked.

When Rob pulled up to the curb, Maggie opened the passenger door and found a mountain of ice where she'd hoped to put her feet.

"Let me move those," Rob said, putting the car in park.

"That's all right."

Maggie threw her purse in the back and climbed into the car. She sat folded in on herself, perched above all the ice.

"That doesn't look comfortable," Rob said.

"It's fine," Maggie insisted. "We're nearly there anyway."

Rob shrugged and carefully veered the car into the flow of traffic.

Maggie settled into a cross-legged position and leaned her head against the headrest. With her eyes closed, her painting floated into her mind. If it had taken her three hours to paint one dome's worth of tiles, she still had nine hours of tile work left. When would she ever get around to the women?

There was a date she was working toward, not that she had told anybody. April 12, the final day students could be nominated for "the grant." The grant, which was mostly mentioned in hushed tones and whispers, was a $30,000 cash prize and gallery show that the university awarded to one student in each discipline. The grant was what Maggie was depending on to prove—to her parents, to Rob, to herself—that she could successfully, financially, *be* an artist. That she was right to have gone to art school. That believing in herself, that listening to the small voice that told her she was talented, had not been totally delusional.

"What are you thinking about?" Rob asked, pulling up to a red light.

"Ceiling tiles," Maggie answered. "And what people look like when they're dying."

Rob's low laugh filled the car.

"What I would give to live in there," he said, wrapping his big hand around the back of her skull. He squeezed, and Maggie could feel the edges of her headache dissipate.

"We can trade," she said.

Rob turned her head toward him.

"What are you thinking about?" she asked.

"The rest of our lives."

The car slowed as they hit a string of traffic, red brake lights as far as Maggie could see. Rob put his hand back on the steering wheel. He looked over at Maggie, not saying anything but blinking more than usual.

"What do you mean?" she said.

"Oh, you know," he said, struggling to embody an element of ease. "Where we'll live, what we'll do."

"Other than live here and do this?"

Rob cracked an amused smile, but Maggie wasn't trying to amuse him. Talking like this, in vague, grand terms, frustrated her to no end, and it was often Rob's preferred way of speaking. Never getting to the heart of the matter, instead alluding to whatever it was that he meant.

"You know what I mean," he said. "When we're going to take the next step."

"And what do you imagine that step to be?"

"Marriage, kids."

"Kids?" Maggie's voice had gone rogue, intonating without her. *Are you insane?* it basically shrieked.

"Yeah, kids." Rob shrugged.

Maggie rolled down the window and stuck her head out for air.

"It's not so crazy, Mags. People who are in love get married and have kids. It happens all the time."

Traffic multiplied in front of them. Everyone seemed to be merging. Maggie imagined the cars *actually* merging, becoming one conjoined metal nightmare, each with its own horn honking and honking.

"Your mom doesn't seem to think it's such a bad next step."

"My *mom*?"

"She called me earlier. She wanted to see how we were."

"Yeah, she called me earlier, too, but we somehow managed to avoid the topic of child-rearing."

"We were just talking. It's not like I said we'd have kids tomorrow. It was just hypothetical. Like what if?"

What if?

Yeah, that's not so bad. What if Maggie went off birth control? What if they had giggly, unprotected sex, and Maggie let Rob impregnate her? What if she had a child growing inside her, draining her of life force and energy, and she had to nap all the time? What if she threw up every day for thirty days straight? What if she never won the grant, abandoned painting altogether, and raised Rob's babies instead?

Maybe that's extreme. What if she *paused* her painting? Only for a little while. What if she got back into it after a year, maybe two? What if they had another kid? And another one? And another one? What if Maggie's life floated right past her? Just for a little while. Just for a year. Just forever.

Rob opened his mouth, but before he could speak, Maggie interjected. "Stop," she said. "I can't do this tonight."

She could feel his fear, her rage, polluting the car.

Rob turned on the radio, and Maggie closed her eyes again and tried not to imagine herself pregnant. A man was singing, his sound thin and tinny. He had the voice of someone very famous whose name Maggie could never remember. Someone everyone knew, and if Maggie were to say "I don't know him," people would lose their minds and let their jaws hang loose. "You don't know *him*?" they'd say. This whiny-yet-sexy voice had practically coaxed these people out of the womb. Maggie bet their parents played his music for them growing up, so that his name was in their heart as much as it was in their head. But Maggie's parents had never played his music. It was so American.

"I love this song," Rob said.

They'd made it through two rounds of the chorus when Maggie felt the car pull over in front of John's building.

"Whoa," Rob said.

Maggie fluttered her eyes open and came to the same realization Rob had. Whoa.

JOHN HAD MENTIONED this in the weeks leading up to their party, that the evening was meant to celebrate the inevitable success of the Artist's show, of course, but also that it would coincide with the unveiling of her sculpture, which had been commissioned by their building. The commission had been issued over a year ago, and Maggie gasped at the sum she'd been offered for her services. They'd paid her $300,000 for a sculpture that Maggie couldn't believe didn't even do anything like spin or light up.

"Let's get closer to it," Rob said.

He rounded the car to open Maggie's door and retrieve two bags of ice so she could maneuver her way out more elegantly than she'd maneuvered her way in. She hopped out of the car and grabbed the last bag of ice herself before approaching the sculpture with Rob.

About the size of a vintage Italian coupe, a round, black cloud was covered in lacquered spheres of varying sizes; the largest was as big as a bowling ball, and the smallest could be mistaken for caviar. It seemed to hover above the ground, because the metal posts it rested on were painted black so at night they'd disappear. It sparkled in the light of the streetlamps and somehow reminded Maggie of a brain.

Rob reached out to touch it.

"It's hard," he said.

He bent down to investigate where the piece was screwed into its posts, curious about its structural integrity.

"How much do you think it weighs?"

"I have no idea," Maggie said, waiting for him to stand again.

Rob rose and gave the sculpture the same approving nod he'd given Maggie's painting just minutes ago. He walked toward Maggie and triggered the sliding glass doors of the building's oppressively modern lobby.

"Hey, boss," Rob said to the doorman, who recognized them both and gave a warm greeting in return.

Maggie and Rob boarded the elevator, the ice beginning to melt in their arms.

"Why do guys always do that?"

"Do what?"

"Call each other 'boss.' Don't you think it's condescending?"

Rob drew in a long breath through his nose.

"So I can't talk to the doorman, either? Your mom. The doorman. Anyone else? How about Can? Can I speak to Can?"

Though he couldn't *quite* say it right, Maggie was stung by the sweetness of Rob's continuous effort to pronounce her brother's name the Turkish way, with a soft starting consonant and the stretched vowel. A subtle difference from the pronunciation of *John*, but one Rob always strived to articulate.

"I'm sorry," Maggie said, looking at the ice cradled in her arms.

Rob spoke again, this time almost under his breath. "You come down so hard on me sometimes. Do you realize that?"

The elevator doors opened, and John was standing in front of them.

"The doorman rang," he said, by way of explanation.

"Hey, man!" Rob leaned into John for a hug as best as he could with an ice bag in each arm. The look that spread across his face was genuine and kind. Rob and John always got along, Rob acting like the brother John never had.

John leaned in to kiss Maggie's cheek, and she handed over her ice. She watched as Rob trailed her brother, both of them tall and buoyant in each other's presence. They bounded down the hall, carrying thirty pounds of ice like it was weightless and not, in fact, frozen solid. She could hear them talking to each other, but they were too quiet and too far ahead for her to make out what they were saying. John threw his head back in laughter before opening the door to his apartment.

"They're here!" he shouted into the living room.

Everything about the apartment was wide open and painted white. As the first to arrive, Maggie and Rob stepped inside the bright, empty living room, which adjoined seamlessly to the kitchen, separated only by an enormous marble island. A narrow hallway to the right of the kitchen led to a suite of three small rooms—the master bedroom with its own bathroom, the guest bath, and a spare bedroom, which Maggie considered to be her own, since she was the only person to ever sleep there.

"The place looks amazing," Rob said to John.

The white couch that usually floated in the middle of the living room was anchored against the white wall, and the heart of the apartment felt, to Maggie, like a vacuous hole.

"Thanks, man," John said, leading them down the hallway. "We can set these down in here."

John guided them to the guest bathroom (also white), and he

poured a bag of ice into the bathtub. Peeking through the mounds of ice were sparkling glass bottles of wine and beer, with colorful pops of Aperol, Cynar, and Campari. The whole setup was charming and elegant, even the smattering of aluminum cans that added their dull silver to all the flecks of gold.

Rob proceeded to pour out his bags, and the crash of ice waterfalling into the tub was deafening.

"You're here!" Maggie heard from behind her.

The Artist appeared in the bathroom as a vision. Like Venus on the half shell, she glided onto the scene with her long hair, coiled into loose curls, blowing behind her. She wore a nude linen dress that pooled at her ankles and dragged behind her like the train of a wedding gown, her pale skin blemish-free and gleaming. For once, Maggie could detect the makeup on the Artist's face. It was luminescent—her cheeks were two round pearls entirely made of shimmer. If Maggie took the Artist's face into her hands, she suspected her cheeks would crumble.

"Maggie!" she said. "I'm so happy you came!"

The Artist wrapped her arms around Maggie, and their hug fell into the category of tender embrace, as was the Artist's theatrical way. Maggie didn't hate it as much as she thought she might.

"We're happy to be here!" Maggie said before breaking apart. "The show was something else. Really. Congratulations."

"You're very sweet to say so," the Artist said, accepting Maggie's praise graciously before turning to Rob.

"Oh, Rob!" She forced the same sort of embrace on him, only briefer. They parted by kissing cheeks.

"The sculpture, too," Rob mentioned as they separated. "It's incredible."

"*The Brain*!" the Artist said, nearly bursting out of her skin. "So you saw it?"

"You can't miss it."

Thus began an animated discussion of mechanics. The Artist explained how she didn't have the proper training to make the largest sphere, so she flew to a factory in China to oversee its production. It was apparently lumpy and hollow until the factory workers filled it with water and explosives. "That's what makes it so smooth," the Artist said, beaming, as if that really explained anything.

Maggie watched as John contentedly observed his girlfriend. He was clearly proud, if still mildly oblivious. The pleasant look on his face never wavered, and he nodded while the Artist spoke about her newfound aptitude for welding.

Rob, continuing to ask questions, discovered that the sculpture weighed about nine hundred pounds and that the Artist welded each of the smaller spheres herself before adhering them. She gleefully recounted her first time using the welding gun, how powerful she'd felt. She invoked Hephaestus and became impossibly giddy.

Rob caught Maggie's glance. Look at how good he was with John and his deranged girlfriend. How he was kind and engaged, even though Maggie had been harsh with him, even though their car ride had been nothing short of miserable. *Just be nice to me,* she could feel him pleading to her.

Rob's phone rang, interrupting the Artist's bubbling enthusiasm.

"I'm so sorry," he said, raising a finger and stepping toward the door. "I have to take this."

Then it was just the three of them in the bathroom, and Maggie had no further questions about *The Brain* or what it took to create such a thing. John and the Artist turned to each other to discuss the party. How would they keep the food warm without overheating the apartment? Did John really think they'd bought enough alcohol? Should she have gone out for more cups like she almost had an hour ago? John laid a hand on the Artist's shoulder, and Maggie saw how this touch was like lifting the cover off a drain. The Artist took a deep breath, and a wash of calm came over her. Everything would be fine, her body seemed to understand with John's hand pressed against her.

Maggie longed for the same feeling. For Rob to lay a hand on her and for all her anxieties to recede. To feel as though all would work out for them. She would win the grant and support herself as an artist. They would, calmly, and not in a rush, get married. Maybe in the years to come they would have a child, and no one would have to give up anything.

Rob reentered the bathroom with an apologetic look. He shifted his gaze from John to the Artist, and finally to Maggie.

"I'm so sorry," he said, shaking his head. "But I have to run to the office."

"Oh no!" the Artist exclaimed before anyone else could. "Is everything all right?"

"It's this project in Tokyo," Rob said, looking only at Maggie. "There's been some kind of miscommunication, and our client is tearing my team apart."

Maggie nodded, her eyes cast down. She forced herself to flick them back up to Rob, not wanting to be childish. Of course he should go. He was the head of the New York office, and he had to act like it.

"I understand," she said, standing up straighter.

"I'll be as fast as I can," he said. "I promise."

"I know."

He apologized one more time to John, and then profusely to the Artist, kissing cheeks again and saying how quickly he'd try to turn things around. Just before he left, Maggie raised her face to him. Rob tenderly ran the back of his fingers against her cheek. His touch drained nothing from her body.

MAGGIE WANDERED OUT of the bathroom to give John and the Artist some privacy before the guests would arrive. She studied the apartment from the edge of the hallway. It looked unlike it ever had before, and she came to realize that part of its foreign feel was that they had taken down everything that had once been hanging on the walls. The apartment had morphed into a gallery with no obvious exhibit.

As she drifted farther away from the murmurs of her brother and his girlfriend and the silence of the apartment fully enveloped her, two chords struck her simultaneously. One was the pain of Rob's pleading glance. *Just be nice to me.* She'd like the chance to be. She'd like the chance to share a moment of peace with him before the party. To apologize and have a pleasant evening and go home early. The other chord was quieter, its opposite. It was her fear that it was actually better this way. That there was something right about being alone.

The doorbell rang, and Maggie's chest tightened, concerned she would be the one to greet whoever the first guests might be. She turned her head to call for John, and, thankfully, he was already making his way to the front door. He paused before answering. John looked Maggie up and down and said, "Is that what you're wearing tonight?"

Maggie had forgotten she was still in her work overalls, which were covered in paint. With her hair in two thick braids going down her back, Maggie looked like an elementary school art teacher. She was about to say *No, of course not,* and that she had a change of clothes in Rob's car, but the Artist's hand appeared on her shoulder.

"Yes!" she shouted past Maggie's ear at John.

Maggie wanted to shrug the Artist's hand off her shoulder, but she saw her brother's eyes glued to where she and the Artist were jointed.

"It's perfect," she went on. "Everyone will think you're the artist!"

Maggie watched John's face. He looked horrified. All this work for a party, and his girlfriend was trying to pull a prank? Maggie pitied her brother. She wished she could stop the Artist, but she knew well enough that there was no stopping her once an idea took hold.

"Please, Maggie," the Artist continued. "I'd give anything not to talk to these people all night—you know how they can be. And we can turn the whole spectacle on them! This stupid fancy party for an artist they can't even recognize! Oh, please."

The word *stupid* punctured John. His Adam's apple made one quick quiver before he could catch himself and recompose.

"I mean, I'm sure they'll still recognize you," Maggie mumbled, realizing she was already doomed. Rob had taken the car, with her clothes still in the back seat.

"Of course they'll recognize you," John said, tacking his dissent onto Maggie's. "They were all at the show last night."

"Can't we just try it?"

Nothing in the Artist's world made sense to Maggie. She stared at John, knowing that he didn't stand a chance against his girlfriend's glossy eyes and shimmering face. She and her brother both fumbled for some version of "Sure," and the Artist squealed in delight as the guests started to arrive.

4

JOHN SIDLED UP next to Maggie at the kitchen island and refilled her glass with something that bubbled. The party swirled around them like they were an oil spill.

"Should we tie your hair up with chopsticks or paintbrushes?" John said as he rubbed Maggie's back. "Do you think that would sell it better?"

Maggie rested her head on his shoulder.

"Maybe I should sit on the counter and shove the hors d'oeuvres up my vagina."

John laughed and bent forward at the waist, bringing Maggie forward with him. Her shoulders softened, relieved that her brother was on her side for once.

"I mean, Jesus Christ, did she really think this was going to work?"

Maggie looked around at the guests flocking toward the Artist. They fell mostly into two camps—artists and patrons—and they differentiated themselves by how they dressed. The former fanned their plumage: a shock of lime-green hair, intricate designs shaved into the sides of their heads, color vomiting forth from all of them. The patrons were gaunt and dressed in black. They had pointy, architectural accessories, which Maggie imagined gouging her eyes out with.

She picked at a fleck of paint that had hardened in the lining of her pocket, knowing it would never come loose. Maggie took a sip of whatever John had poured into her glass. "I look like an asshole."

"You don't look like an asshole," John said, giving her a little squeeze. He rocked gently from his laugh. "You look like you!"

"That's even worse."

John took a long sip of what had turned out to be champagne.

"What's up with you and Rob?" he asked out of nowhere. They both looked ahead at the crowd. People were beginning to get drunk.

"What are you talking about?"

"I was just wondering," he said. "You were kind of cold to him earlier."

Maggie rolled her lower back against the lip of the island and thought about Rob's way of things. Talking around in circles, trying to sense her mood before saying what he meant. If he wanted to talk about their future, did he have to do it in such an obtuse way? Did he have to involve her mother?

"We kind of had a fight in the car," Maggie said. "That's all."

"Oh?" John looked at his sister with kind eyes. He wielded this delicate ability to oscillate between stoic and masculine to tender and loving in a matter of seconds. He could go in either direction, back and forth, in perfect accordance with any feeling in any room. Sometimes it frightened Maggie how quickly he could shapeshift.

"What were you fighting about?"

"About how I can't have a baby, Can," Maggie said. "Not right now, not next year."

"I delivered a fourteen-year-old's baby this afternoon," he said matter-of-factly, already switching from sweetness.

"Right."

John was looking out at his guests again. His every move felt exaggerated and ridiculous, like a captain surveying his ship. "Rob's a good guy, you know?"

"I do know."

"He really loves you."

"Are you saying I'm supposed to have a baby because he really loves me?"

"No," John said, slowly turning back to Maggie. "I'm just saying he loves you."

John left her at the island while he gravitated toward a pile of depleting cocktail napkins.

Was someone out there telling Rob how much Maggie loved him? Was someone in the office now, reminding him of this, in case he had forgotten? How absurd that Rob's love was supposed to mean something to her here, at a party he couldn't even bother to attend.

Maggie checked her phone to see if he'd sent her any messages, but there were none.

Where are you?:(she texted.

She slid back into the pool of guests, the temperature of the apartment rising from their body heat. She tried to act normal. Maggie recognized the head art critic for *The New Yorker*, a long woman named Valentina, who was the first nonartist to arrive wearing something colorful—wide-legged silk pants that depicted fields of rice paddies awash in tones of blue, green, and brown. She brought herself close to Valentina to see if the two could possibly make a meaningful connection.

"These pants," Maggie heard herself saying. She reached out and lightly grazed Valentina's elbow.

"Vintage," Valentina said, and swished them to one side.

Maggie couldn't believe how casually this had come out of her, how easily she could feign normalcy. Conversation flowed quickly from there. They talked about clothes—their most coveted finds, how picked over a lot of their usual vintage haunts had become. Their back-and-forth felt so effortless that it occurred to Maggie that she and Valentina *should* be talking. It was building to a place where Maggie was about to mention her work when Valentina stopped and reached for Maggie's arm.

"You have such strong arms," she said, squeezing Maggie's bicep. "It doesn't seem natural."

Her arm, thick in Valentina's grip, made Maggie wonder if despite being too stressed to eat lately, she'd somehow been expanding. Her skin bulged between Valentina's skinny fingers. Maggie felt cherubic in the worst way possible.

"How did you get these?" she asked without looking into Maggie's eyes.

"I do one hundred push-ups every day."

Maggie had not done a single push-up since high school, but Valentina's red nails digging into her skin demanded an explanation.

Valentina nodded to herself. "Push-ups," she said to no one in particular. She excused herself, and Maggie was left to search for a small cluster of people who might house her. She recognized a group of gossiping graduate students and hovered near them until a hole emerged and she filled it.

Maggie felt obliged by the unspoken social contract of gossip to contribute fledgling bits of salacious information. She'd heard that Eros—a name this girl had given herself upon entering art school—had slept with the director of photography at NYU, a man nearly thirty years her senior. Maggie didn't feel bad saying so, because she had seen Eros smoking a joint in the park the other day, telling a group of first-year students how grotesque it had been. After shooting out smoke through her nostrils, Eros had described how every move he'd made was slow and sloppy, each progression unfolding as if by horrible, clumsy accident.

After Maggie relayed as much, Galileo, an Italian student studying sculpture, gasped. Maggie had always suspected he had a crush on Eros, and this was confirmed when she saw the look on his face. He was shocked and sullen, like the long stem of a wineglass had snapped somewhere inside him.

"That doesn't sound like her," he said, looking down and shaking his head of curls.

Maggie, feeling guilty for what she'd done to poor Galileo's spirit, faded into another group of chattering guests.

Now with her back to the Artist, Maggie was poised to eavesdrop on her and John. She overheard the Artist excitedly whisper to him, "So international!" after introducing herself to Dawn, an art critic in town from London, who had brought a couple of friends. They were also Londoners, though, as Maggie heard, to the delight of the Artist, Ovie was originally from Nigeria and his partner, Faheem, was from Sudan.

"I thought I sensed an accent!" the Artist said, though the two were from different countries.

Maggie peeked over her shoulder to see the couple entertain the comment without a change of expression.

Ovie and Faheem looked sharp in their dark suits that had been tailored perfectly to their opposite bodies—Faheem's, long and lean, and Ovie's, short and dense. They were prickly around the Artist but softened when she excused herself. Faheem leaned into Ovie to say something in his ear. Close enough to touch, but they didn't.

Maggie shifted her gaze back to the Artist and saw that she, on the other hand, touched everyone. Always holding an elbow as she leaned forward for a kiss on the cheek, or pressing into flesh with her delicate-boned fingers. She leaned in and laughed often. She was entirely unlike how she was at last night's show. Where there she was steely and metallic, here she was fleshy and sensual. In that moment, Maggie understood that last night the Artist had tried to make herself something nonhuman. She wasn't mimicking birth; she had sterilized it. She didn't scream or produce Lamaze-taught breaths. She didn't ask to hold the watermelon when she was done. The Artist was a medium for the audience, living and breathing only if you caught her. Maggie didn't know what to make of the show anymore, because she had seen the pink soles of the Artist's feet and the beads of sweat forming along her hairline. She had seen her suffering.

"What do *you* think?"

A man with wiry silver eyebrows and almost no hair was looking intently at Maggie. She had no idea what he was talking about.

"I don't know," Maggie said, and the paltry circle she had been a part of quietly disbanded.

John caught Maggie's glance and waved her over to a group of grave-looking White women and their slightly baboonish husbands, all with the kind of papery skin that Maggie's mother constantly told her to be grateful she didn't have. Maggie appeared by John's side, and he hung an arm around her shoulders.

"This is my sister, Maggie. She's also an artist."

Maggie smiled and bowed her head. It was kind of John to introduce her like this—as an artist in her own right. The group received her with barely a murmur, and Maggie immediately wished he hadn't.

"Sister?" one of the women said, somehow incredulous. "I would never have guessed."

"What do you mean?" Maggie asked.

"Well, you two hardly look alike."

Maggie searched John's face for traces of herself. She saw her thick eyebrows over his light eyes, honey-colored like their father's and Sofia's. They were the pale ones, while olive undertones colored Maggie and her mother beige-ish, with dark-brown eyes. She observed John's nose—the nose they all had, even their father, the only one from a region far, far north. It was delicate and narrow as you traveled down to the tip, where the slope fell harshly. John had their father's thin and serious mouth, sure, while Maggie's was more like her mother's, full and feminine. But he looked like her John, her brother. They looked like they belonged to each other, because, of course, they did.

"Maggie's Turkish genes are strong," John said, smiling. "Mine are all recessive."

These people found humor in this, and Maggie was overcome with the feeling that she should defend John: *Look at this hair!* Coarse and dark and strong enough that it would outlast all of theirs. *Look at this mouth!* Look at this mouth and tell her this wasn't Atatürk's mouth!

"Turkish!" exclaimed the same woman who had doubted their affiliation. A few of the surrounding guests' interest was sparked, along with hers. They wanted to know about where was best to vacation and which cities were safe for tourists.

"If any," another woman added with a horrified flare.

They directed all their questions to Maggie, even though John was the one who had actually been born there. Maggie wiped the sweat forming on her upper lip and dried her hand on the leg of her overalls. The relentless heat was beginning to make her feel faint.

"Excuse me," she said, retreating after having given polite answers to their questions about the Middle East. No one seemed to mind her departure. They resumed chatting, all livelier and more animated than they had been when Maggie arrived.

Setting her drink on the counter, Maggie made her way to escape for some fresh air. She could feel John's eyes on her and caught his glance before exiting. Like in a cartoon, he jerked his head back and mimicked getting shot. *Leaving?* he said without saying.

Call, she mouthed in return, and held her fingers to her ear to resemble a phone.

John gave a quick nod, and Maggie ducked out of the apartment otherwise unnoticed.

THE SHOCK OF cold air nearly choked Maggie as she wound her way toward *The Brain*. Earlier in the evening, she'd overheard the Artist explaining a complicated root system beneath the metal posts. She had apparently designed an entire network of poles beneath the soil that served as a mirror image to *The Brain*. She'd welded each rod individually, modeling them after an in-depth study of ginkgo roots. The structure beneath *The Brain* was simultaneously delicate and indestructible.

Maggie reached out to touch it. Just as Rob had said, it was hard. And freezing cold. And undeniably marvelous. Infuriating, the Artist's understanding of the world. How finely she articulated the line between human and inhuman, science and nature. How she could invoke the real through the false.

It became obvious to Maggie suddenly that she was drowning by her own hand, too fiercely dedicated to the real. That was what plagued her painting. Because of her devotion to these women, making them as real as possible, people couldn't see the height of their suffering. They just looked like women.

Maggie's phone buzzed in her pocket with a message from Rob.

I'm so sorry, Mags.

Then another.

It's going to be a while.

And another.

Trying to hurry xx

What was there for her to say, really?

Take your time, she typed, then erased.

She thought about apologizing for snapping at him in the car, but then she felt confused about why she should have to.

I'm not sure the Artist knows the difference between Nigeria and Sudan, she could tell him. Or *Apparently, I have unnaturally strong arms.*

She tucked her phone into her pocket without responding. Instead, Maggie stared at *The Brain*, willing it to tell her something.

"Party's that bad, huh?"

The voice was unmistakable. The low, confident drawl that never asked a question it didn't already know the answer to. Maggie turned her head and saw Rakib's long strides drawing himself toward her.

"You're all alone out here, kid," he said.

Maggie's body moved in all the familiar ways it did around Rakib—soft and subdued, utterly succumbed to his spell.

"Not anymore."

5

Kissing Rakib is like kissing God, Maggie had once texted her friend Grace their sophomore year of college.

The first time Maggie saw Rakib was at a Halloween party. She had just failed a test, which would end up being the score that stripped her of any chances she had to minor in chemistry—something she'd been secretly striving for in hopes that when they announced it at graduation, her parents would shed tears of joy alongside their tears of despair. But she had not gotten a single point. An absolute zero. Even Maggie hadn't thought she was capable of such failure.

Determined to turn the night around, Grace convinced Maggie to stuff herself into a corset two sizes too small, adorn cherry-red horns, and call herself the devil.

"Even your eyes are red," she said when she stepped back to observe Maggie, who had not stopped crying for the past hour and a half.

Over the course of the evening, Maggie drank her body weight in grain alcohol and kept threatening to call members of her family to tell them she was dropping out of school. With her crooked horns atop her head and her breasts pushed up nearly to her nostrils, she had abandoned her self-pitying tears and instead adopted a throw-caution-to-the-wind attitude. Who needed a degree anyway? Who had even come up with a concept as stupid as college?

When they arrived at the house party, it was like every other social event they'd attended as undergrads. It was loud and dark, and Maggie was touching at least three people at any given moment. Separated from Grace, she'd spent a considerable amount of time on a search-and-rescue mission through the bedrooms, when, eventually exasperated, she gave up and found she was touching Rakib all over.

He was tall, dressed in a black suit, and wearing sunglasses inside. His thick black hair formed a unanimous wave that swooped backward. Maggie asked him who he was supposed to be dressed as. A character from a movie, apparently. He said the title, but she couldn't hear him over the roar of the party.

"And what are you?" he asked.

"Isn't it obvious?"

Rakib cocked his head to the side. Maggie couldn't see what his eyes were doing behind his sunglasses.

"I'm the devil," she said, and reached to click her nails against her horns. Her hand landed flat against her head, and she discovered that her horns had disappeared, probably trampled beneath their feet.

"I see it now," Rakib said. "Very dangerous."

A laugh she didn't recognize as her own peeled from Maggie. *So dangerous*, she thought. Dangerous to herself and those she loved.

Rakib lowered his sunglasses to reveal startlingly dark eyes, peering into Maggie.

Her stomach turned, and a hand appeared on her shoulder. It was Grace, her fingernails bitten down to the nubs.

"Where *were* you?" she wailed.

Maggie discovered that Grace was now the one weeping uncontrollably.

"What do you mean?" Maggie asked, bewildered by what sounded more like an accusation than a question. "I'm right here."

"She's *here*." Grace's voice had become raw, stripped of any quality that made it human. "She's here with *him*!"

Immediately, Maggie understood. The love of Grace's life was in this crowded, sweaty hellscape, with the man she'd left Grace for after realizing her lesbianism was really just a phase.

"Oh, Gracie," Maggie said, wrapping her friend in her arms. Grace's snot bubbled into Maggie's chest.

"Let's go," she said, already pulling Grace toward the door. Her small frame stayed clinging to Maggie as they hobbled down the hallway.

Maggie turned her head to look for Rakib. He had pushed his sunglasses back up the bridge of his nose and was watching her drift away.

She tried to give him a pathetic look. *Take pity on me and my poor friend,* it said. *I never would have left if it wasn't obviously dire.* Maggie's gaze was heavy. *Isn't love terrible,* it said, *how it absolutely debases us?*

Rakib's chin dipped in a low, understanding nod, seeming to pick up on everything Maggie had telepathed to him.

Just as they reached the edge of the party, he gave a little wave. It was Grace who made the final push that propelled them through the crowd and out the front door.

IN THE WEEKS after Halloween, Maggie's life traced a faint line around Rakib's. Occasionally, she spotted him sitting outside a café by Washington Square Park, with his legs crossed and his thumbs hooked between sections of *The New York Times*. Once, she saw him waiting in line at the library to scan something at the copy machine. Usually, he was surrounded by a group of male friends who all appeared much younger than him, though Maggie recognized their faces and knew they were in the same year. Rakib stood stick-straight among them. He walked slowly and with purpose. The boys all closed their slack jaws when he spoke. He was their alpha, his voice deeper and more resonant than the rest.

Maggie began to conduct private, but elaborate, research on Rakib. She found out that he was a finance major who dabbled in art history and Italian. He spoke fluent Bengali and had "Limited Working Proficiency in Italian" listed on his résumé, which Maggie had sourced through her part-time job at the Student Resource Center. Photos of him peppered several social media accounts—those of gorgeous, thin, mostly White women and those of rich students with richer parents—but it appeared he had no account of his own.

Though her sightings of him were sparse, they completely altered Maggie's approach in how she presented herself. She stopped wearing leggings to class and started blending concealer to mask her under-eye circles. Rakib could be anywhere, and she never wanted to be caught wishing she had tried a little harder. It was something her mother had been telling her for years. "You never know where you'll meet someone," she'd say, smudging her eyeliner to go to the grocery store. It was advice Maggie had always ignored until now.

It then felt profoundly unfair that when Maggie was finally forced to encounter Rakib up close, she wasn't wearing an outfit. She wasn't even wearing shoes or a bra. It was nearing midnight, and she was the sole pupil in the studio art building. Dressed in an oversized sweatshirt and sagging jeans, Maggie was deep in the work of a final project for her screen-printing class—fifty miniature self-portraits, all done in varying styles. She had kicked off her shoes as she got more and more into a flow with the press, crushing each print with the totality of her weight, staring straight down into each version of herself she was making.

"Oh," Rakib said when he happened upon her.

Maggie scowled, frustrated that she'd been interrupted. But when she saw who it was, she felt her face drain of its color. Her breath became shallow.

"The devil herself," he said.

Maggie lowered her heels back to the floor. She lifted the screen from her print, pleased that she hadn't stuttered or smudged the ink.

"Maggie," she said, meeting his eyes. "And you're that guy from that movie?"

"Good memory."

Maggie marveled at Rakib's features. How full his lips were, how warmth and shine emanated from his face. His every movement was languid and natural.

"Rakib," he said, his hand quickly pressed to his chest before falling back to his side. He made his way nearer to her.

With her fingers poised delicately at the edge of her print, Maggie pinched the corners and lifted it to where her other pieces were drying. Rakib came to observe the grid she had made. After a moment of quiet, he spoke.

"Are they all of you?" he asked.

Maggie nodded. She was halfway done and felt suddenly shy that there were twenty-five small versions of her staring up at them.

"And you're going to hang them like this?"

"Yes," Maggie said. She motioned her hands beyond the grid's perimeter. "But there will be twice as many."

"Amazing."

Rakib reached for a print that had, thankfully, already dried and lifted it.

"They're so detailed." He lowered the print and reached for another. "And so different."

"Do you think they look like me?"

"Definitely," he said seriously. "All together, too. They capture all of you." He stared at Maggie, whittling his attention down to a sharp beam. "They capture your bigness."

Usually, Maggie would shrink at the notion of being big, but not when Rakib said it. Instead, she was delighted, in total disbelief that this was how he saw her.

Rakib returned the print in his hand back to the grid. His attention had diffused now, more like a cloud Maggie was caught in.

"How's your friend?" he asked. Maggie couldn't produce a single memory from this. She looked at him with her brows fiercely pinned together in confusion.

"If I remember correctly, she was in love."

"Grace," Maggie exhaled, almost laughing. "She's in love with someone else now."

"That's too bad."

It was too bad, wasn't it? All the falling in and out of love they were all doing, sometimes at the speed of light. How it was simultaneously the greatest thing that had ever happened to people and how it also never seemed to be working out.

Maggie glanced down the chute between their bodies. Very little air fit in the space between them. She looked back up at Rakib, hoping whatever would happen next would happen already. He lifted a hand from his side and gently grazed Maggie's arm.

"I should probably let you work," he said.

"Probably."

They stayed remarkably still, and Maggie felt heavy in her bones. Magnetically heavy, like it would be impossible for her to ever move away from him.

"Probably," Rakib said again, nodding.

He took a step toward her, which was really a step past her. He wished her good luck, and when she turned to watch him leave, he'd already made it most of the way to the exit. There was his smoothness again. His long gait, the bones in his spine perfectly aligned. He twisted his head over his shoulder to look at Maggie one more time.

"See you," Maggie said.

"I hope so."

Rakib disappeared around the corner, and Maggie resumed making the rest of her prints, thinking of him the whole time. Thinking of the whites of his eyes, so clear against his harshly defined irises. His one million dark eyelashes made his eyes, if you isolated them, like those of a woman or an animal. There was something too beautiful about them to be considered masculine. She thought of how his mouth moved when he spoke.

Eventually, her thoughts of Rakib mixed with her thoughts of what she was doing. Smearing paint across the page became smearing paint across his chest. Pressing her weight into the print became pressing herself against him to see if he would move. In her imagination, he was like the table, sturdy and permanent. He would stay, no matter how hard or strong or forceful she became.

IT WENT LIKE this for a while, circling around each other with the occasional interaction. But it wasn't long before they'd become entwined. Maggie popping up at his dorm at all hours, Rakib always stopping by the studio. Sometimes he'd surprise her with a single silver-wrapped chocolate from the deli down the block, but that was the extent of his sweetness. Rakib was cool. Not gushy or emotional, in the ways Maggie couldn't help herself from being.

This became torturous for her, all the withholding. She often found herself desperately trying to earn back his affection. Bent down at his knees, looking helplessly up at him. Her beauty, when wielded right, was usually a good way. But it was when she made him feel powerful that she knew she was safe for a while, protected against his cold, uncaring stare.

6

THE SMALL STRETCH of sidewalk between them seemed infinitely long as Rakib strode toward Maggie without rushing. He was stunning, dressed in a smart black suit with a pressed dark shirt. One of those button-downs without a collar. He sported a closely shaved beard, speckled with new gray hairs. When he got to her, they wrapped each other in their familiar embrace.

Maggie arched away slightly and reached for his stubble.

"You got old," she marveled, her thumb grazing his cheek.

Rakib's lips stretched into a smile. "Just a little."

As they unraveled from each other, Rakib tugged at one of Maggie's braids.

"What's this?" he asked, facing the Artist's sculpture.

"*The Brain*," Maggie said.

The Brain loomed large up close, dark and shiny, almost hard to make out each individual sphere in the night. The entrance to the building just beyond where they stood was shockingly bright in comparison, its glass doors gasping open and closed as residents came home from god knows where. It reminded Maggie of a hospital, how permanently illuminated and electric it was 24/7.

She looked over at Rakib, who, like everyone before him, had also reached out to touch *The Brain*. He knocked against it twice with his knuckle, confirming that it was, in fact, hollow.

"One of hers?" he asked.

"Mm-hmm."

"Manufactured?"

"Nope," Maggie said, realizing for the first time the significance of that statement. The Artist, always so small next to John, had made *The Brain* with her two little hands.

"All her, except the one big one," Maggie said. "They made that with Chinese explosives."

"It's stainless?"

"I don't remember."

Maggie considered explaining the piece as the Artist had, but she could already feel the limits of her language and all the ways she would inevitably fail in relaying the details to Rakib. *There's a forest beneath* The Brain, *all crooked, gnarled roots she made by hand. It weighs nine hundred pounds. It's science fiction. Machine and man, nature and metal.*

"Hmm," was all Rakib said before slipping his arm around her waist.

"Should we go in?"

Maggie took a long, deep breath as her answer.

Rakib burrowed his nose behind her ear. "If it's really terrible, I promise we'll find something better to do."

They turned away from *The Brain*, and Rakib led Maggie inside, his hand never leaving the small of her back.

MAGGIE HAD FORGOTTEN what it was like to walk into a room with Rakib. As they crossed the threshold into the apartment, everyone turned toward them, like an entire field of flowers turning toward the sun.

A less than subtle queue formed to rub elbows with Rakib. First, he clapped hands knowingly with Ovie and Faheem, apparently having met them at another event in London. Then he kissed Dawn's cheek and asked about her aunt, who he somehow knew was in between rounds of chemo. Dawn pressed a hand to her heart, clearly touched and suddenly emotional.

Maggie idled at the edge of their intimate moment, unsure of where to look or how to stand.

They touched cheeks again, which gently allowed for Rakib's departure. "Call me next week," he said. "We'll get together while I'm in town."

Maggie wondered how long he'd be in town, and if he'd say something similar to her when they inevitably parted.

John and the Artist were the next to be gurgled up from the crowd.

"Rakib," the Artist said in breathy excitement. "So nice to finally meet you."

"You two haven't met?" Maggie said, confused then how he'd be here at this party. Maggie hadn't invited him, and John didn't even know him.

"We've emailed," she told Maggie before addressing Rakib. "We're, of course, crushed you couldn't make it to the show last night," she said, invoking the royal *we*, "but we're thrilled that you're here now!"

"I was sad to miss it," Rakib said, after explaining how he landed from Milan just this morning. "Sounds like it was unforgettable, though."

The Artist blushed.

"You'll come to the next show," she said, raising a glass, and they all toasted to the next show, which Maggie couldn't believe there was already an idea for. It had basically been twenty-four hours since the last show.

"Hey, man," John said finally. He reached out a hand, which Rakib shook in one sure motion. John had been standing silently behind the Artist, his eyes flicking back and forth between Maggie and Rakib.

"This is my brother, John," Maggie said.

"I can tell," Rakib said. "You're practically twins."

John's mouth remained a still line.

"We don't want to keep you," Maggie said, softly laying her palm against the Artist's bare shoulder. "It's your party, and we get to see you all the time." She was almost ashamed of her mimicking *we*, but not enough to stop herself.

Maggie beamed at the Artist, and the Artist beamed back.

John shot Maggie a harsh glance before he and the Artist drifted back into the living room, sucked into another conversation about the Artist's work and her illustrious brilliance.

"I think your brother really likes me," Rakib said.

Maggie knocked her shoulder against him. "He's just like that."

They found themselves in the corner opposite John and the Artist, where, somehow, there were more people who were dying to meet Rakib. In the years since Maggie had last seen him, he'd become someone people had heard of. It wasn't uncommon for artists to know who the critics were, sure, but the frenzy that followed Rakib seemed out of proportion. He had become known for his taste beyond his critiques of art. His refinement transcended the medium, casting a liquidy gold sheen over restaurants, cities, people, and parties. His attendance at this party, at the Artist's apartment, made her a marker of his taste. Rakib had now become another one of the ways in which the Artist was anointed.

It was exhausting, this greeting of so many people. Rakib wove Maggie into every introduction, several of which were with gallery directors and managers who she'd met at countless openings. Each

"Nice to meet you" confirmed her suspicion that they didn't remember who she was. But now, under the glow of Rakib, people seemed open to receiving her. If Rakib hadn't let go of her in the thirty minutes since he'd arrived, they figured Maggie must be interesting.

"You should see her work," he said to more than one critic. "It's breathtaking."

Maggie tried to be gracious as Rakib continued to shine the spotlight on her, but she squirmed every time he referenced her art. Maggie's work had changed so much since Rakib had seen it last that she worried his praise no longer applied. She couldn't even conjure the last piece he'd seen of hers. Undoubtedly something nascent and embarrassing from undergrad. Still, Maggie blushed and smiled and thanked Rakib at every complimentary turn.

"Valentina," he said in a low and joyous voice. Rakib wrapped his arms around her, and she nearly disappeared.

"Rakib!"

Valentina took Rakib's face in her hands and kissed both his cheeks. He pulled Maggie toward them by her wrist and began introducing her.

"Ah ah ah!" Valentina stopped Rakib mid-sentence, placing a hand against his chest. "I've already met your girlfriend with her spectacular arms."

Neither Rakib nor Maggie bothered to correct her. Instead, they all broke out into flirtatious grins. They sipped their drinks and slipped into the conversation Maggie had hoped to have with Valentina the first time she'd approached her. Rakib mentioned Valentina's latest piece in the magazine—which Maggie, thankfully, had also read and loved. It was a review of the newest installation at the Gagosian, and Maggie was able to slip in a few meaningful comments that drew Valentina out even more. Maggie could tell she'd had a few drinks since their last encounter. Her touch was more frequent, but lighter. Her face had flushed, and she hadn't stopped smiling since Rakib had held her in his arms.

Valentina was about to exchange emails with Maggie when a stout gray-haired woman with Lucite glasses tugged on Rakib's arm. Before Maggie could piece together what was happening, their trio was severed. Valentina drifted into a new cluster of guests.

Apparently, this woman with lenses as big as coasters remembered Rakib from a show he'd reviewed in Miami. She was the gallery's director, and he'd eviscerated the show. In his review, Rakib called the artist pedantic and said his work lacked nuance regarding the experience of migrants appearing at borders around the world. Now, he and the director were alternating between terse jabs and backhanded compliments. Maggie was fading in and out of the conversation when finally, she decided she'd had enough. She whispered in Rakib's ear, "Bathroom," and escaped down the hall.

The best part of any private room during a house party was the quiet. Maggie peeked over the ledge of the tub to see half-melted ice still floating. She dipped her fingers in and considered how she'd never taken an ice bath before, but she could now see how it might be appealing. How the water coming up like a collar around her neck might feel like a relief. She patted her fingers dry, then held her face in her hands to cool down. She looked in the mirror and saw how her fingers, thin and red, contrasted with her face.

Maggie had forgotten the absurdity of her outfit until she saw the overalls in her reflection. She tilted her head and unclipped one of her straps. *Is this chic?* she wondered as she left the strap hanging down by her waist and eyed the lace from her bra peeking through her white tank top. It was decidedly not chic, so she looped the strap back over her shoulder and was clipping it into place when someone knocked on the door.

Maggie hadn't even begun to say "One second" before Rakib walked in.

"Oh," Maggie said, confused. "Hi?"

Rakib mirrored her knotted brow. "You said 'Bathroom.' I thought— "

Maggie laughed and pressed her hand flat against his chest as she shook her head.

His eyebrows jumped, and he smirked at the miscommunication. "My mistake," Rakib said, stepping toward her.

Maggie let him hug her.

"It's not so bad, is it?" Rakib asked.

"It's terrible," Maggie said into his shirt.

She could feel a rumble in his chest when he laughed.

"I know," he said. "It really is."

Another knock came at the door, and Maggie pushed her body from Rakib's. It turned out that tearing herself from him was as painful as it ever was.

At the edge of the bathtub again, Maggie plunged her hands into the ice, searching for whatever drinks remained. The water reached up to her elbows, and still she could find nothing. Rakib encountered the person entering the bathroom, talking with them in animated tones, though Maggie didn't bother trying to make out what they were saying. Eventually, she stood, holding two cans.

"Last ones." Maggie's voice was completely flat, unsure if what she'd said was even true.

It was the Lucite woman blocking the doorway. Her cartoonishly wide smile and stretched red lips made Maggie feel like they were in a fun house, everyone's image completely distorted and disturbed.

She and Rakib squeezed past her into the hall.

"Here," Maggie said, turning suddenly. She steered them into the bedroom.

Maggie set down the still-wet cans and sat on the edge of the bed. Rakib stayed standing, taking in the room. Scattered all over the floor were the paintings John and the Artist had pulled from their walls in preparation for the party. Rakib began pacing around, observing all the work at his feet.

He refrained from speaking as he passed from frame to frame. Occasionally, he lifted a small piece to examine a detail. The most he'd said was "Hmm," until he got to an abstract triptych, which came up to his chest. Painted directly on slabs of wood, it was too heavy to lift, so he squatted to eye level.

"Have you seen this?" He looked up at Maggie, whose arms were crossed. The bathwater had soaked through the denim overalls, leaving a dark horizontal trail across her stomach. Rakib's tone did not suggest whether he liked or disliked the piece.

"Yeah," Maggie said, afraid to tell him that she had painted it for John and the Artist as a housewarming gift.

It had been nearly impossible to come up with something that would move her brother. He hated realism, claiming the paintings looked too literal and, usually, unsettlingly religious. He didn't like abstract work either, because, in his words, he never knew what he was looking at. "I just like things that are easy on the eye," he said with a shrug. Then, of course, she had wanted to appeal to the Artist, too.

Maggie had come up with a gentle abstract that spanned three panels. Each a swirl of monochromatic shades—pink, yellow, and green—resembling a flower Maggie had researched with meanings like friendship, longevity, and peace. She had painted them on wood she'd snuck out from their old apartment as it was being demolished, preserving some of the old in what was new.

The Artist had cried when Maggie presented it to them. John had said the wood was "pretty cool."

"Hmm," Rakib said in the same tone he'd uttered it a few minutes ago. It was the most disinterested sound in the world. Maggie instantly wished she were dead.

"It's beautiful," he added.

Standing up, Rakib spotted John's stethoscope on top of the chest of drawers. He lifted it toward Maggie. "Real," he said, "or art?"

"Real," she said, her cheeks taut and rosy, unable to contain the pleasure that came with his approval of her piece. Rakib swung the stethoscope from his finger. John must have had a late shift recently; it was the only reason Maggie could imagine that his belongings would be in this room. He only ever slept here so as not to disturb the Artist.

Rakib plugged the stethoscope into his ears and closed the gap between them.

"Let's see if you're right," he said.

He planted the metal disk against Maggie's chest, and she pulled away with a little gasp.

"Cold?" Rakib asked. Maggie nodded as she looked up at him. She could feel her eyes widen and her pupils dilating. Rakib pressed the stethoscope against her lips.

"Can you hear me?" Maggie asked in the smallest whisper. Rakib nodded.

She skimmed her parted lips against the disk and asked, even softer now, "What's my name?"

"Müjde," he said without blemish. He lowered the stethoscope and let it rest against his torso.

Maggie didn't remember telling him her real name—not in college, not over text, not tonight. She searched her overalls, illogically, thinking perhaps it was written somewhere, though she knew it wasn't.

"How'd you know that?"

"We're old friends, Müjde," he said. "I know a lot of things about you."

The more he said her name, the more she felt like she was drunk.

"Like what?" she asked.

"Well, I know your name. And I know Rob is on his way, *baby*."

The way he said it—*baby*—punctured her. It was cruel to make fun of Rob like this and, almost worse, mortifying to think that she was someone's baby.

Rakib produced Maggie's phone from his pocket.

"It was on the floor in the hallway," he said, handing it over to her.

The screen showed a text from her mother, a text from her father—addressing her by name instead of *kızım*, his usual term of endearment—because she'd ignored the text from her mother, and a text from Rob. Maggie returned the phone to her pocket.

"Does 'baby' mean it's serious?" Rakib asked.

Maggie nodded gravely.

"That's too bad, Müjde," Rakib said, saying her name for a third time.

7

JOHN BURST INTO the guest room without knocking.

"Oh," he said.

Maggie leaned to see past Rakib, who was blocking her view of the door.

"Hey," she said.

Rakib eked through the narrow passage at the foot of the bed and buried himself into the back corner of the room.

"Everything okay?" John asked. His eyes flicked to the stethoscope next to Maggie on the bed. "Worried about your heart rate?"

Maggie bunched up the stethoscope and put it on the bedside table.

"Not exactly," she said.

"Trouble breathing?"

Maggie stood up and walked toward John.

"Dying of boredom, actually," she said, and pushed her way through to the hallway.

She expected he'd follow her, peppering her with more annoying quips, both of them reverting to their ten- and eleven-year-old selves, but Maggie didn't hear John's footsteps behind her. She turned her head, figuring he was ready to bellow at her from afar, but John had disappeared into the room and closed the door.

The party had not dwindled as the hours stretched toward midnight. The living room was the same cauldron of guests, constantly mingling in different permutations. Now among them, however, was Rob. He looked tired but happy. He was in a group of artists, standing heads above them in his navy suit. Someone had taken his jacket, and his hair was mussed. He ran one hand through it, the other hand holding a beer. He broke into a smile, the one slight gap in his teeth, off to the side, was exposed. Maggie snuck over to him, slid her arm through his, and clung tightly to his torso.

"Hey!" he exclaimed.

"Hi." Maggie nestled into the space beneath his shoulder, which over the years had become tailored to her frame. "You made it."

"Of course he made it!" the Artist said loudly, nudging into their circle.

Rob leaned down to Maggie and pecked her quickly on the lips. She stayed facing him, waiting for perhaps a second kiss, or even a third, but none followed.

Previously hidden behind the Artist and now emerging was Maisha, a particularly bohemian sculptor who, though cool in her own right, often trailed the Artist as her groupie. Rob and Maggie always found her pleasant even when she was being grandiosely laid-back. Tonight, she wore loose-fitting olive-colored pants and an oversized cream cardigan that had no buttons, but was tied together just below her flat breasts. She must have freshly shaved her head, because Maggie could see her scalp.

"Maisha," Maggie said, untangling her arm from around Rob.

"Hey, babe," Maisha said, welcoming Maggie in her low register. The sheared hairs on her scalp tickled Maggie's cheek as they hugged.

"Maisha was just about to do a reading for me." The Artist reached for both of Maisha's hands and squeezed them in excitement.

"A reading, huh?" Maggie said, thinking of the only time she'd let Maisha read her tarot. She had just begun dating Rob and was feeling uneasy about their union. They'd connected in most of the big important ways, but Maggie was worried about the small things they kept missing. At a party, not unlike this one, Maisha pulled three cards for Maggie and looked into her eyes. "The man you're asking about is trustworthy," she'd said, seemingly moved by her own discovery. Trustworthiness was not exactly one of Maggie's concerns about Rob, but the omen felt like such a firm affirmation of his character that Maggie figured she should keep dating him.

"Be careful," Maggie said to the Artist. "Maisha is powerful."

The Artist squeezed Maisha's hands tighter and made a high-pitched, gleeful sound. They hurried away from the group and found an open spot on the floor to sit.

Rob's hand traveled up and down Maggie's spine.

"What'd I miss?" he asked, surveying the crowd.

"Nothing," Maggie said, leaning deeper into him. "Just a bunch of snobs."

John and Rakib emerged from the guest bedroom. John looked drunk, red-faced and sweating slightly. Rakib, walking behind him, looked unchanged, the same combination of handsome and stoic that he'd been all evening. Rob ticked his head toward them.

"Who's that?"

John had made his way into the kitchen while Rakib continued straight toward them. Maggie tried to consider how best to describe him to Rob. Which paths she would lead him down, which details she'd obscure from him.

"I know him from undergrad," she began. "He's a critic now. Hardly stays in one place for more than a month."

"What's his name?"

"Rakib," Maggie said, and suddenly he was upon them, sticking a hand out to Rob.

"The famous Rob," he said.

Rob detangled himself from Maggie and shook Rakib's hand for longer than was usual or necessary.

"Rakib," Rob said, finally releasing his hand. "Maggie says you're old friends. College days?"

"Yes," he said, smiling. "Long time ago."

Maggie felt sick to her stomach, each of them performing a bizarre ritual of laying their claim to her. Rob announcing Rakib's stats, saying *See? Nothing she's hidden from me.* The fondness in Rakib's voice as he said "Long time ago," knowing it was a time Rob could never access. Flaunting that he had known a version of Maggie she would never be able to show Rob.

Rakib flexed a vein in his neck. Rob cleared his throat.

As Maggie ran through every excuse she could possibly bring up to take them away from here, the Artist streamed past in a blur. She was holding on to her dress with one hand and wiping the skin beneath her eyes with the other. Maisha stood by the door, talking solemnly to John. John's brow was furrowed, and he kept leaning closer and closer to Maisha, so much so that his body threatened to topple over and crush her.

"Sorry," Maggie said in Rakib's direction, already turning toward her brother. She excused herself and approached John and Maisha to split them apart.

It took Rob a moment to catch on, but eventually he followed and took John aside to sit on the couch while Maisha and Maggie stayed close to the door.

"What's going on?" Maggie asked Maisha, who kept her eyes cast down.

"I told her that not every reading is spot on." Maisha spoke quickly, still not looking at Maggie. "I told her that if the conditions aren't right, if I don't do them in my studio or if I'm not surrounded by the right energy, the reading could be thrown." She kept repeating how she'd *told* the Artist.

"I'm sure it's fine," Maggie said. "What did you tell her?" *All this hysteria for tarot cards,* Maggie thought. *What would they do if real tragedy struck?*

"There was death, obscuring of the self, and flames. Everything was in flames." Maisha reached into her satchel and pulled out a pack of cigarettes. "I'm gonna go, babe," she said, finally meeting Maggie's eyes. She looked panicked, like an animal that had been stepped on but survived.

"Sure, sure," Maggie said in the most soothing voice she could summon for something so absurd. "I'm sure she'll be fine."

Maisha hugged Maggie goodbye. As the door closed behind her, Maggie made her way to John and Rob. John, slurring his speech and mumbling nonsensical threats about Maisha, kept trying to get up to check on the Artist.

"You guys stay," Maggie said to them. "I'll make sure she's okay."

Maggie let the party fade behind her as she made her way back to John and the Artist's bedroom. Everything felt so trivial and stupid. Her overalls, her relationships, her chosen career. Now, tarot cards. What would she even say to the Artist? "Cards you can order online cannot actually determine your future"? Isn't this something every human being should know intrinsically? She knocked against the bedroom door.

"Can I come in?" Maggie asked, cracking the door open an inch.

She could see the Artist leaning over a chest of drawers, looking at her reflection in the mirror that hung above. Two images of the Artist pressed tears from her eyes. Maggie knocked again and slipped half her body through the door.

"Hey," she said gently, bringing the rest of herself into the room. "Everything okay in here?"

The Artist let out a puffy sigh that suggested she was laughing at herself.

"I know I'm being ridiculous," she said, rolling her eyes. She kept twisting her tissue into a tighter and tighter spiral and dabbing it into the inner corner of her eyes.

She plopped down on the bed, and Maggie sat next to her. The Artist threw herself backward with surprising force and lay down, though she kept her knees bent and her feet on the floor. Maggie made her body into the same shape beside her.

"When Maisha said 'flames,' I just saw the whole apartment go up." The Artist waved her hands around before folding them on her stomach. "John, all the paintings, my whole life—I just saw it all engulfed and— " She cut herself off to steady her breath.

Maggie waited to see if she'd keep going.

"And it scared me that my mind could make that image. That my mind could set John on fire." Her voice cracked when she said John's name.

As if acting of its own accord, Maggie's hand reached over toward the Artist's. Their fingers folded together neatly, like shutting a paper fan, and Maggie squeezed. They both looked at the ceiling.

"Do you think it'll all go up in flames, Maggie?" the Artist asked, turning to face her.

Maggie met her eyes and saw up close how glassy and blue they were, threatening to overflow. She squeezed the Artist's hand again.

"I really don't," Maggie said. "I really, really don't."

The Artist smiled with her lips shut tight. She clearly didn't believe Maggie, though Maggie could tell she wanted to. They both looked at the ceiling again. The Artist rustled to sit back up, though she seemed to struggle with whether or not sitting back up was actually what she wanted.

"We can stay here a while," Maggie offered, lying perfectly still.

"Yeah?" the Artist said in a small voice. Her lower lip flapped into her mouth as she tried to settle her crying.

"Of course," Maggie said.

They lay like that, holding hands and staring straight up, for an hour. They listened as the din of the party grew softer and softer until all the guests had left and the apartment was finally quiet.

8

EVERYTHING ABOUT COMING home contributed to disturbing what felt like a perfect silence. The keys jangling in the door, the heavy clunk of the lock coming undone. Even things that didn't have sound, like the light flooding in as the door split open to their apartment's dark hallway, felt like the harsh crash of a cymbal. Maggie stepped in first, followed by Rob, and when the door shut, they stayed in the dark, unzipping their coats and removing their shoes. They were relieved to be home, the lights off, the floor unsticky from guests they hadn't had over.

Maggie padded into the kitchen while Rob struggled to take off his boots, one hand on their freshly painted wall, the rest of him hunched over and exhaling in effort. By the time he made it into the kitchen with her, she had flicked on the overhead lights and slid the dimmer to its lowest setting. Maggie pulled two glasses from the cabinet and filled them with water.

"Was work okay?" she asked, handing Rob a glass. "I forgot to ask when you came back."

"It was fine." He sighed. "Fine."

Rob had fitted himself onto one of the stools at their kitchen counter and rounded himself forward, his elbows on the counter and his head in his hands. Everything about him was softened by the lights' orange glow.

"You were gone a while. I figured it must have been bad."

He stared down at their stone countertop, dark and textured, and passed his fingertips over the granite. Slowly, he pushed his body upright and opened himself to Maggie, stretching his arms wide and resting them on the seats on either side of him.

"Come here," he said.

Maggie stood above him, tucking herself into his spread wing. He tilted his head back and exposed his throat. Maggie thought about John saying how much Rob loved her. He must be in love with her to expose himself like this. Arms spread, neck bared, his soft underside stretching up at her. Only something made stupid by love would present itself like this to another, completely unable to protect itself should one decide to strike. Maggie reached for Rob's neck, wrapping her hand delicately around it, passing her thumb over his Adam's apple.

"That feels nice," Rob said.

He closed his eyes, and Maggie slid her hand to the back of his neck, supporting it like one would a child. She kept her thumb to his lips now, parting his lower lip slightly.

"So it was bad?"

Rob nodded.

"Did you fix it?"

He shrugged.

Maggie's hand grazed his entire face, moving from his mouth, across his stubbled cheeks, and landing gently against his ear. She ran her fingers through his hair, swirling it in different patterns.

"And you came back anyway?" Her voice was small, almost girlish with disbelief.

Rob opened his eyes.

"Of course I did," he said.

Rob pulled Maggie into him. Both arms were tight around her waist, and his cheek warmed her stomach. When he released her, she bobbed only slightly away from him.

"Do you paint tomorrow?" he asked.

Maggie nodded.

"Even though it's Saturday?"

She nodded again.

"I have to finish the ceiling."

"And the women," Rob said, his voice low and serious.

"Yes," Maggie said. "And the women."

Rob stared up at her, his head still tilting backward. Maggie leaned down and kissed him. Once, then twice, then again, a third time. Behaving as if she could teach this to Rob so that when she gave him that same wide-eyed look, he might do the same.

MAGGIE WOKE UP in an empty bed. She dressed for a day of painting—not in her overalls again, but not in anything much nicer—and found Rob in the kitchen. He was standing in front of the coffee machine, already drenched from a workout and on the phone. Maggie maneuvered around him to make herself a cup of coffee and sat on the couch while she waited for his conversation to end.

He was frustrated, his voice loud and demanding, every sentence ending in a strongly punctuated stop. Maggie could tell he was talking to Tim, who they both generally liked, but who had lately become a sour topic of conversation. Rob was now saying that Tim needed to "step up," and "prove himself" if he really wanted to make partner at their firm.

Rob hung up the phone with a heavy sigh.

"Sorry," he said, turning to join Maggie on the couch.

"That's all right," Maggie said. She draped her legs over his lap when he sat down. "You're going in now?"

"After I shower," he said. "I'm meeting Tim in an hour."

Maggie felt bad hearing the way Rob said his name. Before Tim needed to "step up," his name was synonymous with having a good time. Rob and Tim were always getting beers after long days at the office, hitting the gym before morning meetings, or playing basketball on the weekends. Now, Rob could hardly say Tim's name without groaning.

"Think you'll be long?" she asked.

Rob looked over at her, already beleaguered before the work had even started.

"I have no idea."

KNOWING IT WOULD take at least nine hours to complete her ceiling tiles, Maggie hurried to the studio, hoping to avoid another day turning to night while she painted. She'd developed a way, an order, that made her work pass faster. If she connected certain strokes with a certain flick, dipping for more paint only when absolutely necessary, it almost became like painting the tiles two at a time. She sped through two domes' worth in the same amount of time she'd spent detailing the first one. The sun was still up when she finished, illuminating the whole piece as Maggie stepped back to look at the work she'd done.

The ceiling was perfect. Symmetrical, dimensional, and not distracting in its perfection. The way the sunlight streamed into the studio reminded Maggie of what shading work still remained. She'd have to darken certain tiles to show what time of day it was and to accentuate the inner curvature of the domes, but otherwise she was done.

Then came her women. Maggie was taken by how damned they all were. Meek in their small number. Seven was nothing in the center of her humongous canvas, the width of which was so vast that its negative space never seemed to end. The dark background swallowed them whole and created the illusion that they were shrinking, being sucked into the painting's core.

Maggie could feel the constraint of time pulsing all around her. It encroached on her neck, pressing itself into all her soft crevices. It was beginning to fill her nose and mouth, threatening to block her air supply. She could feel it pounding against her head in a constant low-grade headache. She had one more group critique before grant nominations would be announced. Then if by some miracle she was nominated, it would be a few more weeks before she knew whether or not any of this was worth it.

Avoiding her women was no longer an option. Maggie drew herself toward one she affectionately considered her almond-eyed girl. Her eyes were wide-set, making her a bit fishlike. She had thick eyelashes and a full upper lip that did not quite dip at the Cupid's bow. Her lower lip curved dramatically, weighted almost, so that her mouth cried open. Delicate wispy lines made up her eyebrows, which were archless and harsh. She had features, yet no distinct expression. This felt true for nearly every woman Maggie had created. They were incomplete, which cast an uncomfortable feeling of restlessness over the painting.

Maggie lost almost an hour to studying their expressions, no actual progress made beyond thinking. She considered the Artist and wondered if invoking the absurd could heighten the reality of their conditions. She thought of making their faces into drooping puddles, like a Dalí clock, or stretching their mouths into contorted, disturbing caverns, all yelping and shrieking. How could she draw their pain closer to the surface? How could someone look at her painting and think *Whoa*, the same word she and Rob had uttered when they saw *The Brain*?

With so much to consider, Maggie couldn't commit to abandoning realism just yet. Instead, she packed her things and hurried to catch the last moments of dusk before getting on the train. By the time she'd get home, everything would be dark.

THERE WERE NO signs of Rob in the apartment. All the lights were shut off, and the condition of the kitchen was the same as when she left—half a pot of coffee and their two mugs, left soap-filled in the sink.

"Rob?" Maggie called out.

She opened their refrigerator and poured herself a glass of wine. Crawling into bed with the wine and her phone, Maggie spent the evening scrolling online shops for things she half wanted but didn't need, clicking on articles that sounded interesting and leaving them open to eventually read. She periodically checked her messages with Rob to see if she had missed any, but there were none. He was still trapped with Tim, managing a mess Maggie couldn't even begin to fathom, apparently. Or he was elsewhere. With no way of knowing, Maggie finished her glass of wine, and then another, before washing her face and going to sleep.

9

"THEY'RE NOT VERY pretty, are they?"

Wade Richardson was the first to speak in Maggie's critique. Wade had very pale skin that shimmered blue under harsh light and a long, straight nose whose tip looked like a coiled piece of wire.

"If they were pretty, you wouldn't look," Camille said calmly, and the comment settled over the students encircling Maggie's painting.

Maggie thought of how hard it had been to look away at the Artist's show. Even though she had found the whole thing totally absurd, and occasionally disgusting, Maggie had watched the rind of each fruit make its way in and then out. They all did. There was something about suffering where everyone had to look.

Camille snuck a glance at Lorrie, who, through her thin, pressed lips, emitted a long, affirming "Mmm." A satisfied glimmer sparkled in Camille's eye. None of them were immune to the drug of impressing their advisor.

"Light strokes," Nadia said, sitting up. "The figures are harsh, but their strokes are light and subtle." She returned to her slouch, saying "Beautiful," before fully closing in on herself.

"Right, Nadia. Very nice," Lorrie said, and Wade scanned the painting with a knotted brow as if to find what he had been missing. "And you're right, Wade," she said. He snapped to attention, confused by how they'd all been right since they'd all made different points.

"They're not very pretty," Lorrie said. "They're not very anything."

This was not how Maggie had envisioned her final group critique. Admittedly rooted in fantasy, she had pictured more awe, more fawning over technical prowess. She'd hoped for grumblings of the grant, either an outright nomination from Lorrie or the jealous murmurs of her peers. "Not very anything" was not something she'd anticipated. Maggie felt her lungs straining to expand, heavy with doubt.

Anxiety among the graduating student body was at an all-time high as nominations had begun trickling through the grapevine. A photography student from Lebanon was nominated for her drone shots of the crisis in Syria. *War,* Maggie thought. *Another thing we all turn our heads to watch.* Performance Art had a few front-runners, but all neck and neck so far, none eking out ahead. Fine Arts in Drawing and Painting had no obvious nominees, no whispers, no gossip. There were so many students, which Maggie feared would be to their detriment.

"Not very anything," Lorrie said again of the women. "They're too subtle, Maggie. And where are the rest of them?" She lowered her head and peered over her glasses.

"Working on it," Maggie said feebly.

"I certainly hope so."

Maggie chewed at the inside of her cheek. A few one-on-one meetings with Lorrie remained for each advisee, but soon they would all arrive for the final critique—an abbreviated version of what they'd been doing all semester, except Lorrie would bring a tin of cookies and they'd leave early and drink themselves relieved at a bar nearby. Until then, Maggie had to make thirteen more women appear out of nowhere. And had to make them *something*.

Wade's painting was nearly finished, light reflecting off it like a Vermeer. Nadia would show them a final cut of her mixed-media project in two weeks. Everyone was falling neatly into the timeline except for Maggie. And Camille. But majoring in two disciplines meant Camille wouldn't be graduating for another year. She had no idea what it was like for the others, on the precipice of the rest of their lives.

"Disappointing," Lorrie said, issuing her verdict. "I was expecting more this late in the semester."

The taste of blood swirled in Maggie's mouth. She had bitten herself. Lorrie hadn't hinted at this in any of their earlier meetings. It had been the complete opposite, even. Lorrie had been encouraging, seeing the promise in Maggie's ideas and execution, always saying how she was on to something. *Disappointing* shattered every notion Maggie had built about how well things were going.

Camille gave her a sympathetic look, which Maggie both appreciated and hated. Without a final project to destroy her spirit, Camille was free to be lovely. Her fleshy, round face and thick-lashed doe eyes were totally unencumbered. She was also twenty-two, and as smart as she was and talented as she was, her brain had not yet fully developed, and Maggie resented that. She was soft and malleable, her hands constantly shaping herself.

Discussion perked up as Wade mentioned the painting's proportions. When Maggie was still in the early stages of planning, several in the group thought the women would seem too big for the space at three and four feet tall. The consensus now seemed to be that they filled the space naturally. The room they were in felt real and the women life-sized, even though, of course, everything was scaled down. It would be interesting to see if that "natural" element remained when the canvas was stuffed with women, Lorrie quipped, reminding Maggie of their absence for a third time. Nadia and Camille bickered about the feelings the figures evoked. Nadia felt they looked hopeless, a skilled portrayal of how society tears down women until their spirit is beyond repair. Camille was not ready to give in to darkness. She saw the women as dying, yes, but there was hope. How could there be so much light illuminating them if they were supposed to be hopeless? Nadia was then drawn back to how many there would be. With twenty women dying from edge to edge, how could the message *not* be hopelessness? Their back-and-forth eventually quieted, and everyone looked at the painting instead of each other.

"The tiles are nice," Wade conceded. "Good symmetry."

"Yes," Lorrie agreed. "Well done on the tiles."

Lorrie folded her notebook, and it became clear that this was the parting thought. Nice tiles. They all began to pack their things and wrap their scarves.

"You're next, Nadia." Lorrie said. "Two weeks, yes?"

"Could we push it to three?" Nadia asked. She mumbled something vague about editing issues and hard drives.

"Yes, fine, fine." Lorrie sighed. "Three weeks is fine. Wade, will you switch with her, or do you both want to go in three weeks?"

"We can both go," Wade said, like he was sharing the day with Nadia instead of admitting that he, too, needed the extra time.

"Maggie, I'll email you for our check-in," Lorrie said. "And then we're all ready for the end of next month?"

Collectively, they made general sounds of agreement, all nodding, all supposedly ready for the end of next month, when really, they all felt sick to their stomachs.

"All right, then," Lorrie said with the distinct air of dismissal. "Go and be young."

They shuffled toward the door, Maggie and Wade the last to be fed through.

"I'm sorry I said they weren't pretty," Wade mumbled behind her.

Maggie looked up to see that his face had drooped into seriousness.

"That's all right," she said.

"I don't know why I say things sometimes. After listening to you guys, you're all so"—Wade rolled his lips together as he sought the word—"thoughtful."

Maggie placed a hand on Wade's shoulder.

"Don't worry about how you said it, Wade." She wasn't sure she had ever said his name aloud to him before. "You were right. They're not very pretty. And you want to know something else?"

Wade cast a nervous look at her.

"They're going to get even worse."

Wade swallowed. Unsure of how to respond, he moved cautiously around Maggie, passing ahead of her to get to the stairs.

"See you," she said as he started his descent.

"See you," he said back, spiraling down.

Maggie stood at the top stair, watching Wade's floppy hair pop up and down before he disappeared around a curve. She turned around and reentered the studio. Finally, in the wake of them all, she could get back to work.

WHERE ARE THE rest of them?

Maggie brought herself next to one of her women and began making her a friend. *A sister,* she thought, before shaking off the idea. *No, a stranger. A beggar. An enemy.*

Maggie made the woman's torso long, like her own, looming slightly over the figure beside her. She would generate three more bodies to make up for lost time. Three a day for however many days, never mind their faces. *Get the bodies in the room. The pain can come later,* she said to herself. Maggie needed them there on the canvas before she could ruin their beauty.

Beauty had not really occurred to her until Wade's comment. Were they not very pretty? They abided by the same symmetry as the tiles, eyes level with one another, not freakishly wide apart or close together. Maggie had delighted in their mouths, most of which were full and plump in a way hers would never be without cosmetic intervention. She hadn't made them *ugly*, she'd thought. She'd made them real.

Maggie outlined three new bodies. A tall, grim-reaper-ish woman and two twins, heavyset, hands swollen with arthritis, standing next to each other like bowling pins, staring down the alley at whatever was coming to knock them over. Maggie sketched the folds in their necks, knowing the real work of their flesh would take time and shading.

But suddenly, over the course of a few hours, there were ten figures instead of seven and the painting became a more serious thing in the room. Like the women were going to step out of the work and join her in the studio. Maggie imagined them confronting her, demanding answers. They all spoke different languages, and yet she could still understand them. Why had she brought them into this world? Couldn't she see that they had things to do? Mouths to feed, places to go, work to be done? Why was she making them a spectacle? They were just trying to live. Couldn't she leave them alone?

JOHN LISTENED AS Maggie let out a dramatic sigh.

"I am trying to unclench my entire body," she said into the phone.

The sun had set, and all its light had drained from the studio. Maggie had packed her things and cleaned up, and now was lying on the floor, with her head against the wall that held her canvas. She lay there with her eyes closed, because every time she opened them it looked like the painting would fall on her. Sometimes she opened her eyes just to make her heart race. When the feeling became unbearable, she closed them again.

"And how is that going?" John asked.

"I think it's working."

Maggie imagined being absorbed into her piece, the chemicals in the paint dissolving her bones and turning her into something soft and gel-like.

"Is this why you called?" He sounded more tired than annoyed.

"No," Maggie said. "I just wanted to see how you were."

"I'm fine."

"And how's the Artist?"

"She's also fine." John took an exasperated breath. "How are you?"

"My fingers hurt." Maggie squeezed her hands open and closed.

"Vocational hazard."

"I suppose so."

She imagined telling John about her critique. How awful it had been, but that she had spent the day working and now felt like she had overcome feeling totally sorry for herself.

But then he took a mocking tone. "And how's Rob? How's Rakib?"

"Don't do that."

"Do what?"

"Ask me how Rakib is like he's somehow attached to me."

"Are you two unattached? I couldn't tell."

Maggie opened her eyes and let the painting make her heart race.

"What are you trying to say?"

"That you should be careful."

"Careful of what?"

"I don't like him, Müjde. He's no good."

"No good? Jesus, when did you start talking like Uncle Mehmet? Should I cover my shoulders, too? Remind me, what direction should I point toward to pray?"

"I'm just saying he's an asshole. And prior to dating Rob, you were, unfortunately, naturally drawn to assholes."

"You don't know what you're talking about."

"It's late, Müjde. I have to go."

Without further explanation, John hung up. Maggie dropped the phone onto her chest. She rolled the hard curve of her skull against the linoleum floor. She thought of her painting, her life. Nothing to do but so much to be done.

IO

ROB TRIED TO be quiet as he entered the apartment, but Maggie could hear him peel off his shoes at the front door after it clicked shut, the slow shuffle of his socks coming down the hall. When he made it to the kitchen counter, Maggie shut the refrigerator.

"I'm up," she said softly, trying not to startle him. "You don't have to be quiet."

Maggie strained to see without the light of the fridge, but she caught something shedding from Rob. His body became slumped and heavy, his steps leaden as he walked over to her and wrapped his arms around her waist. She absorbed him without thought, shouldering the entirety of Rob as he buried his head into her neck.

"It's so late," Maggie said. She arched away to look at him and pushed his hair back from his forehead.

"I know," Rob said, his voice was low and wrought. "They are killing me with this project in Japan." He fell back into Maggie, and they began to sway. She ran her thumb over his highest vertebrae, all the tension gathered at the base of his skull.

She spoke barely above a whisper. "I hate it when you come back this late."

"I know."

"Do you have to be up early, too?"

Rob's head, still pressed against her, nodded yes.

"Do you want to go to bed?"

He shook his head back and forth. Then after a moment, he said there in the dark, "I don't want to be anywhere but here."

"I THINK WE should go to Turkey." Rob's voice had the intense, gravelly quality it only had immediately after sex.

Maggie made a humming sound. Her eyelids were heavy as she focused on the feathery touch of Rob's fingertips running up and down her arm. He had been so sweet, swaying with her in the kitchen. A small part of her wondered, though, if there really was a project in Japan. She shuddered as she considered this, and Rob pulled her closer.

"Cold?"

Rob traded the gentle glide of his fingertips to the full, warm friction of his palm. He showed no signs of being with someone else. He smelled like himself, vaguely sweet and emollient. Like almond oil. He wasn't flighty or nervous or strange. He'd even remembered to ask about her critique, rolling his eyes at Wade and pressing her close when she said how awful it had been. She told him how Lorrie said her women weren't "very anything" and how she wanted to sink into the center of the earth. By then, Rob had enveloped her, taking on her whole being, the way she had when he'd first come home.

"So," he said. "What do you think?"

"What do I think of what?"

"Of going to Turkey."

"I think... *why*?"

"Because it would be nice." Rob tucked a strand of Maggie's hair behind her ear. "We haven't been since the wedding."

Her cousin Serdar's wedding had been a production. Hundreds of people in the oppressive heat of late summer, never-ending platters of food served on round dishes the size of truck tires. The whole ordeal ended with a fireworks show that felt like it was ushering in a new millennium. Serdar's father, Mehmet, and Maggie's mother wept every other day, lamenting that their mother hadn't lived long enough to see the first grandchild get married.

Rob had come with Maggie and seen it all. He'd listened patiently to all her family's memories, secrets, and gossip. Had his coffee grounds read by Maggie's painfully thin Aunt Gökçen. They went on long meandering walks around the city every night for a moment away from all the people Maggie was related to. They had been together for just under a year, and Maggie had never felt so in love.

"Are you up for that again? My whole crazy family? Because you know if *we* go, my parents will go. I doubt John can get the days off, but even if he can't, Sofia would sooner die than be left behind."

Rob laughed, which jostled Maggie's head from side to side.

"They're only crazy to you. They actually like me."

They adored Rob. How strong he was, how willing to help with every task. To them, every Turkish word he butchered sounded like honey. "He's getting good," they said at least once a day.

"Okay," Maggie said. "We can go to Turkey."

"When you graduate," he said.

"Maybe."

"Maybe," Rob said back to her, letting his hand fall still tangled in her hair.

IN THE DAYS leading up to her meeting with Lorrie, Maggie had become obsessive. So determined to turn her fate around, she spent every waking hour at the studio. Her hoard of women had grown to fifteen and the canvas began to feel cramped. She had measured it, of course, made sure there'd be room for five more figures. But looking at what space was left, more felt impossible.

The world around her morphed as Maggie spent her days in the studio. John had all but disappeared. Maggie knew this was less about him being busy and more about him having "caught" her with Rakib. Caught her doing what, it was unclear. All she had done was sit, but John was running with whatever he thought he'd seen.

It was not the first time he'd punished her like this. Whenever Maggie veered from "the path," John would exert a sort of brotherly vengeance against her. Couldn't she just be easy? Her whole life—couldn't she just get good grades, and be on time, and respect Mehmet's wishes as a guest in his house? Why wouldn't she just marry Rob already? He really loved her—did she know that? Was there a reason she insisted on being so difficult?

But did it not occur to anyone that Rob had yet to even ask her to marry him? The likelihood of which felt like it was slipping away. The more time Maggie spent in her studio, the later Rob stayed at work. Most nights she was already asleep by the time he came home. They'd practically stopped having sex, other than the night Rob said they should go to Turkey. Which had been that sweet, sort of wild, speechless sex that happens in the dark, and everything is a tangled blur. But that felt so long ago now. Lately, Maggie slept so deeply that she didn't even register when Rob slipped into bed or when he'd snuck out again in the early morning.

Rakib had texted her twice, but Maggie hadn't responded. John had effectively spooked her with his ominous "be careful," even though she knew there was nothing to be careful about. No matter how well-meaning he may have been, John had no clue what Rakib was really like. No one even came close to knowing Rakib the way she did. None of these emerging-artist darlings, none of these gallery owners or art collectors. And still, when he'd texted—once inviting her to drinks and then to an industry party—Maggie was inexplicably paralyzed. She stayed in the studio. There was work to do, and even if she was confident Rakib wouldn't derail her, it couldn't hurt to stay focused.

The constant in Maggie's world, regardless of whatever state anything was in, was her mother. Texting and calling despite Maggie's inability to answer.

The thing everyone had in common was that they really couldn't understand. They had no idea how much was at stake. How hard she'd have to work to win the grant. How she was already behind, and how Lorrie was disappointed. How the women didn't just come to her; she had to find them. How five more was a lot, even though fifteen were already there. How far away she was from done. How deeply afraid she was that none of it would work.

Maggie had the sneaking suspicion that no matter how much she poured into her painting, it was too late. Her fate had already been decided.

THE LIGHT FLOODING through their windows meant Maggie was late. Lorrie would beat her to the café, and there was nothing Maggie hated more than making a professor wait. It made her look young and frivolous and stupid, all of which she might be, but she didn't want Lorrie to think so.

She pushed herself from the bed and launched into her closet to put together an outfit that might convince the world, since she could not convince herself, that Lorrie was spending time with her out of desire rather than out of obligation.

Wrapped in her nicest coat, Maggie emerged from the bedroom to find a full pot of coffee with a note beside it.

Breakfast with Can, be home after xx

It was nice that her brother was at least speaking to one of them, she figured. Maggie left the coffee on the counter and rushed out the door.

A TRAIN PULLED away just as she arrived at the station. Maggie looked at the schedule, then at her phone, and saw that she was on the verge of being fifteen minutes late. She debated texting Lorrie but decided against it, figuring she didn't have her phone on her anyway.

"If I'm not at home or at work, I probably don't want to be reached," Lorrie had said in one of their first meetings. "So I make myself unreachable."

In their early days, Maggie had wanted to be like Lorrie. She wanted to throw her hands up and give her phone to whoever passed her on the street and continue on phoneless and free. However, being young and inextricably tied to the digital world, Maggie couldn't bring herself to give up her phone entirely, so she went through a phase of "forgetting it at home." Over time, she realized how naive and ridiculous this made her, so she loosened her grip on the dream of becoming Lorrie. Now, Maggie only wanted to impress her.

A train pulled up, and Maggie found a seat next to a window, stared into some middle distance, and thought of how much had changed over the course of a year. She had been so afraid to ask Lorrie to be her advisor that Maggie drafted six versions of an email before awkwardly stumbling through a speech in her office.

"Where do I sign?" Lorrie had asked, peering over her glasses, already reaching for the form before Maggie had finished asking.

Now they were into their final meetings, and Maggie felt a pang at how much she'd miss Lorrie. Her sharp yet generous critiques, the way she talked to the piece as much as she talked about it. Maggie would miss their Saturday morning debriefs and the ritual of them: Meeting at the café, the one cigarette—sometimes two—that Lorrie smoked on the way to the studio, the comfort of seeing her intimidate new baristas with her direct demand for a small black coffee. She was the type of person people referred to as a pistol. Lorrie didn't say much, but what she did say was clever, and she was impeccably chic. She was serious, which people could get lost in, and if they did, they missed out on the fact that she was funny.

The train lurched to a stop between stations and sat in a dark tunnel. Maggie caught a glimpse of herself in the window. She was shocked by how deeply set her under-eye bags were, and she could hear her mother's voice. *You even had them as a baby.*

Maggie pulled concealer from her purse and placed a single dot beneath each eye, using her reflection to guide her. She blotted the makeup with her ring finger until the dark rings were at least tended to if not remedied. Maggie stopped blotting and took a moment to give herself a once-over. She could see a man across the train watching her. She raised her eyebrows at him, but when he refused to break eye contact, she looked down.

A man's voice came onto the intercom to announce they had been halted by a train stalling at the next station, so Maggie closed her eyes and waited. Dread flooded her body as she thought of her painting. *Disappointing,* she could hear in Lorrie's voice. It seemed such a harsh edict, impossible for her to claw away from.

When Maggie opened her eyes, the man across the train was staring at her. He had opened his mouth to say something when the train jerked forward suddenly and they were moving again. Maggie focused on her lap as they pulled into the station, and the man got up. "Pretty bitch," he muttered as he passed her. She leaned her head back and clenched her teeth. Only one stop away from whatever Lorrie would say next.

LORRIE WAS SHARP, but not unforgiving of her lateness.

"I suppose no one befriends an artist because they are punctual," she said to Maggie. Lorrie offered her a quick smile before ushering them both into the warmth of the café.

"Small black coffee," Lorrie said to a barista with a metal spike emerging from her forehead. She turned to pour Lorrie's coffee, and Lorrie whispered into Maggie's ear. "She'd be perfect for my godson."

Maggie laughed, though she wasn't really listening.

"Red eye, please," Maggie said when it was her turn to order. "With an extra shot."

The spiked barista raised her eyebrows. When Maggie failed to waver, she asked, "When we pull one shot, it automatically makes two. You want both?"

"Sure," Maggie said, and she paid nine dollars to potentially give herself arrhythmia.

When the barista handed over the drink, Maggie could see how dark it was. Peering down into it, it looked like the coffee would swallow her instead of the other way around. Maggie fitted a lid over the cup and looked around for Lorrie. She spotted her outside again, one gloved hand holding her coffee and one ungloved hand fussing with a lighter for her cigarette.

"Let's go," Lorrie said as Maggie exited the café. "A student I failed is inside, and he keeps asking what he can do for extra credit. He's driving me crazy." She ticked her head back, and, sure enough, there was Stephen Gordetsky, a first-year drawing student who was dying for Maggie to set him up with the Artist so the two could collaborate and make something he kept calling "next-level." Stephen stared at Lorrie from his table and began clamoring over his friends to make his way to the door. Lorrie turned the corner and began walking toward the studio, with Maggie just a few steps behind.

Maggie had a hard time speaking during their walk. Lorrie

occasionally filled the air between them with humorous anecdotes and cutting asides, but mostly she smoked. Maggie *mm-hmm*ed when necessary between sips of her intensely bitter coffee. She was distracted by thoughts of whatever job she'd have to get if the grant fell through. And then immediately began berating herself for essentially planning her life around the equivalent of winning the lottery. She felt like a fool. Like she deserved the emotional beating that came from her brother. If only something like that would change everything and make her a different person.

When they reached the front of the studio, Lorrie turned to look at Maggie straight on.

"Something on your mind?"

She took a drag of her cigarette that drew her cheeks in so close together Maggie imagined them actually touching inside Lorrie's mouth.

"It's nothing," Maggie said, waving a hand, then fitting it in her pocket to turn off her phone. She shrugged. "I think I'm just nervous."

Lorrie took one last drag before she stamped out her cigarette.

"Well, let's pull the Band-Aid off, then."

MAGGIE'S PAINTING WAS loud. It had always been big, but in its inception, the colors were so muted that the work hardly announced itself. Now, illuminated by the studio's three enormous windows, the piece was cacophonous. The dark-crimson backdrop overwhelmed at first but then acclimated the viewer, somehow immersing them in a welcoming aura. It felt as though the figures whooshing around behind the women in the foreground were really moving. She had made so many people, Maggie realized as she watched Lorrie take in the piece. She could feel them in the room with her.

Lorrie's method of assessment was like a show in and of itself.

Maggie stayed perched in a folding chair as Lorrie walked to the center of the piece and slowly took steps backward, to bring more and more of the canvas into her field of vision. From the center of the studio, Maggie knew, she could see everything. Lorrie stood still for several moments before reversing her trajectory and observing everything up close.

When interrogating a piece she found truly consequential, Lorrie would tuck her hair behind her ears and lean toward whatever it was that interested her—a photograph, a sculpture. Sometimes in her office, Maggie would see her reading a newspaper like this, the print hovering inches from her nose. This gesture became the metric with which Maggie measured her success as an artist.

Lorrie's hands were buried in her pockets, and the wispy hairs framing her face remained painfully untucked as she approached each of the women in the painting, scanning their faces from top to bottom. Lorrie got to the woman that Maggie thought most resembled herself and stood straight up.

"You have to do something about their faces," she said, turning to Maggie as she finally spoke. She freed her hands from her pockets to wave one of them at the women. "All their mouths are open."

Maggie looked to her women and realized Lorrie was right. All their mouths were wide open. It was not something she had done intentionally. It was as if each woman, as Maggie made them, had taken a deep, gasping, breath.

"It's like they're all shrieking the same shriek," Lorrie said.

"Isn't that kind of what they are doing?" Maggie found herself saying, shocked to be speaking during a critique, when she usually kept to herself, furiously scribbling notes. "They're all crumbling beneath the same kind of suffering," she continued. "They all are shrieking the same shriek."

"The suffering can be the same," Lorrie said, "but they can't all *look* the same."

Maggie couldn't decide if she agreed or not.

"You need to go out and see them," Lorrie said. She had now abandoned the painting and was solely facing Maggie, who was confused.

See who?

Lorrie leaned closer to her, flinging her wrist in a small circle.

"Go to the communal spaces you're trying to evoke. Go to museums, watch movies. You need to see what all sorts of women look like. You'll see what I mean."

Lorrie turned back to the painting, contemplating, and Maggie realized that Lorrie was scanning the piece for herself. *I'm not in here,* she was saying. Lorrie's mouth was not open. She was not letting out some long, wretched screech.

Lorrie pulled her glasses from her face and began cleaning them with the edge of her charcoal woolen shawl.

"It needs work," she said definitively, which seemed to Maggie only a minor improvement from "Disappointing."

Lorrie placed her glasses back on her face and spoke again. "If you can get it into decent shape, I'd like to submit it for the grant."

"What?"

"I haven't nominated a student in years, so it would really have to be something else." Lorrie's eyes traveled the length of Maggie's body, then the length of her canvas, and landed back on Maggie. "Something outstanding."

"Of course."

Maggie almost hugged her, but she stopped herself when she realized they had never hugged before. Instead, Maggie thanked her again and made another appointment to meet in a few weeks.

Lorrie took a long look at Maggie, like she was searching for something. She narrowed her eyes, her gaze darting all across Maggie's face. Maggie leaned back and waited for it to be over.

"Don't get lost," Lorrie said to her.

She left the studio without waiting for Maggie's response.

Alone now, Maggie walked toward the center of her piece, just as Lorrie had. She took slow, even steps backward and tried to see the work with new eyes. In the center of the studio, Maggie took a deep breath. She thought of Lorrie's critiques and saw them each in sharp focus, glaring in error on the canvas.

"Don't get lost," Maggie said aloud to herself, and headed to the sink to mix new colors.

II

MAGGIE COULD HEAR Rob inside the apartment. He must have been on the phone, laughing. She twisted the key in the lock and walked in.

"Of course she doesn't know," Maggie heard him saying.

Light flooded her vision. The apartment was warm and bright and entirely dizzying. She kicked off her shoes, hung her coat in the closet, and made her way toward Rob's voice.

"I'm home," she called from the hallway.

Rob said something indecipherable and quickly hung up. His phone was already in his pocket when Maggie reached the living room. He leaned down to kiss her before she fell into the couch.

"Who was that?" she asked. She pulled a pillow to her aching lower back and crossed her legs.

"Tim," Rob said, giddy and strange. Maggie had to squint to see him. He was fully dressed and wearing dress shoes.

"Who doesn't know what?"

"Lillian. He's planning some elaborate surprise for their anniversary."

"Romantic," Maggie said, lolling her head back and closing her eyes. Tim, though Maggie liked him well enough, was anything but romantic. And Lillian, who Maggie liked not at all, was like a wet cat. Imagining her on the receiving end of so much as a box of chocolates or a heartfelt card could turn the world on its axis.

Rob was watching Maggie from the step above the sunken living room.

"How was your day?" he asked. "What did Lorrie say about your painting?"

"She said it needs work."

"Jesus," Rob said. "Is she as hard on everyone else as she is on you?"

"I don't know."

Maggie rubbed her fists into her eyes. She debated telling him she might get nominated. Rob was the only person in her real life who knew the grant existed. It was the reason he'd told her to quit her day job. Insisted, really. He offered to support them both for the year so she could have more time to paint. Rob was a true romantic.

"She thinks I'm on to something," Maggie said, dropping her hands. "Like I'm close."

Rob slowly fit himself into the negative space her body made on the couch so that they looked fused together. His cheek was pressed against her forehead.

"I'm sure you are," he said softly.

"It doesn't feel like it."

Maggie stared into the dark gray of Rob's slacks. She picked a thread and snapped it between her fingers, rubbing the spot to eliminate whatever small hole she may have created. She pulled away to look at him.

"It's Saturday."

Rob furrowed his brow.

"You're wearing work pants," she said.

"I have to go in," he said apologetically. "Just for a little while."

Maggie could feel her eyes widen, filling with tears in a way she couldn't resist. She tried not to blink.

"Are you avoiding me?"

"Mags, are you being serious?"

Rob strengthened his grip around her, but Maggie kept the distance between their faces. She could hardly speak.

"You're always leaving."

They sat, half fused half pulled apart, and stared at each other until Rob spoke again.

"I'll be quick," he said. "An hour max."

Too exhausted to do anything but believe him, Maggie coiled into Rob. He held her on the couch for a few minutes more before detaching himself and making the long walk down the hall.

"I'll call you when I'm coming back," he said from the front door, his voice strong and booming.

"Okay," Maggie murmured. Her throat had begun to ache. And when Rob finally closed the door, she pulled her knees into her chest and fell asleep.

MAGGIE WOKE UP to the buzzing of her phone in her purse.

"Hello?"

"Well, well, well." Rakib's voice streamed into her ear.

Maggie looked around the living room. She had fallen asleep with all the lights on.

"Who is this?" she asked.

Rakib laughed. "Don't be cruel, Müjde. It's not in your nature."

"Oh? And what is my nature?"

There was something so pitiful and hopeful blooming inside her chest, waiting for Rakib to tell her what she was like.

"It's been so long I'm beginning to forget," he said. "You've been ignoring my texts. Also not in your nature…"

"You're right." She laughed. "That's not like me at all."

"I'm covering a show downtown. Come meet me."

She could hear the traffic speeding all around him. Maggie turned to face her phone. It had gotten late already. She opened her texts with Rob to see if he'd said anything about coming home soon, but he hadn't.

"You there?" Rakib asked.

"Yes, sorry," Maggie said. "What time?"

"Come whenever," he said. "I'm wrapping up drinks nearby." Rakib's voice was clipped from her as they hung up.

Maggie texted Rob.

Going to a gallery opening, may be home late

She rolled from her position on the couch to put on fresh clothes. Maggie was careful in how she dressed—first for Lorrie, and now for Rakib, hoping to look chic and remind him of her nature, whatever it was. She sprayed herself with perfume and combed her hair well enough that she could wear it down. As she was setting foot out of the apartment, Rob texted her back.

Sounds good, he said. *I'll miss you*

Maggie was more restrained than Rob when it came to the word *miss.* There were years where she hadn't seen her parents, and they'd never once uttered "I miss you." Not because they didn't miss her, and not that they didn't acknowledge her absence in other ways, but *miss* was such a strong word. *I long for you,* it sounded like. Maybe Rob had meant it that way, Maggie considered, but lately, it did not seem like Rob was the one who longed.

IT WAS A quick train to the gallery. A bulky man in a suit held a clipboard and dutifully checked in the couple ahead of Maggie. She stepped up to him once they'd disappeared inside.

"Name?"

"Maggie," she paused as she watched his eyes scan the page.

"Arif," she prompted. "Maggie Arif."

"Müjde?" the man asked, furrowing his brows hard toward each other. Maggie thought about the harsh line it would carve in her own forehead if she did the same.

"Yes, that's me."

He moved aside and allowed Maggie in, where she was greeted by the humid, wet heat of a crowd.

At first, she swiveled her head to look for Rakib, ready to tease him for using a third party to flirt with her. The poor security guard, having to confront her real name for Rakib's agenda. But the pieces were so beautiful she became easily distracted. Because of her own painting, the word *big* had lost most of its meaning, but the paintings were sizeable, maybe three feet by three feet, and the artist had achieved a grainy quality that made it seem like the viewers were looking at scenes through a fogged window.

Maggie was staring at a scene by a lake, a misty day but still with enough light to be considered nice weather. There was a couple close to the water, a man and a woman, and their construction amazed Maggie. They were somehow perfectly articulated yet thinly veiled in something that felt like gauze. You knew exactly what they looked like, yet you couldn't tell for sure.

"Found you," Rakib appeared by her side. It took Maggie a moment before she could look away from the piece.

"They're amazing," she said. Her tongue felt slack in her mouth, her jaw finally relaxed for the first time since she'd started her painting. Being in the presence of something so beautiful had stupefied her.

"Aren't they?"

They stood side by side, not touching or speaking until Maggie could feel Rakib inch himself closer to her. The flesh of their arms pressed together—hers bare, his sheathed in a black suit jacket. Sometimes it felt to Maggie like this was the kind of thing that would keep her alive. The subtle acknowledgment of her body by another.

"This is what it feels like," she said, still not looking at Rakib, though she could feel him looking at her.

"What do you mean?"

"Making things," she said. "This is what it feels like. Like you have this perfect and clear idea—it's almost holy in how perfect it is, like God beamed it down into you. And then you try to make it, little obedient human that you are, and you can't. You can't make it even half as good as God instructed, so it has this slimy, dusty film over it. And you can see through the film, but you can't see how perfect it really is."

Maggie turned to see Rakib smiling at her, shaking his head.

"I love the look you get when you're being serious."

Maggie wilted away from him, snapped from her earnestness.

"No, no," Rakib said, pulling her back with both hands. "You're right. It is serious." Rakib had lowered his voice and somehow sharpened it to a point.

"It's incredibly serious and you look beautiful illuminating it for me." He made sure to stare directly into her eyes. "Sometimes it feels like you're the only person forcing me to be smarter."

Forcing felt like such an odd word to Maggie. Like she was beating Rakib into understanding, like listening to her was somehow unpleasant or medicinal.

They returned to the painting, and Maggie felt newly crushed by its beauty.

"They're so far away," she said, and she could not hide the sadness in her voice.

Rakib wrapped an arm around her waist, and Maggie leaned her head against him. He rubbed her side, and she felt soothed by the back-and-forth of his touch.

RAKIB AND MAGGIE were like two trees that had been planted next to each other four hundred years prior. As time slowly seeped past them, they bent further toward each other. Their limbs curled into loops, locking into each other in a way that felt natural and eternal. They rooted themselves in front of a grid of miniature pieces and scanned for which piece would strike them hardest.

"You made something like this junior year," Rakib said, pointing to the third row of paintings. They all depicted women obscured by the artist's masterful fog.

"The middle one," he said.

Maggie stared at the middle woman, articulated well enough that it was clear she was all bone. Knobby and skeletal.

"My ghost," Maggie said, remembering their nickname for the small piece she had painted.

"She was beautiful. The crags in her face like the side of a mountain," Rakib said, turning to look at her. "You had that natural skill for faces even then. Like you were born with it."

Maggie was unsure of how true this was. Or worried if it was once true that now, according to Lorrie, it no longer applied. Maggie's eyes narrowed as a man came to stand next to Rakib, who, staring intensely at Maggie, didn't notice until the man tapped him on the shoulder.

"Mimmo!" Rakib's voice was filled with surprise and delight.

He unentwined himself from Maggie and forcefully pulled the man into a hug. They fell into a hushed, emphatic string of Italian.

"This is Domenico Ricci," Rakib said, eventually pulling Maggie in. "We met the first year I lived in Milan. He's the artist."

"Bella," he said, leaning in to kiss both her cheeks.

Maggie was struck by how young he was. He must have been a scrawny teenager when he and Rakib met all those years ago. Domenico was fidgety and nervous and unlike any Italian Maggie had ever met. He had dark hair and dark eyes, and after his two seconds of flattery, she could see he was only concerned about the work. Maggie touched her chest and gestured toward the first piece she'd seen, the couple by the lake.

"It kills me," she said in the rustiest Italian. She had taken an intro class the semester Rakib was abroad so she could sprinkle her emails with embarrassing confessions of affection and yearning. She hardly ever spoke the language aloud.

Domenico touched a hand to his heart and bowed his head. It was the only moment he'd stood still since they started talking. Rakib gave Maggie a look of pride and satisfaction. He turned once again to Domenico, and they continued in their clipped Italian.

Domenico broke from their conversation to look directly at Maggie. "Party?" he asked.

Maggie let out an airy laugh. There was something delightful in how straightforward they were forced to be with each other without a common language. She shook her head.

"Not tonight," she said.

Domenico's face fell, but he shrugged. "Next time," he said.

"Yes," Maggie said. "Next time."

Domenico gave Rakib details before kissing them all goodbye.

"You can't swing by? Just for a drink?"

"I should get home," she said. "Rob's waiting for me."

"Right," Rakib said. "I forget that you're practically a married woman."

Maggie rolled her eyes. She leaned into Rakib for one last embrace before tearing herself away.

"There's another show I think you should see. It opens next week," he said as they parted. "I'll send you the details."

As Maggie spun around to leave, she wondered if he would know that artist, too. It was beginning to feel like the only way for her to break into this world, the world in which she supposedly already lived, was Rakib.

Maggie caught one last glimpse of the couple by the lake and sighed, marveling at the talent small, fidgety Mimmo had.

THE APARTMENT WAS black when Maggie returned. She tried to be quiet, taking her shoes off noiselessly, as Rob had done the other night, but when she entered their room, the bed was made. No one was home.

She flicked on the overhead lights and let herself make noise, moaning as she entered the bathroom to wash her face, letting the full rush of the tap flow instead of a polite dribble.

"Where are you?" Maggie asked aloud to the empty room once she'd slid into bed.

She checked her phone. No new messages from Rob, just the last one he'd sent:

I'll miss you

12

ROB HAD COMPLETELY floated away from Maggie. She'd tried to ask him what happened the night she came home from the gallery, and his excuse was work. It was only supposed to be an hour, but things ran late. Couldn't she understand? Work late, work late, work late. Work drinks. Projects in Tokyo, Paris, Dubai, and Sydney. Time zones.

Maggie wondered how big work's breasts were. If work was kind or smart. What if the worst was true? That work was completely ordinary and bland. That Maggie couldn't even compete with someone plain. The thought of work left Maggie exhausted and husked from herself. She was now only the shell.

MAGGIE STARED UP at the ceiling as Rob got dressed. Threading his belt through its buckle, he told her it would likely be another late night at work.

"We've got a big presentation this week and then the client dinner on Friday."

The haze of sleep hung over Maggie. Her eyelids bobbed open and closed like a doll's. Phrasing it like this—"*the* client dinner"—was Rob's way of reminding Maggie that she was also expected to attend.

"Who's we?"

"I'm splitting this one with Tim," Rob said. "It's a big account. More than enough to go around."

"Ah," Maggie said, her head crinkling against the pillow as she moved. "I take it he'll be at dinner, then?"

"Yes, and Lillian, too."

Maggie remembered the first time she met Tim. He was easy to like, always smiling and saying something pleasant and unremarkable. She felt an immediate fondness for him, for how simple he made life out to be. Maggie met Tim at one of the several rec basketball games she had attended to support Rob. He was one of twelve mostly White, corn-fed, corporate-American men on the team, all of whom were generally good-natured, easygoing guys. They put on suits in the morning and pretended to be men, but in their real lives they were just boys, same as they were out on the court.

And then there was Rob, who fell into the same categories, but who was different in ways that Maggie clung to for reassurance that she'd picked someone well suited to her. Rob read three different newspapers in the morning and always told Maggie what was happening around the world. He liked obscure films that Maggie had never heard of and ate anything that was presented to him. Never one for creature comforts, Rob was always willing to brave something new.

While there was nothing wrong with his teammates—Maggie liked them well enough—she could never marry any of them. And what she really understood was that they could never marry her. She was from another planet. Men like Tim married women like Lillian—slightly stuck-up brunettes who at some point in their youth had issued an ultimatum: Grow up and marry me or I'm leaving. The men didn't want to get married, but they didn't want the women to leave, so one summer, Rob dragged Maggie to a million weddings of Tims and Lillians all over Connecticut and the Hudson Valley. They all made Maggie incredibly depressed.

"Can you grab the dry cleaning at some point?"

"Mm-hmm," Maggie said.

A sudden sweetness came over Rob, and he came to Maggie's side of the bed and kissed her neck.

"I'll try not to be *too* late," he whispered. She heard clicks and zips and the grabbing of keys. Rob was gone.

Maggie rolled onto her side to see if she could sneak an hour more of sleep, but her phone pinged with a hieroglyphic text from Lorrie.

Hv you heardd of her? Smarter than she looks…

What followed was a link to an artist profile: NEW YORK'S LATEST DOWNTOWN GIRL. What a headline—latest, as if it wouldn't last. Another girl already champing at the bit. How long did one have to be New York's latest girl. A year? Two if they were lucky?

Maggie opened the article, and her brother's girlfriend's face filled the whole screen. All Maggie saw at first were her piercing blue eyes staring straight ahead like that one cover of *National Geographic*. The Afghan Girl, everyone called her. Except the Artist wasn't a refugee, with "haunted eyes." She lived next to Battery Park and did yoga on the rooftop gym of her building. Maggie scrolled lower, and a ball gag appeared in the Artist's mouth. Instead of a shiny red ball clamped between her teeth, it was a Magritte green apple. Bright and waxy and almost too apple-like to be real.

I know her, Maggie began typing to Lorrie. *I know her well, actually. She's fucking my brother and I've seen her fake-dilated!!! All 10 centimeters!!!*

Maggie erased the message. Instead, she sent:

Thanks for sending! I've been meaning to read.

Lorrie responded immediately.

Too much fluff in some of hr stuff but the idesas r good

Some n convo w your piece

There was a rush of relief in Lorrie's minor criticism of calling the Artist's work "fluff." Finally, another person who thought seeing this woman's every orifice was maybe a little much. Perhaps it even got in the way of her point. But the thought that their work was "in conversation" made Maggie's eyes roll. She cleared the article from her screen, unable to bring herself to read even a single sentence.

MAGGIE STOOD BEFORE her painting and sought which woman was supposedly in conversation with the Artist. *Which of you freaks is it?* Maggie thought. She had a sickening feeling that it didn't even matter. The piece was full of inadequacies—the veil between the viewer and the painting felt thick and woolen. The question was, how to thin it out. How to bring its perfection closer to the surface.

Maggie could feel herself losing her grip on reality, unable to see how good or bad her work had become. Whose mouth was open, and whose ought to be sewn shut? Was it the woman in the center ruining things, or the ones fanned out to either side? Was it their faces, or had she lost that "natural" element by making them all too big?

She glanced at the clock on the wall and saw she had lost the entire day to interrogation and doubt. It was 6 p.m. She remembered the dry cleaning, only then to realize that the cleaners had closed an hour ago. Rob had texted to say *Eat without me*. Work.

The thought of Rakib floated into her mind. He had disappeared after Domenico's show into the shadows of an after-party. Likely into the skinny arms of a young coked-out fashion-week model. He never sent Maggie the details for the next show. Days came and went, the opening unattended and unmentioned. She was tempted to text him: *Dinner tonight?*

She considered making Rakib an elaborate meal like the ones she'd tried to create on his electric dorm-room stove. Mini versions of her favorite dishes from home. He once said he'd only consider marrying a White girl if she cooked like Maggie. She remembered feeling proud but defensive.

"It's not like I'm *White* white."

Rakib frowned, as if to consider this, but said nothing. He just continued eating as Maggie brought her dishes to the sink.

Instead of texting Rakib, Maggie called her brother.

"Hello?" John answered the phone dopily, like nothing had been wrong between them.

"Are you done ignoring me now?"

"Ignoring you? When was I ignoring you?"

"I haven't heard from you in weeks."

"I have a job, Müjde."

This was as if to say she didn't. That she was twirling around in all the free time she had. How fanciful and silly her life must be.

"Are you there now?"

"No, I just got home."

"Do you want to come over for dinner? I'll cook."

John idled.

"She can come, too. There will be enough for all of us."

Maggie had given up her resistance of their union. John and the Artist had been together so long now, what was the point?

"Do you need me to bring anything?" John asked.

"Wine."

JOHN BROUGHT A weird, buzzy energy into the apartment. He kept bumping into things and asking "Was this always here?" as if he had never been invited over before. He struggled to open the bottle of wine he brought, and sloshed red all over the counter when he finally wrested the cork free.

"Jesus Christ," Maggie said, running a towel over the mess. "What is your deal tonight?"

"I'm fine."

John poured himself a glass he could swim in. Maggie poured herself half as much.

"And where is *she*?"

"She'll be here," he said. "She's just getting her head sized."

Maggie raised her eyebrows, but her brother didn't elaborate.

"Well, let's get started, then."

John reached into the paper bags on the counter and pulled out the pink hunks of ground beef and lamb. He unwrapped the cellophane packaging carefully and placed the meat into a mixing bowl. Now with a task, he had become relaxed and focused. He knew where things were again, pulling open a drawer full of spices and crushing dried mint between the heels of his hands.

Maggie chopped onions for rice. She should have used day-old rice, since that's what her mother added for dolma, but she hadn't cooked much lately. She hadn't eaten much, really. Mostly protein bars and glasses of water she never seemed to finish. Tonight, for the first time, she'd add uncooked rice to the meat and see what it yielded.

"Don't mix it too much," Maggie said to her brother, thinking of how their mother always issued the same warning. How if you overmixed the meat, it would become tough.

John didn't say anything and instead cleaned his fingers off into the bowl and ran the tap to wash his hands. He appeared next to Maggie again, ready to core the vegetables and dice their insides.

"Is it the Artist?" Maggie asked.

Her brother refused to look at her.

"Is it bad?" she asked.

John shrugged and reached for a tomato. He delicately carved out a ring where it had been severed from its stem.

John didn't like to cook—it was too much work and took too much time—but all his medical training made him an excellent companion in the kitchen. Each slice was precise and exacting. He cored out the vegetables with just enough skin intact that everything would still hold while cooking. Their diced innards went in with the meat, all eventually to be restuffed into their shells.

John mixed everything together. Gently, Maggie could see, just until combined. She hung an arm around him and hugged him from the side.

"Whatever it is, I'm sure it will be okay," she said. She ran her hand across her brother's shoulders. "You know she loves you."

Just as she finished speaking, the apartment buzzer rang.

MAGGIE TRIED TO stifle her gasp as the Artist appeared in the kitchen. She had a semisheer metal globe fitted around her head that fastened around her neck.

"Hey," Maggie said, hoping she sounded friendly.

John just looked at the Artist. His eyes, beginning to water, pleaded with her for some show of affection or kindness.

"Hey," she said softly and only to John. She used a voice one would use to hush a child, assuring him that everything was all right. "I just have to take this off," she added, jostling the cage a little, from side to side.

"Sure, of course," Maggie said, finding an unalarmed tone. "The bathroom is just down the hall."

When the Artist disappeared into the bathroom, Maggie kneaded an elbow into John as if to say *Go help her.* Sullenly, he followed in the Artist's footsteps.

Maggie began the delicate process of stuffing the vegetables, saving the onions for John, as she was known in the family for cracking their fragile shells. Once everything else had been stuffed, Maggie sliced potatoes in thin rounds to line the bottom of the pot. Her mother left them a quarter of an inch thick, while Maggie liked them thinner, so they'd crisp up and form a crust beneath the dolma.

Her mother had scoffed when Maggie first made them this way. "You must be my *Persian* daughter," she'd said, claiming Turks would never do such a thing. "We like our food to taste and feel like food, not burnt and crisped like coal."

The Artist emerged from the bathroom, cradling the medieval contraption in her delicate hands. John was not far behind her, his shoulders softened and his face rosy. Whatever the Artist had said to him seemed to bring John back to himself.

"How can I help?" the Artist chirped, setting the headpiece on the counter.

Maggie wiggled her beef-covered fingers. "You can pour the wine," she said as she cleaned off her hands.

The kitchen was lively in a way it hadn't been in months. The three of them milling around the island, John fishing another wineglass out of the cabinet for the Artist, the Artist opening and closing the fridge as ingredients were required, Maggie telling them all what to do and where to go. Suddenly they were on each side of her, and she was flanked by their warmth. All three glasses were full again.

"To Maggie," the Artist said.

They clinked, and Maggie could feel her edges expand to press into both her brother and his girlfriend. John eyed the hollowed onion skins. He looked at Maggie, and without her having to speak or move, he understood. He set his wine down and carefully began stuffing the onions. As he finished each one, Maggie nestled them into the pot with the rest of the vegetables.

She snapped a picture of the dolma all together and sent it to her mother.

Perfect, her mother responded.

And the tiny ones! Maggie sent back, proud of the skinny, innermost layers of onion John had managed to stuff without splitting.

Even better than me now

This made Maggie's heart ache. She wanted the praise and approval, of course. But she couldn't fathom either of them surpassing their mother in skill. The thought of it made her jittery and sad.

Maggie found the lone onion she had stuffed before deciding to wait for John. The skin had split, and she'd had to sew together with a toothpick. She plucked it out of the bunch to take another picture to send to her mother.

Not yet, she sent.

Maggie returned the onion to its rightful place and let John pour in the crushed tomatoes.

"And now we wait," Maggie said.

The three of them retired to the living room with yet another bottle of wine, the apartment slowly filling with the scent of bubbling tomatoes and freshly fluffed rice.

WHILE THEY WAITED for the dolma to cook, John became noticeably restless and kept disappearing into different rooms as Maggie and the Artist chatted on the couch. First, he went to the bathroom, shouting through the closed door that they didn't have any hand towels. Then he made it known that he was doing all the dishes that Maggie had left soaking in the sink, by clanking every lid against the side of every soapy pot. He ran the faucet and shouted over the racket that the rubber gloves were too tight on his hands. Finally, he ran out to grab something for dessert, even though Maggie and the Artist both protested—they hadn't even had dinner yet and they weren't really that hungry.

Maggie heard him pocket the keys from the counter. The lock in the door clicked, and Maggie and the Artist took a collective breath, both feeling guilty for relishing the silence John had left behind.

"Is everything all right with you two?" Maggie asked. A grainy film coated her teeth, sediment from the wine.

The Artist took a deep breath that made Maggie nervous.

"We're fine," she said. Her voice floated to a register Maggie had never heard come out of her.

"What does that mean?"

"Maggie, you have to know that I know how this sounds. Okay? I know it sounds preposterous." She paused and looked seriously into Maggie's eyes. Maggie thought immediately of the Afghan Girl.

"Ever since Maisha's reading, I feel like I've had a vision. Like my third eye has been blasted open."

The suggestion of this struck Maggie as violent and unsettling, but the Artist was buzzing. She looked like she was actively rejuvenating in front of Maggie. Old energy was sloughing off her, and she was being replenished with something lilac and new.

"I know what I want for myself, and I'm just trying to chase that."

"And my brother?"

The Artist slumped in her seat, the mention of John puncturing her high.

"And your brother..."

"He's freaked out," Maggie said, matter-of-factly. "If you go off and chase this thing, he thinks you'll leave him behind."

"Yes!" The Artist bounced in her seat. "Yes, exactly."

She rocked back against the couch and stared at the wineglass in her lap. Maggie went quiet, suddenly self-conscious that she had been open about John like this when he wasn't around. It felt like conspiring against him in some way, though Maggie hadn't meant it like that. He could just be so obvious sometimes.

Maggie folded her arms and pulled her legs up to sit cross-legged on the couch. She was about to speak, come to John's defense somehow, but the Artist interrupted her.

"I wouldn't sit like that if I were you," she said.

"Like what?"

"All folded up. You're closing yourself off to the universe."

Maggie uncrossed her legs and placed her arms by her sides.

"See?" the Artist asked. "Don't you already feel more open?"

Maggie nodded slowly, in constant disbelief that this was likely who John would marry.

"Definitely."

They endured a lull that felt like it stretched the space between them, pulling them into opposite corners of the room. They both drank more wine.

"Where's Rob?" the Artist asked.

"Work."

"Oh," the Artist said. "Isn't it sort of late?"

Maggie nodded, at a loss as to how to defend Rob, who she didn't even wish to defend. She looked around the apartment at all of Rob's things. Every sleek, curved shelf nearly empty. Architectural sculptures in black and silver and dark hammered copper. Maggie found his minimalism oppressive. *There's nothing here,* she thought. What a bleak message to send.

"Are you okay?" the Artist asked.

No one had thought to ask her such a question. Maggie was surprised that the one to ask would be the Artist, whose gaze usually curved so harshly inward that it formed a never-ending spiral.

"I'm okay," Maggie said, testing to see if this was the correct response.

"You two will find your way through. He really loves you."

"That's what I've been told."

The Artist scanned Maggie from top to bottom. She leaned back, lifting her glass from the low table before speaking again.

"Rakib seems quite fond of you, too."

"Oh? And what makes you say that?"

A smile spread across the Artist's face.

"Just from watching you the other night. Valentina asked me about you two—if I thought Rakib was going to propose." She laughed, and Maggie discovered that the ancient feeling of wanting Rakib to propose still lived somewhere inside her.

"Maybe in another life."

"Not this one?" The Artist raised her eyebrows.

"Not so far."

The Artist kept her unblinking eyes on Maggie.

"He spoke highly of you, anyway," the Artist continued.

"Is that so?"

"Said he's never seen anyone with more raw, natural talent. And of course, he mentioned how beautiful you were. He said Rob was a lucky man."

"Rakib certainly knows how to talk."

This released a giggly laugh from the Artist.

"You're right," she said, lowering her eyelids.

"Should I tell Can?" Maggie said.

"Tell him what?"

"That you're quite fond of Rakib, it seems."

The Artist covered her reddening cheeks with her hands.

"He's so handsome," she said, her voice low. Like this fact was dark and serious.

Maggie couldn't contain her own amusement. No one could resist Rakib, even the most bizarre among them.

"He most certainly is," Maggie agreed, drinking her wine in long, indulgent sips. "Handsome and dangerous."

A key turned in the door, and John's heavy footsteps made their way toward the living room. Maggie looked up to see he had completely mellowed from his outing and was pleased to return to his girlfriend and sister still drinking on the couch.

"What did I miss?" he asked. He brought his face to the Artist's and kissed her cheek quickly before popping up again.

"Just stuff," the Artist said.

Maggie leaned her head back against the couch and closed her eyes. She could tell John had lifted the lid to the pot on the stove. The smell wafted its way to the couch, and Maggie and the Artist sank deeper into the cushions. It smelled so good it felt like the scent alone could sedate them.

"It's ready," Maggie said, not motioning to stand. "Can you take it off the burner?"

She heard John slide the heavy pot. The Artist stood first and held a hand out for Maggie. As she pulled Maggie up, she squeezed her hand with a force that proved she was stronger than she looked. While it had surprised Maggie at first, the fact also felt like something she already knew. Slowly, they made their way to the kitchen together, their bodies warm and swaying slightly from the wine.

13

MAGGIE DID NOT have to open her eyes to know Rob had not come home. As her body slowly grew accustomed to waking, it sent her all the signs. The covers were tight around her, still tucked on his side. The bed was cold. Nothing smelled like man.

When she fluttered her eyes open, sure enough, his absence was confirmed. There would be a plate of aluminum foil-covered dolma on the counter. The bathroom would be dry, spared Rob's drippy morning shower. Everything would be still. Maggie was alone.

LORRIE HAD TOLD Maggie to go look at them. Go look at women. So Maggie went to the movies. The women at the theater were varied. Not a lot of young women going to the movies in the middle of the day, Maggie noticed. There were young women working the popcorn machine, though. One had chubby hands and short fingernails with chipped baby-blue polish. She was wearing a black short-sleeved polo with the theater's logo embroidered over her breasts, which were threatening to tear through the fabric.

Older women were there to see whatever was playing; they weren't picky. They wanted to be clued in to what was happening "in the culture," they kept saying. One woman wore exclusively leopard print. She had red lips and shimmering white eyelids, with mascara tracks above and below her creped eyes. She revealed crooked yellow teeth when she smiled at Maggie.

The women on screen were gorgeous. Hollywood. No wonder women were riddled with complexes. No wonder Maggie hated the curvature of her nose and debated, every other menstrual cycle, whether she should dye her hair blond. No wonder she had begged her mom to wax her arms in fourth grade. No wonder she'd tweezed her eyebrows into nineties oblivion in middle school. She still had patches that wouldn't grow back. No wonder none of the Tims would marry her. Even if Maggie could get herself close to Hollywood thin, she could never get herself to Hollywood hairless. Or Hollywood White. She couldn't fit into Hollywood ethnic, either. She was too White, really, to be that mysterious kind of beautiful, though the word *mysterious* had been lobbed at her and Sofia over the years. Secret orientalist code for *Why am I attracted to you?*

The movie ended, and Maggie felt dead and numb. The beautiful White man gets the beautiful White woman. Their vaguely ethnic friends, one Black, are happy for them and make up the most impossibly diverse wedding party to be seen.

Maggie had come out to see women, and somehow she got the sense that, in addition to being a woman wrong, she had come to see the wrong women. She left the theater and went in search of more.

GRACE CALLED MAGGIE, and Maggie ignored the call. *Can't talk,* she texted. *Looking at women.*

Grace texted back immediately. *I always knew your heterosexuality was just a phase.*

Maggie laughed. *FOR WORK,* she wrote.

Sure... Grace responded.

Then came another text. *Call me whenever. I miss you.*

Maggie went to MoMA and found more women—most of whom were misshapen and faceless. More suggestion than representation. Severe black blobs that haunted the canvas. Pale, pale, pale wives of painters.

The crowd was magnificent, however. Everyone speaking a different language, pointing at something and whispering to a loved one. Countless funky glasses, with colorful ropes keeping them safe and secure around necks. Women were every age, and some were exhausted, carting around disinterested children who were also exhausted, and vocally hungry. Some of the very young women, girls, were lovely. One girl was spinning and spinning in front of Matisse's *Dance (I)*. Her mother clapped as she spun, bobbing her head up and down in the same rhythm as her daughter's delighted hops.

A young woman had her arm hooked into the elbow of a stooping elderly woman, who had every plaque read aloud to her by her companion. The young woman was slow and gentle, carefully guiding them along the museum's perimeter, stopping as often as the older woman needed. Maggie was suddenly emotional, thinking of how far away she'd flown from her mother, wondering who would guide her when the time came.

Maggie called her mother as soon as she stepped out of the museum, aching for her closeness. To smell her warm motherly smell. To hook her arm into her elbow and walk and walk and walk. The phone rang only once.

"One second, canım." Her mother was shouting.

Maggie heard rustling before her mother returned on the line.

"Okay," she said, restarting.

Her mother was busy and frantic and nowhere near needing someone to gently shepherd her through a crowded space. She launched into the list of everything she had to do before Sofia would come home for spring break. Apparently, Sofia was bringing her roommate, Lisa. Lisa was an international student from Stockholm, who couldn't travel all the way home for just a week, so Maggie's mother had insisted she come home with Sofia instead of staying alone on campus. Now on the phone, Maggie's mother was so wrapped up in what Lisa would and wouldn't like to eat that she was too distracted to pick up the minor tone of Maggie's voice. Relieved that she would get away with missing her mother, Maggie let the frenetic ramblings wash over her as she began walking to the studio.

"What about pork?" her mother shrieked. Maggie could hear a shopping cart rattling and rolling as she spoke.

"She's Swedish, Mom, not Jewish. Besides, you don't even make pork."

"I'm saying what if she *only* eats pork, heh? What then?"

"Nobody only eats one thing, Mom."

"What about that silly girl your cousin almost married? New York. She only ate vegetables! What kind of wedding were they supposed to have? Everyone would think we had no money for food."

Before Serdar married Zeynep, he had dated a girl named Brooklyn during his last year at Oxford. She was there for her year abroad, and the whole family was simultaneously obsessed with and horrified by their relationship, none of them able to understand why she was named after a place. Serdar and Brooklyn were never even close to being engaged, let alone married, but that didn't stop the family from churning out baseless concerns that Serdar had been brainwashed and might propose to an American vegetarian.

Maggie transported herself next to her mother in the grocery store. She imagined slumping against the parked cart while her mom argued with the butchers. Their disputes always stressed Maggie out until she could see them laughing as they exchanged whatever was wrapped up that week. Three pounds of ground beef, enough lamb chops for ten people, even though they were only five, twenty chicken thighs to be roasted and shredded. Whenever Maggie ran to the store without her mom to pick up whatever had been forgotten, the butchers always asked about her. "Where's Mom?" they'd ask, as if she were the universal mother. Maggie didn't know this until she'd returned from college one summer, but once all the kids left home their mother started bringing the butchers leftovers from her elaborate meals and teaching them how to make Turkish dishes.

She came to know every butcher's name and their stories. Vincent, who strictly went by Vin except for with Maggie's mother, had just enrolled in classes at the community college and worked as many extra shifts as he could during school breaks. Maggie's mother was always asking him about his grades, telling him if he needed more time to study that she'd tell Frank to give him a day off. Frank was the veteran butcher. He'd been there the whole time Maggie was growing up and had always been sweet with her, even when her mother was being impossibly demanding. Frank had a wife and four boys, two fully grown and two who lagged far behind—ages nine and twelve. Maggie's mother snuck sweets to them whenever she baked. Finally, there was Milo. Milo was a stunningly handsome twentysomething, with ice-blue eyes and tattoos that crawled up his arms and threatened to take over his neck. He had started working there in Maggie's later high school years, and she refused to let her mother go up to the counter when Milo was working. It was Maggie's only chance at flirting before college, and she exercised those muscles whenever she could, insisting her mother go on to produce while Maggie ordered veal and batted her eyelashes.

"Three pounds, Vincent. Not two." Maggie's mother's voice boomed through the phone.

Lisa was lucky to be stuck with this woman for a whole week. She would make her whatever she wanted.

"I am sure whatever you make will be fine," Maggie said, wishing she could actually transport herself to her mother. Just for one dinner, just for one second of comfort.

"How was the dolma?" her mother asked, turning her attention to Maggie's world. "Can stuffed them so *nice*." She poured praise so lovingly over her son.

"Not as good as yours. It was too dry."

"We will make again when we go to Istanbul."

"What?"

"Rob told me yesterday. Tickets for end of May. We're looking. Baba is going to buy them this weekend."

"Mom, that was just an idea. We're not sure we're even— "

"Okay, canım, you go." Her mother's voice lapped over hers. "Vincent is weighing the lamb."

Maggie heard a muffled voice on the other end. "Hey, Müjde." Vincent's voice was low and cheerful. Having been introduced to Maggie by her mother, Vincent only used her real name. At first, the butchers chewed over her name like cud in their mouths, until one day it just came out smooth.

"Hey, Vin!" she shouted, unsure if he'd even hear her.

Maggie's mother had stopped talking to her. She pulled the phone away from her mouth so that the last thing Maggie heard was her talking to Vincent. Something about how he was cheating her with the price of the lamb.

MAGGIE ARRIVED AT her studio swirled in a strange, panicked trance. When had Rob told her mother about the trip? Last night? Texting her mother from the office but not bothering to text Maggie that he wasn't coming home? Anyway, hadn't Maggie said 'maybe'? It was all happening too fast, her life rushing toward her. She wanted to focus on the work, not flights. Not whether or not Rob would come home. Not whether or not Rakib would text her. Maggie just wanted to fix her painting. To see the women Lorrie had told her to and transpose them onto the canvas. To win $30,000. To have her own show and embark on the rest of her life.

She opened the door to the studio and flicked the lights on, newly arrested by her painting. She approached the piece. On the first day she started working on it, Maggie swore to herself she wouldn't paint her mother. She wouldn't paint her mother, or Sofia, or herself. Not her grandmother, her aunts, or any woman she had ever met. They would be universal women, women she knew without knowing. But as she came closer to the piece, she held her breath. There she was. Her mother. The central figure had her mother's mouth, full lips with the edges turned down. She was stoic and powerful and strong. And Sofia. Sofia showed up in the slight woman clinging to the edge of the group. Maggie's grandmother was the sturdiest among the painted women. Small in stature, but strong, with hands that had been worked to the bone. She stood off-center, with her hands folded in front of her and her eyes cast down, the way they were whenever her grandmother was thinking.

Horrified, Maggie found herself in the work. She stood next to the figure most closely resembling Sofia. As they did in life, the two looked similar. The same almond-shaped eyes, small ears like their father's. Maggie stood in contrast to Sofia with her slightly darker complexion—something that had always been a topic of conversation in their family. Porcelain Sofia was kept inside to preserve her pale skin while Maggie spent summers crisping in the sun. "Help Mommy inside, canım," she'd said. "Your sister is already ruined."

Her mother always claimed Sofia would thank her one day. But the summer Sofia was sixteen, she had a meltdown because Maggie looked more Turkish than she did. She even cursed their mother for giving her a name that was "so boring," in her words. Sofia never saw her name as the gift it was. Even if the only gift was being asked fewer questions. "No one here knows I'm not like them! That I'm different!" she'd said. Sofia was obsessed with being different, obsessed with her dark hair and light eyes and the few occasions she'd been mistaken as Persian or Arab. She desperately wanted everyone to know she wasn't like every other White person in America, while Maggie mostly just wanted to be left alone.

After the outburst, Maggie tried to be gentle with Sofia. She tried to understand her and resisted the urge to tell her she was being ridiculous. Their mother was at a total loss. To her, the kids weren't even Turkish. Other than John, they'd been born in the United States, their pronunciation was abysmal, and they had visited the country only a handful of times in their lives. "But you are Americans!" she'd said to Sofia, whose tears she couldn't understand. Maggie didn't fully agree with her mother's sentiment, either. They were obviously something in between.

Maggie looked at the version of Sofia she had painted. Her lost gaze, her pleading eyes looking around for someone to recognize her and love her, came across the canvas as a near-violent need. Of course Maggie had painted herself next to the image of her sister. Her figure held Sofia's upright, showing her the way. Showing her that there was a path for women like them. That she didn't have to despair.

14

MAGGIE CAME HOME to find Rob had laid her dress on the bed. It was a long silver sheath with a low back. Excessively beautiful for a client dinner, she thought, but Rob had liked it for this reason. "I want them to see how gorgeous you can be," he'd said when he suggested it. He had also suggested she wear her hair down. All Maggie heard in this was that she was somehow squandering her beauty with overalls and greasy braids. Maggie had warned Rob that one more "suggestion" would send her over the edge, and he backed down. When Maggie walked into the apartment with her hair trailing down her back in loose curls, he thanked her and apologized for asking in the first place.

"I'm just nervous," he said.

"I know," Maggie said, running her long, freshly manicured nails through his hair. They felt like foreign objects after an eternity of short nails with nothing coating them but a thin layer of grime. Rob shook her off and continued getting ready.

He was becoming threadbare from his late nights—irritable and always rushed. The whites of his eyes were sullied, and he was losing definition in his face. It was now sort of puffy and sallow.

He hadn't hugged Maggie in how long? She couldn't remember. He paced around the apartment, talking to himself, but only every few words were audible.

Maggie slipped into the dress while Rob made himself a drink in the kitchen. The fabric slid over her like a second skin, draping and pooling in beautiful platinum droops. She stepped into heels that would keep the dress from skimming the ground and held up the fabric that was supposed to wrap around her neck. She emerged from the bedroom to ask Rob to help her with the buttons.

"Whoa," he said, looking up from his glass.

Maggie just smiled.

"Can you help me?" she asked. "The buttons are so tiny, and my nails are too long."

She presented her back to Rob. He looped a fine thread over the three satin-covered buttons cinching the band around her neck. His head appeared next to hers, and his arms wrapped around her stomach.

"Thank you, Mags," he said.

Maggie turned around to face him and gave him a brief kiss on the lips.

"For what?" she said softly.

"For everything."

Rob released her. He went back to his drink, and Maggie disappeared again into the bedroom for earrings and a purse. For *everything*? Maggie was at a loss, feeling like nothing between them made sense to her anymore. At what point had they stopped speaking the same language?

Maggie was fitting her things into an impossibly small bag when Rob appeared in the doorway.

"Ready?" he asked.

Maggie looked up and saw that his face was getting red, sweat emerging at his hairline. She nodded.

"Great," he said. "Let's go."

TIM'S WIFE, LILLIAN, had just returned from the bathroom when the heavier of the two middle-aged clients was reiterating, for what must have been the fourth or fifth time, what an exotic beauty Maggie was and how Rob was such a lucky man. He was starting his third martini and spat a little as he spoke.

Exotic was the word Rob's mom had used when she first met Maggie.

"You didn't tell me she was so exotic!" she had said to Rob, meaning it as a compliment, though her voice was affected with a tinge of horror.

Unable to control his curiosity any longer, the client finally set his elbows on the table and asked, "Where are you from?"

Maggie looked to Rob, whose forehead was taut and shiny with sweat, so nervous that she'd make a scene. That she'd proudly declare "I'm *from* California," with a flourish he had once called obnoxious.

"I'm Turkish," she said, reaching for her glass in an attempt to drink any further questions away.

Lillian rolled her eyes, and Rob's forehead began to relax.

"My wife and I love Istanbul," the client said after yet another gulp of gin. "The Turks are such a warm people."

This made Maggie think of every screaming match she'd ever had with her uncle. Usually over where she was going, how she was dressed, and why couldn't she take Serdar and John with her? She felt so far away from them at this table, its white linens weighted with pebbles in the corners. Everyone drinking but nobody laughing.

"That explains the brows," the client's wife said. She winked at Maggie from across the table.

"But still beautiful," her husband added, chewing with his mouth open. "European."

Stunned, Maggie just smiled with her lips pressed tight. People felt comfortable with her like this often, like she would understand their casual disdain of the Middle East. How she, too, must be afraid of how *dark* it all was, in every sense of the word. She looked to Tim, who seemed not to notice anything, then to Lillian and the client's wife, neither looking up from their plate. Maggie was hoping someone would say something about another foreign city, and they could move on. But the man persisted, mentioning Topkapı, with intense force on each consonant, and lamenting the heat but fawning over the stray cats. Charming, he called everything.

"And the food!" his wife chimed in, feeling it safe to look up again.

"You have to have Maggie's baklava," Tim said to a less than subtle groan from Lillian. The attention feeding into Maggie—her appearance, her culinary aptitude, her *anything*—seemed a personal affront to Lillian, though Maggie wished it would stop more than anyone. And now with the fucking baklava.

Maggie and Rob had brought a tray to Tim's house when he first got promoted and he had invited them over to celebrate. People kept marveling in the same tone to Maggie, "You *made* this?" They were so effusive that Maggie quickly became uncomfortable. She kept repeating, "It's a lot easier than it seems," but no one cared to hear her. They asked how she got such flaky layers and went for seconds and thirds. Lillian's catered profiteroles were virtually untouched, and when Maggie went to claim one, Lillian told her not to bother. "Probably stale by now," she said.

Rob's shoulders finally dropped, and he ordered another round of drinks for the table, then chimed in about the baklava's syrup and how Maggie never used honey. This was always his line, the absence of honey. But no one used honey. It wasn't an ingredient she was omitting for something more labor intensive or innovative or pure. It simply wasn't called for. Maggie never understood what he was trying to say by mentioning it.

"We're actually going back in the spring," Rob said as he poured himself a glass of sparkling water.

"That's good," the wife said. "Beat the heat."

Maggie could feel her throat closing up. She looked into every face for something to ease her. But the client and his wife were besotted with her exoticism, Rob was besotted with himself for conducting the perfect evening, and Lillian was besotted with her rage. The other client—a cold, wiry, unmarried Frenchman who'd hardly spoken since they'd arrived—kept his eyes on Maggie as he muttered under his breath.

"Barbaric," he said above a whisper.

"Oh, Paul!" a voice chided.

Paul leaned back and flung his hand over the conversation.

"The whole Arab world, really."

Rob placed a sweaty palm on Maggie's thigh and squeezed. Lillian could hardly contain her pleasure, smiling into her wineglass as she sipped.

"Don't be nasty, Paul," his business partner said, scolding him like one would a child.

"It's disgusting what they've done to France."

Paul was getting louder as his rant became more involved. His hands swung back and forth as he cited the rise in crime with the rise in Arab asylum seekers, calling them "predators" and "thieves." His speech even tore down Lillian's amusement, and she waved away a busboy, to spare him from the cross fire.

Maggie tried to think of how best to stop the conversation from spinning further out of control. She opened her mouth to counter him, but her voice was shaky.

"Turks aren't Arab," she said, which was entirely beside the point.

Rob squeezed her thigh again as she spoke. *Don't,* he seemed to beg with every ounce of himself. Maggie shot him a glance. Rob lifted his hand to the top of the table and turned a fork around nervously while Paul hmphed and retreated to his drink.

Most of the other restaurant patrons had ignored them, though the nearest two-top had gone still to eavesdrop. Rob stopped flipping the fork and tried to change the subject.

"We're excited by all the opportunities in France," he said. "Maybe after we get a few projects off the ground, we'll reopen the Paris office."

"Don't waste your time," Paul said. "Paris isn't what it was."

Maggie excused herself to go to the bathroom, and the other two women looked down when she stood. They were ashamed of their male counterparts. *As they should be,* Maggie thought.

She passed the busboy who Lillian had waved off. She tried to apologize to him with her eyes, though she knew she must have looked ridiculous. Maggie hoped he'd clear the table while she was gone and that they would hurry to pay the bill.

There was something comforting about the dim light of the bathroom. Like Maggie could look in the mirror but she didn't have to see her reflection. She thought of her father, always a pacifist, who would have clicked his tongue at her for speaking back to Paul. *He's ignorant, kızım. He doesn't know,* she could hear his easy voice calming her. Immediately contrasted with her mother, who would question why she didn't say more. *So teach him! Who is this foolish man?* Show your teeth, go for the kill. That was Maggie's mother.

Barbaric, Paul had called them. And his partner had agreed, just in veiled terms about how wonderfully European Maggie appeared. Maggie had never wanted to call her father so badly as in moments like these. To have someone who would let her be fragile and weak and, in his words, peaceful. Her mother was always teaching her how to fight, how to build her armor. If Maggie called her mother, she'd tell her to throw a drink in Paul's face, spit on the round client, and leave. She'd rile herself up until she was flaming mad, cursing them up and down in English and in Turkish, leaving Maggie to calm *her* down instead of the other way around.

Maggie pressed her hip bones against the cold sink. There was no one to call, no one to come and retrieve her from the bathroom. No one to sneak her somewhere safe and warm. Maggie stared at herself until someone walked into the bathroom. She whipped her head around.

"Sorry," the woman said, apparently afraid of Maggie.

She quickly disappeared into a stall, and Maggie continued staring at the mirror, wishing she could hit herself.

MAGGIE'S PHONE BUZZED in her tiny purse while Rob laid down the company card to pay for dinner. The clients sparred under their breath in French while Tim and Lillian sparred under their breath in English. The table had never found easy footing after Paul's tirade, though everyone managed to force a pseudocalm frequency from themselves. At some point, Lillian mentioned losing her mother, which cast them further into uneasiness, but it freed something in Maggie, who still had a mother. She wished she could give something to Lillian that would mean something, some small bit of kindness, but she feared it would be like the baklava all over again.

All the miniature espresso cups were empty, left only with brown foamy rings along the inside. The men shook hands, and the evening was finally over. Outside, Rob shepherded the clients into a black town car, leaving Maggie, Tim, and Lillian to form an uncomfortable trio.

"Lots of late nights on this one, huh?" Maggie said to fill the silence that lingered between the three of them.

"Not really," Tim said. "This was pretty much a slam dunk."

It was like he'd thrown a dart into her throat. Before Maggie could pluck it bleeding from her mouth and question Tim further, Rob had returned, slipping his arm around Maggie's waist.

Tim gestured north and said, "Well, we're this way."

"And we're this way," Rob said, gesturing south. They clasped hands and made plans to meet in the office early on Monday to iron out the details. Lillian and Maggie bowed their heads at each other, and the couples split off.

As soon as their backs were turned, Maggie wrested herself from Rob.

"Don't fucking touch me," she said through her teeth.

"Maggie," he pleaded.

She huffed a cloud of air from her nostrils. It was still that time of year where her hot breath could make steam. Maggie hopped a few steps to get ahead of Rob and threw her arm up to catch a cab.

"Maggie!" he called out from behind her.

When she didn't reply, he kept shouting. "What's wrong?"

Maggie stopped trotting forward and turned to look at Rob. "What's *wrong*?" Her mouth hung open. "I don't know, Rob. Maybe it's the two hours of sickos drooling over your barbaric Arab European girlfriend, or it's that Tim just let me know there haven't been many late nights over this deal."

She swung her focus back out toward the street, flicking her wrist in the air, trying to see whose lights were on.

"First of all, Tim doesn't know what he's talking about."

"I know Tim doesn't know what he's talking about." Maggie was shocked to hear that she was screaming now. "You're all fucking idiots!"

"C'mon, Mags," Rob said, thinking tenderness here would be the answer. "Let's go home."

"I'm not going anywhere with you."

"You're making this a bigger deal than it needs to be."

With her arm still in the air, Maggie caught the tail end of Rob rolling his eyes. "I can't even look at you," she said.

Maggie finally flagged down a cab, and when Rob reached to open the door for her, she grabbed the handle and slid the door open. She gave the driver the cross streets of her studio and looked back at Rob.

"Will you be coming home?" he asked, suddenly small in his suit.

"Don't count on it," Maggie replied. She closed the door, and the cab pulled into the traffic speeding down Second Avenue.

MAGGIE RESTED HER head against the cool window, which was slightly wet with condensation. The hard glass pressed against her head hit a deliriously satisfying pressure point, and she let her eyes shut briefly. She stayed like this for long enough that when she lifted her head from the glass, she found the relief felt nearly as good as the pressure.

Despite enduring three courses of red meat and thick martinis, Maggie realized she was starving. Her skin felt vacuum-sealed against her bones. She took in a cold shock of air as she inhaled. The cabdriver had rolled down the window on the passenger's side.

A slam dunk. Maggie imagined Tim's and Rob's sweat-dripping bodies dribbling up and down a court. Tim's legs bent as he swung from the rim. Where had Rob been all these nights if not at work?

She imagined whoever the woman must be. Someone small, no doubt, not giant and towering and enormous, like Maggie felt. Certainly not *barbaric*. She probably had small breasts held up by pale-pink lace, Rob's hands skimming over them before trailing her waist, her hips.

Maggie's mind spun with all the characters from dinner. Cold, motherless Lillian. The pale, fat client. How he had looked at Maggie's breasts when his wife was giving her order to the waiter. Maggie imagined slicing into him with a chef's knife, splitting him in half as his innards oozed out of him like a steaming lava cake. *The Turks are such a warm people.* His wife saying Maggie had great brows. *You should see my bush,* Maggie desperately wished she could have said. Rob and Tim conjured up the image of those plastic-teeth toys that chattered when you wound them up. And Paul. Wiry but handsome. French and mean. Maggie thought of what sex might be like with him. How Paul might hurt her, and the dangerous possibility that she might like that. Maggie rolled down her own window and let the cold wind whip its way into the cab.

Maggie's mother was always making a case for Rob. "Things will be easier with him," she'd say. "He's an American." She said *American* like it glittered in her mouth. Her mother loved Rob's blue eyes, like he was born with the natural protection of the evil eye. And she loved that he always ate double portions when he visited. But her main selling point was that he wasn't Muslim, and because of this, she said, he wouldn't try to control Maggie. "Americans believe in freedom. That's why I married Baba," she often repeated. "He's not so crazy like your Uncle Mehmet."

All this reasoning felt so absurd to Maggie, because they *were* Muslim. Not practicing, not even in Maggie's youth, but technically they were Muslim on both sides going back to whatever generation started them all. Whenever Maggie pushed back on this point, however, her mother would give out a high-pitched "Heh," as if to say *You'll see.*

Her mother would have been so disappointed had she seen Rob's performance tonight. Flashing a smile at every mention of her as his exotic beauty but unwilling to step in and defend her. Her mother had never seen how weak he really was.

The cab lurched forward in a stop as standstill traffic appeared out of nowhere.

"Sorry, miss," the driver said, flashing Maggie a look in the rearview mirror.

"It's okay." Maggie smiled, and she was surprised by how genuine it felt, her lips stretching across her face. The driver's reflection also showed signs of a smile. Deeply grooved crow's feet embedded next to both of his eyes flashed and then fell as his focus returned to the road. This was the only exchange they'd had, but Maggie felt somewhat comforted by it. They were friends now, in a quiet, knowing way.

Maggie could feel her phone vibrate again in her purse. A call from Rakib.

He was with people. She could hear them bumping into each other in the background. Glasses clinked, and Maggie imagined an amber light surrounding everyone. In her mind, they sparkled and were mid-laugh. Heads thrown back, hands grazing each other's bodies. An evening entirely unlike her own.

"Hello, Müjde," Rakib said. She could feel him reaching for her through the phone.

"Hello, Rakib."

Maggie sounded like a different person than the woman she'd been at dinner. She was looser, her voice mellowed like a glass of wine that had been left to breathe.

"Where are you?"

"I'm in a cab."

"Great. Tell him to take you to Sixty-Second and Central Park West."

In the split second she was given, Maggie weighed her options. She could continue on to her studio and paint—though she had no new ideas of how to approach her project. Working in spite of this would undoubtedly make things worse and would likely create more work to do in the long run. She could go home and confront Rob, find out which hotels he'd been using for his late nights. Hound him until he admitted it was multiple girls or just one. They could fight until they each passed out, her on the bed and him on the couch. Or. Maggie's head fell back against the stiff headrest. Her body softened and told her the answer.

"Okay," she said to Rakib. "I'm coming."

15

HE WAS WAITING for Maggie on the corner, standing tall and easy beneath an umbrella with the rain falling everywhere but the two-foot circumference surrounding him. He had spotted her in the back seat and waved the cab over. Now that they had formed a friendship, the driver raised his eyebrows at Maggie in the rearview mirror as if to ask *Is this okay?*—to which Maggie nodded. *Yes, he's waiting for me.* She wondered if this millisecond of an exchange made the driver complicit in her bad behavior. She was already looking for someone with whom she could share the blame. As if he could have driven her there without her telling him the address.

Through the open passenger window, Rakib thanked the driver and handed him the fare in cash. Maggie slipped out from the back seat and pressed her side into Rakib's, under the guise of shielding herself from the rain. His arm wrapped around her with his palm landing flat against her hip bone. Like this, Rakib could wield her any way he'd like, and Maggie would happily let him. Curled up into his neck, Maggie lifted her lips to Rakib's ear.

"Thank you," she whispered.

"Of course," he said as the cab sped away. She could tell that he relished in the innate sense that he had saved her. "C'mon. Let's get inside before we're soaked."

They turned as one entity and entered a marbled lobby that felt more Las Vegas than New York. Rakib handed the now-collapsed umbrella to one of the doormen and led Maggie onto an elevator that skipped the first twenty floors.

"Are you still afraid of heights?" Rakib asked.

"Just keep me away from the windows, okay? And no balconies."

"I think we can manage that."

Rakib's voice was low, and every move he made was languid and erotic. He laced his fingers between Maggie's and squeezed. Her ears popped as they soared past 20, 25, 30, until finally a ding sounded at 33 and the doors opened. Maggie followed Rakib into an apartment. She had forgotten to ask who it belonged to and why they were there. Ultimately, she didn't care.

Someone handed her a champagne flute, and Maggie smiled at the people in the crowd, who were sparkling just as they had been in her ideation of them. She had glass after glass after glass, until she was no longer afraid of heights and stepped out onto the balcony.

THE RAIN HAD thinned itself into a mist, and even those droplets were beginning to dissipate. Pinpricks of moisture tickled Maggie's bare shoulders as she took a deep breath and brought herself up against the railing. *Now this is a place to scream,* she thought, looking at the view.

Central Park spread out before her in dark-green expanse. Spring was just starting to usher in new blooms, but Maggie could not help but fixate on the fact that summer was not far off. The idea of hot, unending days sent her spiraling. If she didn't get the grant, Maggie had no plans to fall back on. She would graduate and slink into adulthood with her tail between her legs. She had enough money put away to survive until August, but after that there was no telling what she'd have to do. Returning home was not an option, and letting Rob support her indefinitely was even less of an option. "I will die before I let him bankroll me," she'd said to John one night. Maggie felt suddenly emotional as she remembered her brother's confidence in her. "You won't have to," he'd said. "I know you."

Maggie turned east, toward their apartment, looking for Rob. Their neighborhood was well past what she could possibly see from the balcony, but she could feel the red needle of a compass always tilting toward home. Maggie felt stupid looking for him, and she quickly realized he might not even be at home. After all, she was supposed to be at the studio, and here she was at some stranger's party. They had spun so far out that anything could be a lie. Could he be with someone now?

Maggie leaned her chest slightly over the edge of the railing and looked straight down, to see how far up thirty-three floors was. She let out a little gasp.

Rakib placed his hands on her hips and tugged her backward. "I thought you said no balconies," he said, holding on to her from behind.

"I just wanted to see the view."

Safely contained within Rakib's arms, Maggie took a few shaky breaths before turning around to face him.

"You looked like you might jump there for a second." Rakib's face had fallen, and his dark eyes were harsh and unblinking.

"I'm not that bored," Maggie said, giving him a gentle nudge. She hoped this might bring back some levity, but he remained stoic.

"I'm kidding! I just wanted some fresh air, and then the view, and then I guess I got a little too bold." Maggie cupped Rakib's face with one hand and placed the other against the bare patch of skin exposed beneath his throat. "I'm fine," she whispered.

She pulled him closer and kissed him. She could feel Rakib's worry drain away and his muscles became molten. He melted into Maggie and hardened his arms around her. She squealed in delight, her teeth grazing his lower lip before she laughed and threw her head back.

"See?" she said, grinning wider than felt natural. "I'm just fine."

Rakib lifted Maggie and spun her toward the door.

"We're going inside," he commanded into her ear.

Returning her to the ground, Rakib escorted Maggie through the door, and the two of them waded into the warm crowd of beautiful people.

THE ROOM WAS full of women. Wealthy women, mostly over fifty, of all persuasions. Many of them were there with partners and husbands. Few of them were artists, most of them collectors, directors, and donors. They had elegant partners, arrogant partners. Some were alone—widowed, never married, no children. Some of them had grown children, a few of whom attended the party with them. The women all had beautiful lines engraved in their faces, showing the wear of their storied lives. Maggie felt outside of them. Outside of all the secrets they knew.

Over the course of the evening, Maggie came to understand that they were in Cathy and Don's apartment, and they were celebrating Cathy's retirement from some thirty-odd years of curating shows for museums all around the world. Her husband, Don, was standing in the living room as Maggie and Rakib reentered, tapping his crystal glass with a silver spoon. Don was easy to watch. He commanded attention without giving off the sense that he needed validation. Gray hairs sprayed the side of his closely shaved head, though the longer strands up top were mostly black. He was handsome, olive skin with light eyes, tan and somewhat weathered. Like in another life he had been a ranch hand, or in some other profession that spent every day under the unforgiving sun. An aura radiated from somewhere deep inside him, and it drew people to him, both men and women. He was like Rakib in that way. People liked bathing in their light.

In his speech, Don kept calling Cathy "my Kitty," and this was taken by his audience as a show of his sweetness, though it made Maggie uneasy. There was something aggressive in using the diminutive in front of all his wife's colleagues. They'd now be forced to reconcile Cathy with Don's "Kitty" in their view of her, and Maggie couldn't help but feel like Don did this on purpose. Her agency, which Maggie assumed to be hard-fought, was slowly being peeled from her, one "Kitty" at a time.

"So, to Kitty," Don said finally, raising his glass. "She may be retired, but she's still the boss."

Forced laughter flooded the living room, and Don flashed Maggie a look, followed by a quick wink. She turned to see if Cathy was behind her, thinking she had wrongly intercepted the gesture, but Cathy was on the opposite side of the living room, hiding a wince behind a raised glass. The pained look on her face lasted only a second and faded with the applause of their guests. Cathy graciously bowed her head and mouthed, *Thank you*. She touched a few fingers to her chest in real or feigned gratitude. She was the picture of grace. Maggie hoped she would never have to be as good of an actor.

Rakib leaned over. "They're so in love," he whispered to Maggie.

As the party resumed, Rakib and Maggie bounced off each other like particles in motion. They'd conduct themselves individually for minutes at a time, collide briefly, and pass on to new groups. Each collision included a touch. Hands grazing in the refreshing of a drink, Rakib trailing his fingertips down the open back of Maggie's dress, her lips grazing his stubbled cheek as she whispered jokes they had formed at the expense of other guests. Rakib periodically checked on Maggie from across the room with a glance, to which she returned her lowered gaze or a smile. They could go on like this forever, Maggie thought.

In their last collision, Rakib and Maggie decided they'd leave in half an hour. This would give Rakib enough time to do his elaborate round of goodbyes, and Maggie could either attempt to make one last meaningful connection with someone or hide in the bathroom. She sidled up next to Don, figuring she'd thank him for hosting and Rakib could make Don his last goodbye before whisking her away to wherever it was they were going next.

"It's been a beautiful evening," she said, looking out over the guests, as Don was.

"Yes, it has been. And nice to have some young people come liven up the crowd."

Maggie never knew quite how to handle her youth. She was made to acknowledge it as some sort of power, but it was simultaneously something that made her vulnerable. "Never discount being young and beautiful," Lorrie had said to her once in a meeting. It was the first time Maggie had sensed tension between them, as if the adage was to serve as both a threat and a warning. Whatever it was supposed to mean, holding a club in each hand had never made Maggie feel like she was armed.

"I was not particularly lively until I arrived, actually," Maggie said, her voice deepening as she remembered Paul's diatribe and Rob's hot hand clamped on her thigh.

"I highly doubt that," Don said, looking directly at Maggie for the first time since she had pulled up next to him. It was the same powerful glance he'd shot her earlier, confirming that his wink had been meant for her.

"So," Don said, looking away from her again. "Rakib says you like to paint."

"I *do* like to paint," she said as if it were her chic hobby and not her desperate attempt at securing a livelihood.

"What do you paint?"

"Women, mostly."

"Ah, so we have something in common," Don said, smiling.

"And what is that?"

"We're both drawn to beauty."

Maggie eyed Rakib, who had just kissed both of Cathy's cheeks. She had the look on her face of having been seen, relaxed and elated. It was the look she should have had when Don gave his toast. Rakib moved on to bid another group goodbye. Don shifted slightly so that his wrist was touching Maggie's.

"I'd love to show you some pieces around the apartment. That is, if you're not leaving."

Rakib was talking to an older Bangladeshi woman now. Maggie could hear him calling her "auntie" and flattering her nearly to death. She was smiling, but Maggie saw her narrow her eyes at him. The woman had seen through Rakib, puncturing his charm. Wounded, but not dead, he left her to clap hands with a youngish man and lift a dainty, pale wrist to his lips.

He wasn't even halfway around the living room and would clearly be going over their agreed-upon thirty minutes. Without Rakib arriving as her out, Maggie was stuck. So she said yes. She'd love to see some pieces around the apartment.

CATHY AND DON'S collection was eclectic. In one room, they hosted a Hockney, seven African tribal masks arranged in a circle, and miniature pottery by various Indigenous groups spanning North America. Don was keen to point out the texture of each piece, how it influenced the space and made the experience tactile and sensual. "You can touch it," he repeated often.

Maggie touched a few pieces, but mainly she looked at the silver watch on her wrist, waiting for the moment Rakib would notice she was missing and would come and find her.

They passed three paintings in the hallway that Maggie was tempted to linger in front of, but she didn't want to give Don an excuse to stand next to her and explain each piece, hinting at its price but never revealing the actual cost. They had been blessed by Cathy's profession and had received many gifts in her years of curating. "No one could afford this otherwise" became another refrain. However, what Maggie had also gathered from hushed whispers among the party's attendees, was that Cathy was independently wealthy. Her father had invented the adhesive on the back of Post-it notes. No one could afford this otherwise.

Precious hand-blown glass figurines were secured to podiums with wax, and as Maggie brought her face close to them, she was asked for the first time *not* to touch something. Feeling drunk and mildly defiant, she lightly pressed a fingertip against a piece of glass that looked like it was melting. Maggie looked at Don as she felt the tacky release of her fingerprint. He smirked in amusement.

"Don't tell Kitty," Maggie said.

Don moved toward her slowly. The click of his shoes hitting the floor echoed with each step. Maggie noticed the crisp line of his shoulders as he neared. He was broad, athletic probably, and lightly swung his arms by his sides.

She stood perfectly still while she braced for his approach, her glass balanced by her long fingers. He stopped just behind her, standing so he could turn his head into her ear. With his breath steaming against her neck, Don ran the back of his fingers down her arm.

"There are plenty of things I don't tell Kitty."

Maggie swayed away from his touch, but his hand followed her and landed on her shoulder.

"Maggie?" she heard Rakib call from down the hall.

Her chest swelled with relief, only to fall when she realized that Rakib's instinct was to call her Maggie. It was the first time she had ever hated herself for teaching her body that this was its name.

Don released Maggie's shoulder, but as she stirred to move away from him, he cupped her breast. With two strong fingers, he pinched her nipple, making it hard and obvious beneath the sheath of her dress. Don never strayed from his casual confidence, like groping her was as innocent as shaking her hand. He squeezed her breast again, hard, before letting go.

"We're in here," Don called out, straightening his tie with a flick of his wrist. Rakib appeared in the doorway, more shadow than himself, blocking the light filtering in from the hall.

"Hey," Maggie said with little power in her voice. She wanted to slip her hand into her dress and soothe the tender spots Don had dimpled with his grip. She imagined bruises already forming.

"Ah," Rakib said, lighting up and leaning back. "You're in good hands, I see."

The corners of Maggie's mouth twitched up in a quick half-hearted smile. She strode over to Rakib, trying her best to look unaffected. He placed his arm around her and hooked his thumb into the low, open back of her dress.

"Ready to go?"

"Yes," she said, figuring out how to sound like herself.

Rakib left Maggie to shake Don's hand and thank him for inviting them. She saw how easily they moved with each other. Rakib made a joke, and Don laughed, clapping a wide hand perfectly against Rakib's shoulder. They'd do tennis next time Rakib was in town. "Be good until then," he said.

Rakib returned to Maggie and drew her even closer, as if sensing that she could not be without his touch. They were on their way out when Don called after them.

"Oh, and Maggie . . ."

Her body refused to turn, so she glared at Don from over her shoulder.

"I'd love to see your work sometime."

"Sure," she said, without blinking. "That would be great."

MAGGIE SAID NOTHING as the cab sped downtown. Don grabbing her breast was not the worst thing to ever happen to her. A professor once groped her during office hours when she was a sophomore. That had been worse. And there was the barista she'd let drive her home when the coffee shop closed. He wouldn't unlock the car until she had felt how hard he was. How hard she had *made* him. There were a handful of forceful, drunken kisses from men at bars that were all worse. At least Don hadn't hurt her. She didn't have to feel the strain of her neck against a palm pushing her down or a wad of spit thwacking against her face. There had been worse cab rides home.

"You okay?" Rakib asked, squeezing her thigh.

"Yeah," Maggie said, shaking herself from the memories stored in her body. "Just been a long night."

Rakib let out a long sigh in agreement. He talked about how great the apartment was, though. Had Maggie seen the guest bathroom? Apparently, the sink was gold. And what about the art everywhere? Unparalleled.

"I'm glad Don could show you some of the pieces himself."

Maggie felt her body tighten.

"He's not so great, you know." She sought Rakib's gaze, but he stared ahead.

"Kind of arrogant," Rakib said. "Showy." He shrugged. "But not so bad, either."

"That's not what I mean," Maggie said, trying to make him understand that she was serious.

"What *do* you mean?"

"Don't you think he's a creep? Getting the youngest girl alone at the party?"

Rakib's face morphed into a grin not dissimilar to Don's.

"Maggie," he said. "It's not his fault you're the most radiant person in every room you walk into." His eyes were glistening and dark and completely devoid of understanding.

Maggie looked out the window. Everywhere felt cruel and unfavorable. Every building she looked at, the thirty-third-floor apartment, their conversation. It reminded her of something she'd told her mother once: "When you're a woman, there's no such thing as safe—only safer." Maggie closed her eyes and leaned against the headrest.

She felt Rakib's hand squeeze her thigh again. Maggie opened her eyes to find him staring at her intently. She gave a slight nod, and Rakib wrapped his hand from the top of her thigh inward and upward. She couldn't tell if this was what she wanted until he had slipped his fingers inside her. With his free hand, Rakib tossed his jacket over Maggie's lap.

"Spread your legs for me," he whispered into her ear, and she did, straining against her seat belt. The edge of the strap dug into the flesh of her thigh as Rakib maneuvered his wrist so as not to be at an odd angle. Maggie decided that she did want this. She took a deep breath and closed her eyes while Rakib slid his fingers in and out.

She could feel her drunkenness bubble up to the surface, rosying her cheeks. She had not let herself be this drunk in years, and once she realized this, she felt flush with the warmth of youth and recklessness and every light in New York City. Her skin was hot to the touch, and a single bead of sweat dripped from her hairline into her ear. The wetness of it made her shiver. Then the pressure of Rakib's thumb against her made her shiver harder. She thought of Cathy.

Formidable Cathy, who had blazed an incredible trail for herself, and how Maggie wanted to rage and flame as she had. She wanted to set herself on fire.

Maggie's face grew hotter, and as Rakib sped up, she drew in a succession of airy gasps. She slid her own hand beneath Rakib's jacket and touched herself as he continued to finger her with surprising force. Rakib leaned into Maggie's neck until his teeth were by her ear.

"Don't come until I tell you to."

Her mouth fell open as Rakib pulled his fingers away. She drew a sharp breath, wondering why he had stopped. But then she realized the cab had pulled over. She didn't recognize the street they were on, but Rakib nodded when Maggie turned to him for affirmation that she should open the door.

She readjusted her dress and stepped out onto the curb. A breeze pushed her hair from her neck. Maggie closed her eyes and faced the wind, relishing the cold air washing over her. She prayed her body might keep a record of this, too.

Rakib corralled Maggie with an open hand, careful not to touch her with his fingers until they were in the elevator. There, he trailed them across her lips. Catching him by surprise, Maggie bore her gaze into his and opened her mouth, unafraid to taste herself.

THE APARTMENT WAS tidy and nondescript, and Maggie said as much to Rakib upon entering. Apparently, tidy and nondescript was like winning the lottery of short-term rentals. But she could see the almost-invisible ways Rakib had made it his. There were blood-red tapered candles in a modern interpretation of a candelabra. They were all half melted, and Maggie could imagine the dinner party surrounding them when they were lit. Or, worse, if he'd lit them for a date.

Maggie tried not to picture anyone gorgeous while she surveyed the apartment further. He'd bought a decanter with two dramatic curves that made up its neck. It was upside down, balanced between plates drying on the dish rack. His wire-rimmed glasses were on an end table next to the couch, unfolded as if he'd just pulled them from his face to see who was coming in. *Just me,* Maggie imagined herself saying as she came in with her own key. Bringing in wine or ingredients for dinner.

"You have to see the view," Rakib said, leading Maggie to the bedroom.

He clicked a button, and a whirring noise made her jump. The blinds rolled up to reveal the Hudson, shimmering with all the lights from the West Side. Maggie walked to the windows and pressed her fingertips against the cold glass. Taxicabs flickered below, and even though it was close to 2 a.m. people were still out hailing them.

Rakib ran his fingers along Maggie's shoulder blade. She waited for his hand to trail lower, but it simply traced and retraced the curve, back and forth and again. She looked at him from over her shoulder.

"Is this what you do with all your girls? Give them lots and lots of champagne and then show them a romantic view?"

"C'mon," he said rocking gently against her. "All my girls? You make me sound cheap."

She looked down again at the glossy river. "Surely, it's something that has worked before."

Rakib gathered her hair and drew it to the side. He began undoing the buttons around Maggie's neck.

"Is it working now?" he asked.

Had they been in college, Maggie would have lied and said no. In their youth, she'd poured ceaseless effort into obscuring the power

Rakib held over her. But she was tired now. Too tired to stand up straight and resist. So in a low, small voice, she told him the truth.

"Everything you do works on me."

MAGGIE WAITED FOR the front of her dress to fall as Rakib undid the last button. He found the hidden zipper embedded on the side, and suddenly Maggie was naked. She hung herself from Rakib's neck like he was the bow of a ship.

"I forgot how soft you were," he said as his hands moved from her ribs to her waist. Maggie wanted to be absorbed into Rakib. Wanted not to have a body of her own but to be a part of his.

They maneuvered Maggie onto the bed, and Rakib stood above her, unbuttoning his shirt. His eyes lingered on her nipples, hard and dark without the lights on. She pinched one, then began circling it with her fingers. Rakib's lips parted, and his shirt floated to the floor. He ran his hand over his inseam as he watched.

"It's so funny," she said.

"What is?"

"It's like you're hypnotized."

Rakib was naked now, touching himself as Maggie pressed her breasts together. The one Don had grabbed was sore, but not terribly. Maggie soothed herself by massaging it. There wouldn't be a bruise, she could see so now, and she admonished herself for being so dramatic.

Rakib stayed standing, observing Maggie. He shook his head in disbelief. "You are very, very beautiful."

Maggie kept one hand on her breast and moved the other between her legs. "You think so?" she asked. She smiled and tilted her head.

"Jesus," he muttered.

Quickly, Rakib clasped Maggie by her ankles. He ripped her

through the air, and she landed, startled, at the edge of the bed. Rakib leaned down and whispered to her, his lips grazing her ear.

"Yes, Maggie. I think you're very, very beautiful."

He pulled Maggie to the exact edge of the mattress and entered her slowly. She made a sound that if it had ever been replayed for her would have made her suicidally embarrassed.

Rakib smiled, and as he sank farther in, he groaned. "You're so fucking wet."

Maggie let Rakib crush her beneath his weight. She wanted to suffocate with how much she wanted him. He could have plugged her nose and filled her mouth, and still, Maggie thought, moaning beneath the palm of his hand, she would have asked for something more. *Weigh me all the way down,* she thought. *Fill me all the way up.*

Rakib was severe and stony. It hurt to have his hips grinding into hers, but Maggie's mind had succumbed to speechlessness. She opened her mouth to say something, but it only curled around vowels and muddled everything into a series of *ah*s. Eventually, her tongue formed the word *yes*, which she said over and over in place of actual speech.

Maggie screwed her eyes shut, and Rakib's hand found a gentle grip on her shoulder, his thumb occasionally dragging over her neck.

"Open your eyes," Rakib said, his words urgent.

When she didn't, Rakib held Maggie by her face, a hand wrapped around both her cheeks.

"Open your eyes," he said again.

Maggie opened her eyes, and Rakib's gaze shot through her. He came, and though she had been close, too, she finished after he had collapsed next to her. They lay side by side, not touching, not speaking.

Rakib shook his head back and forth.

"Maggie, Maggie, Maggie."

THE ONLY WORD that came to Maggie as she looked at herself in the bathroom mirror was *deranged*. Her face was flushed from sex, red and uneven and feverish. Her nose, somehow more prominent than ever, was straight and harsh, like a beak. Rakib had been lying, calling her "very, very beautiful." After scanning the counter for a brush, Maggie gave up and pulled her hair back, with little attention to detail. She drew her face close to the mirror and turned her head from one side to the other. Who was this sick person, worn thin with rage and sex? There was a clock in the bathroom. It was nearly four in the morning.

"You can stay," Rakib said to Maggie as she clicked off the light and exited the bathroom.

As she rounded the corner of the bed to retrieve her dress, Rakib reached over and pulled her toward him. Maggie collapsed into his chest, and he half rolled her onto the mattress, half held on to her. Her bones felt like they were made of lead, like she should have made a loud thud as she fell. But whatever sound she actually made was absorbed by Rakib's abdomen and the cushy down comforter.

Maggie thought of staying there, with Rakib's hand perpetually against her hip, her ribs, or even between her legs. She imagined waking up the next morning pressed against him, tangled and dozing in and out of sleep while an alarm beeped. She pulled his hand up to her neck and made him place his thumb directly against the well of her throat, spreading the rest of his fingers along her collarbone.

"Stay?" Maggie asked.

"If you want to."

In all their years of sleeping together, Rakib had had early exams, meetings, flights, games, and practices—all likely fake—to avoid spending the night together. Maggie remembered begging him, wincing as he inevitably pulled away from her. On the rare, desperate occasion, she'd stooped so low as to ask for five more minutes.

"I have to go home," she said with weak notes of finality. "I don't live here. You don't even live here."

"For the next few weeks, I do."

"And then where do you go? London? Paris?"

"I guess it depends on how things go here. If you and Rob..."

Maggie whipped her head around to look at Rakib. He was propped up, with a hand thrown casually behind his head. He looked like he was in an ad for bedsheets.

"If Rob and I what?" she asked, almost accusing him.

"I just mean it depends on if you want me to stay." He spoke to her softly, unperturbed by her tone.

"What are you talking about?"

"I don't have an assignment for a while, you know. I have a couple irons in the fire, but nothing set in stone. I could stay in New York for a while, and maybe we could..." His voice trailed off, leaving the idea unformed.

Maggie stepped into her dress. She slid it over her hips and began struggling with the tiny buttons. *Maybe we could*... Maggie felt like she was in a dream. She hadn't seen Rakib for years, and now he thought maybe they could... what?

She had so desperately wanted this when they were both young. She had wanted him to pick her, to stay in New York. Instead, he flew to Florence to look at art and "inform his craft" and fuck beautiful Italian women. The first time he came back to New York, he didn't even tell Maggie. By the time she found out, he had already returned to his jet-setting life abroad. Yet part of her still wanted to pick him. And she still wanted to be picked.

Maggie looped the top button, just as Rob had before they'd left. And what was she going to do when she showed up to their apartment as the sun was coming up, her hair a mess and her makeup run? What was she going to say to Rob, with whom she had already figured out so much of her life?

"I can't talk about this right now," Maggie said. She smoothed her dress and pulled her hair from the lopsided bun she had drawn it into.

Maggie perched on the edge of the bed to slip her feet into her heels. But before she could push herself up, Rakib reached for her wrist and sat beside her. Instantly deflating, Maggie rested her head against his shoulder. A tremor took over her hand, which Rakib squeezed until she regained stillness. Maggie released her grip and stood. She leaned toward Rakib to give him a quick kiss.

"Going?" he asked. Maggie could hear what she thought were trace amounts of relief in his voice.

"Yes," she said.

He said something to her as she passed into the living room, but Maggie couldn't hear him. She couldn't hear anything other than the blood swimming in her body.

16

ROB WAS HOME, sound asleep on his side of the bed and decidedly less ad-like than Rakib had been in the same setting. He had folded his suit and put it in the nylon bag they used for dry cleaning. Maggie stuffed her dress in along with his suit, not bothering with the same care Rob had.

Maggie stepped into the bathroom to take a hot shower and start her entire life over. Under a stream of hot water, she considered the evening. If she could, she would rewind the whole night until she was back in the bedroom with Rob getting ready for dinner. They would decide not to go, Rob would give Tim the whole deal plus commission, and they would do takeout from Wonton King. Maggie wouldn't have to know how cowardly Rob was. She wouldn't have to know he was cheating on her. She could believe that he just loved her, and she could finally let him. She would feel herself fully in her body. She would be able to feel Rob in his. They would both be wholly in their apartment instead of always being elsewhere. Maybe they could fix all that was so broken between them. Maybe he would charm her so effortlessly and they would book their tickets to Turkey, and Maggie would somehow not be annoyed. Maybe she could marry an American and finally make her mother happy.

But Maggie had lived through all that came after Rob buttoning her dress and thanking her for everything. If Maggie could really rewind everything, she'd go back so much farther. She'd go back to her last visit home during the holidays. Maggie would hug her mother and let herself cry for all that was to come. She'd get into a screaming match with Uncle Mehmet that would end with them laughing over sweets. She would beat John in backgammon. She would let Sofia take her black skirt back to college with her, not even under the condition that she had to return it. She could just have it. Maggie would hold her cousin's baby for an hour longer and give her extra kisses and apologize that she was a girl but also tell her there's nothing better.

Maggie washed her face three times without meaning to and remembered that that's what you're supposed to do with dead bodies in Islam. You're supposed to wash them three times before burying them. *Muslims bury their dead, right?* She couldn't remember.

She washed her hair three times, too, and left the conditioner in as a mask. She rubbed soap all over her body and lathered herself over and over again to wash off any remnants of Rakib. She even crouched to run her fingers between her toes. It was during this compulsion that she slipped backward and narrowly avoided hitting her head against the tub. Maggie took this as a sign that her shower was over.

She could hardly see herself in the clouded bathroom mirror, but she got enough of an idea to pull her hair into two somewhat-even braids. Her drunkenness had waned, and Maggie had enough wherewithal to press cream into her face and rub everything upward in a vain attempt to fight gravity. Clean, braided, and naked, she walked into the bedroom and slipped into her side of the bed.

"You home?" Rob asked, almost without moving his sleepy lips.

"Yes," Maggie whispered. "I'm home."

ROB WAS GONE when Maggie woke up that afternoon. He had left a note:

I'm sorry about dinner last night. Make up for it tonight? Anything you want. xx Rob

xx had firmly taken over *I love you*, or even just *Love* for some time now. Maybe that should have told her something, Maggie thought, examining the *x*'s. Were they the kisses or hugs of *x*'s and *o*'s? All Maggie saw when she looked at them now were the *x*'s drawn over the eyes of something dead.

While heating milk for her coffee, Maggie checked her phone, dreading whatever bombs might have dropped while she was asleep.

A new text from Grace following Maggie's continued silence. *Where are you, babe?* she asked. Maggie was overwhelmed with the kindness of *babe*. She had completely ignored Grace, yet Grace had the sweetness within her to let Maggie know with one word that it was okay.

I'm here, Maggie thought. *I think.*

Still evading Grace's text, Maggie played a voicemail from her mother detailing how Sofia's roommate, Lisa, had loved everything she'd made for her arrival dinner. Dolma, lamb chops, plain rice, herb rice, and eggplant. And chess bars for dessert. She'd read about them in the *Times* and thought she'd make something special for "Sofia's friend," as she kept calling her. Her mother hated the chess bars—too sweet—but Lisa ate two.

John texted her twice:

Are you alive???? and *Are you with my girlfriend??*

No and no, she responded.

An email from Lorrie:

Have to reschedule our meeting. I know we said Friday, but let's do Wednesday.

Be a genius under pressure,

L

Maggie had four days to become a genius. Just as her painting flashed in her mind, John texted back.

Was just worried about her last night. Didn't come home until late... I guess while I was sleeping? She was back when I left for the hospital earlier.

At least we always come home, Maggie typed.

She thought of the night she'd had John and the Artist over for dinner and how Rob hadn't come home. Maggie had hardly thought anything of it then. Work, she'd let herself think. She'd let herself think of every possible iteration of their worlds before she'd told herself the truth.

Maggie erased her text and sent instead, *Anything off otherwise?*

No, he sent so fast it was clear his phone was in his hands.

He followed up with a more frantic *Do you think I should be worried?*

Maggie thought of how foreign it was to see how other couples run their relationships. She now knew that her brother and the Artist generally knew each other's whereabouts. Staying out late was unusual. Not coming home was unheard of. She imagined their texts, tender updates throughout the day like *Running to the store* or *Shift wrapping up at the hospital.*

Rob and Maggie were clearly a couple not well run. She never knew where Rob was or what he was doing, and he thought everything between Fourteenth and Canal was Maggie's studio. And now, evidently, they were both fucking other people. To think she could offer advice to someone else seemed preposterous to Maggie.

If you're worried, just ask her. I'm sure everything is fine, though.

John seemed to calm with Maggie's perfunctory assurances. "Talk it through" felt like sound advice regardless of if she followed it herself. She now wished someone would advise her.

The milk heating on the stove boiled over. It hissed as it bubbled out of the metal pitcher and erupted. Maggie rushed to turn off the stove and pull away the pitcher, but she forgot to grab a towel and burned her fingertips.

"Fuck!" she said under her breath.

Maggie lowered herself to the floor and pulled her legs into her chest. She rested her head against her knees, closed her eyes, and played her mother's voicemail again. "Dolma, lamb chops, plain rice, herb rice, eggplant, and chess bars." She played it again to hear her pride swell when she said "And Sofia's friend had two!" And she played it again, not listening to the words—just so she could hear her mother's voice reverberate through the apartment.

MAGGIE LEFT HER phone at home and took herself for a long walk, like she was an old, old dog that could die any day now. *Let's go to your favorite spots,* she imagined the owner, who was also herself, saying to her as she clipped a leash around her neck. *We can take as many breaks as you need.* And a hand, which was her hand, patted her softly on the head.

She set out across the bridge, looped through the East Village, then moseyed west. A damp fog had spread its long, spindly fingers across Manhattan, and Maggie could see tiny droplets accumulating on her clothes. At some point, she'd have to duck in somewhere, a coffee shop or a bookstore maybe. Someplace where she could be alone with everybody and dry off.

A café with a ripped yellow awning appeared and seemed to Maggie as good a place as any to slip inside. She got a cup of coffee from a man kind enough to flirt with her even though she looked like shit. Israel, he said his name was. "Guess how long I've lived in New York?" He had a thick accent, and Maggie felt a desperate yearning for him to speak to her in whatever language was his.

"Ten years?" Maggie guessed.

"I just moved here last week," Israel said, and he smiled, showing off one silver tooth toward the back.

"How long are you staying?" Maggie asked, hoping Israel would keep her in his life for just one second longer.

"Forever," he said.

Maggie batted her eyes and thanked him for the coffee. He said, "Ciao!" and blew her a kiss as she passed through the door, back onto the wet street.

Despite feeling miserable, Maggie found herself wishing every day could be like this one. That every day she could go for a walk, be pleasant with a stranger, drink good coffee, and enter little shops and touch everything and then leave. That didn't seem like such a bad life. Sure, nothing would ever happen, but so much was always happening that things happening began to seem overrated. Maggie wondered how long nothingness could hold its charm. She imagined not very long.

Maggie pulled her coat closed with one hand and carried her coffee with the other. She felt on edge as she neared Rakib's neighborhood, nervous he'd step out and see her like this—wrung out and slightly crazed. But every face she peered into was a new face. No one who knew her or even wanted to know her. What a relief it was to be invisible.

Over the span of her slowly sipped coffee, Maggie veered farther west. She passed by what she considered her undergraduate landmarks. The corner outside the yoga studio where her mother had called to tell her about her father's cancer. The dorm room in which Maggie cried one night while Rakib was going down on her. He'd stopped and left, because Maggie always found a way to be too much. The dorm where she shared a room with Grace, who she missed so terribly she felt like she could die.

Maggie reached into her pocket for her phone to call her now. To make a point of calling her "babe" and saying aloud "I'm here, and I'm so sorry." Knowing Grace, she would give Maggie a hard time for about ten seconds before forgiving her.

But Maggie had left her phone at home. *Call Grace when you get back,* she told herself, though she knew that by the time she got home, calling Grace would be too daunting, too real.

Maggie arrived at the base of Washington Square Park and entered from the southeast corner, which she had always considered her favorite corner. It was darker there than the rest of the park. Maybe the trees provided more shade than trees in other areas, but whatever made this darkness created a mood that Maggie found suited her any time of day, any time of year. It was the sultry corner of the park, and by the time she had come to that conclusion she was at the fountain, wondering when the city would turn it back on after the official end of bad weather.

A skateboarder wove himself through a narrow a path beside Maggie. "Hey, baby," he said to her. Maggie looked at him with her blankest stare, and saw that he was just a child, seventeen at the oldest. Her glazed look had scared him. The toughness drained from his hardened face until all that was left was the rosy fat of his baby cheeks. "*Sorry*," he said, and skated away.

She sat on a bench and held her coffee cup with both hands. She watched a European tourist insist to his wife they were going in the right direction—that it was just a few more blocks *this* way. Then there was a group of young NYU students brimming with hormones, all nervously touching their wrists, necks, and hands while they decided where to go next. There were dogs shitting. Owners feeding their hands through green plastic bags and trying not to make eye contact with anyone but the shit itself. Babies in strollers clasped their hands around the air, which they knew was wet but couldn't see how or why. Maggie thought of spending the rest of her day on this bench, looking out at people who were unconcerned with her own life. But not long after sitting down, a man named

Freddie approached Maggie and asked if he could take a picture of her bare feet.

Maggie made her second stop indoors, this time at a bookstore, and took a deep grounding breath. She patted her coat with the back of her hand to feel how wet she really was. It was her hair that felt most damp, and in her reflection she could see dark flyaways snaking down the sides of her cheeks. Her entire hairline had formed little curls, reaching up, begging for water, growing toward moisture. She raked her nails through her hair in hopes of smoothing things down, always aware of her mother's warning that she could run into anyone anywhere. "Who knows," she'd once said during the many years Maggie was single. "Someone could stop you for directions, and the next year you could be married."

A man in glasses behind the register ticked his head hello, and she returned the gesture as she tucked herself into the far back corner of the store. The books she lifted all felt heavy. Cookbooks, art books, celebrity memoirs. What wisdom came just from being famous? she wondered. But also—wasn't that what she wanted? To be famous. To be a genius, as Lorrie had said.

Feeling guilty, Maggie began flipping through a book about female artists who had shaped the twentieth century. She pressed her thumb against the edge, and the pages fanned open in a whir. She let go, and the book settled on a section devoted to Georgia O'Keeffe. A quote in bold italic letters sat heavily in the center of the page.

> *I have done nothing all summer but wait for myself to be myself again.*

Maggie closed the book, laid her hand lightly against its cover, and left the store wondering who herself was and if she'd ever get to be her.

MAGGIE'S PHONE VIBRATED on her bedside table.

Text from Rakib:

What are you doing?

Texts from Rob:

Just got home

Going for a run

Let me know what you want to do for dinner

Texts from Sofia:

Hey

Mom wants to know if we should send you the box in your room

???

She didn't want to wait to go to the post office so we sent it

Hope that's ok

Text from John:

Turns out she was working and her phone died, sorry to be panicked

ROB HAD SHOWERED by the time Maggie got home, and was dressed in casual black pants and a gray T-shirt. He looked so healthy and alive.

"Hey, you," he said, strolling over to her. Rob wrapped his arms around her, and Maggie fought the urge to jerk away from him. She was small in the center of his hold, like a pearl in the wet, sandy mouth of an oyster.

"Hey," Maggie said into his chest.

"Where have you been?" he asked, releasing her.

"Walking."

"I was worried when I didn't hear from you."

"I left my phone here."

"Ah," he said.

Rob rounded the kitchen island to the fridge. Maggie collapsed onto the couch and looked up at the ceiling. One of the first things

Maggie had noticed about living with a man was that they were always hungry. She turned to see Rob's head buried in the fridge, looking for something to put in his mouth.

He brought a fistful of cherries to the couch and dropped himself next to Maggie.

"Any thoughts about dinner?" he asked.

"We should have it."

This elicited an unexpected laugh from Rob, one that felt easy and free. Maggie wanted to make him laugh like that again, in hopes that it could take them somewhere else. To a place where nothing was wrong.

"What about takeout?" he asked, popping a cherry in his mouth. He gathered the pits in the pocket of his lower lip like chewing tobacco.

"I want really bad Chinese food," Maggie declared suddenly. "And later, when I feel sick, I want you to fan my face while I whine and moan about how bad my stomach hurts."

Part of her wanted this earnestly. She wanted Rob to dote on her after she had put herself in pain, which was something he had done for Maggie many times over the years. Staying up with her when she'd drunk herself sick, holding her hair back and rubbing her shoulders as she vomited into the toilet. One night, she couldn't sleep, and Rob kept flipping her pillow every few minutes so the cool side was always pressed against her face. Another part of her, the cruel and selfish part of her, wanted to ruin the efforts of his run. Maggie wanted to make him eat something greasy and sickening so that the healthy glow would drain from his face and he could be a fraction as miserable as she was.

Rob set the remaining cherries on the coffee table and spit the pits into his palm. With his clean hand, he pulled Maggie over so that she was lying on his stomach.

She wanted to be strong enough to deny him this. To sit upright next to him and not touch. But once she was on top of him, it was an immediate relief. Rob was shouldering her entire weight, which made Maggie feel like she was floating.

He put his hand on the small of her back, where her shirt had crawled up and exposed her skin. There was a patch of hair there that grew sideways. She'd spent hundreds of dollars over the years waxing the spot, but she hadn't bothered lately. Rob had noticed the hairs once while she was napping. He'd kissed them and woken her up to say he loved these hairs the most, which Maggie had found incredibly annoying. He fingered the patch now and made a satisfied sound deep in his throat.

"Bad Chinese sounds perfect."

MAGGIE RIPPED INTO the paper bag, the bottom already blotched with grease, and dug chopsticks directly into a container of wontons. Rob fiddled with his phone until Brazilian samba streamed through the apartment's speakers, and Maggie was plunged into the first summer she lived in New York. Her downstairs neighbor had shown her this album. Manuel was a twenty-six-year-old Brazilian artist, who, after they'd slept together, used to draw charcoal nudes of Maggie in the afternoon, when the light streamed just so into his otherwise dark and dingy apartment. She felt so sophisticated. Of course, she was a teenage girl on a dirty mattress, but she told herself she was *grown*. Samba always reminded her of that summer, living without an air conditioner and sitting on her stoop while her super's hot but mean son growled about the heat and chain-smoked menthol cigarettes. Life had felt like it was about to split open for Maggie. Like she could become anything she wanted.

"Where'd you go?" Rob asked, popping into Maggie's field of vision.

"Nowhere," she said. "I just love this song."

Rob went back to arranging their takeout on the counter.

"Do you remember what you told me when you showed me this album?"

"No." Maggie didn't remember even showing the album to Rob. "What did I say?"

"You said, 'I could listen to this every day for the rest of my life.'"

Maggie crunched into the bubbly fried shell of a wonton, and smooth cream cheese filled her mouth.

"I thought that said a lot about you."

"What did it say?"

"That you really knew how to love something."

Rob stared directly into the container of noodles in his hand. Maggie waited for him to look at her again, but he only tugged at the stretchy strands of lo mein. Pulling and pulling but never actually bringing them to his mouth.

"Do you still think that?" she asked.

"I don't know."

Maggie could feel herself harden against him. Against the idea that they were standing in their ruins because of how unloving she'd become.

"That's convenient," she said before another audible crunch.

"What's convenient?"

"That everything boils down to how bad *I've* become."

"That's not what I'm saying."

"Then what are you saying?"

"I don't know!" Rob exploded in a volume that was unusual for him.

Maggie saw a shamed look settle on his face. He had scared himself.

"I don't know," he said again, barely audible.

Maggie stared at Rob, who looked helpless with his eyebrows

pinned together, quivering. He continued to stare at his food as his shoulders crawled up into a shrug.

"I never know where you are."

"I'm here," Maggie said. The coarseness of her voice sounded like she'd spent her entire life screaming. And in a way, hadn't she? Crying out on her canvas, in the crater she made in their mattress every night she fell asleep without him. Making her presence known every day, dirtying the dishes and filling the fridge with cherries.

"You're the one who's always leaving."

Rob looked up at this, and Maggie saw how deep and urgent his feeling was. It was like peering into a vast desert of black that went on for miles. *This is pain,* she thought. So pronounced that it could name itself.

The mild sounds of samba were abruptly replaced by ringing—a call coming in on Rob's phone. Maggie watched as he deliberated.

"You don't have to answer," she said.

Rob set the lo mein on the counter and reached for his phone.

"Yes," he said. "I do."

The ringing stopped, and Rob was sucked into his other world. Work. Maggie carefully snuck around him and swiped the pork buns from the counter. She dragged herself to their bedroom, where she could eat them cross-legged and alone.

17

ROB SPENT THE next half hour on the phone, and from what Maggie could hear through the door, he was arguing over blueprints for a project in Australia. She was making her way through a book, not really reading it, and staining nearly every page with her oily fingerprints. She pressed her thumb, hard, in a blank margin, leaving a perfect, whole fingerprint. There was something freeing about ruining something without caring about the consequences.

In the book, a girl passes a gaggle of geese, and somehow, they remind her of her dead mother. Maggie kept floating in and out of the story. A sentence about how white their feathers were bled into an image of Rakib sitting up in bed. *You can stay,* he said, surrounded by a million white down pillows. Maybe she should have.

Maggie tried to read on. One goose was slick with oil, and the other geese were trying to clean him. This was supposed to be a metaphor for the mother's cancer and all the doctors trying to help her, but all Maggie could think was, *Is this me?* Who, then, would lick her clean?

She couldn't hear Rob's voice anymore, so instead she listened for signs of his movement. His footsteps were muted, but he was making laps around the apartment. She heard the jangling of his keys, then his footsteps getting louder and louder until he stopped at the bedroom door. He knocked, and the rap of his knuckles was loud. Like someone had come into the room and turned the sound on.

"Come in," Maggie said, pinning the book open with her thumb in the middle of its spine.

Rob cracked the door. He looked wrecked—his whole body tired and sagging, like the luminescent effects of his run had been from another lifetime.

"Hey," he said softly.

Maggie said "Hey" back, and with the wide-open look of her eyes, she offered for him to come in further. Sit down, even. Help fix this. But he stayed clamped in the doorway.

"I have to run to the office."

"I figured," Maggie said. She tried to think of how she could project the most nonchalance—eating, turning the page. She decided to stay perfectly still.

"Okay, then, I'll see you . . . " His eyes darted around the room as if trying to calculate the damage at work and how much time he'd need to fix it.

"You'll see me when you see me."

"Right."

Rob tapped his fingers against the doorframe, gears obviously still turning in his mind. He gave a single firm nod and began walking down the hall.

He had taken only a few steps before looking over his shoulder and speaking again. "Can we start over when I come home?"

Maggie stared at Rob's half-twisted back.

"Okay."

"Okay," Rob said.

Maggie listened to the soft smack of his footsteps until the front door opened and closed and she couldn't hear anything at all.

THERE WAS SOMETHING paralyzing about lying around at the apartment while Rob was supposedly at work. He could be anywhere—with anyone—and Maggie was home, licking her greasy fingers and trying to decide whose pain was greater. Was it the flash of what she had seen in Rob, or was it what was beginning to consume her own body, starting in her chest and radiating outward?

Maggie made a half-hearted attempt to keep reading, but she was fading. When in the next few paragraphs, she discovered that the goose covered in oil died from swallowing too much of it, she gave up. She flipped the book over, leaving it splayed open with its pages against the duvet, and brought the pork buns back into the kitchen. She found that Rob had packed up the rest of the takeout and put it in a neat line inside the fridge, like a lo mein army. Maggie folded the top of the container in her hand and added it to their ranks. *Shoot me,* she wished she could ask of them.

Maggie scrolled through her phone and stared at the text she'd already read from Rakib: *What are you doing?*

She had left his message burning in her coat pocket as she and Rob walked to Wonton King. With her arm linked with Rob's, Maggie had debated what she'd respond, and if she'd even respond.

Halfway through their walk home, Rob had waved at a baby wiggling its fist in ecstatic greeting over its mother's shoulder. Maggie saw how Rob's face lit up, how his eyebrows flashed up and down and an unselfconscious grin splashed across his face. "Hi! Hi!" he kept saying to the baby. This had made Maggie think that Rob might be able to save himself from the damage he'd done in her life. That perhaps he'd be so sweet that she would never text Rakib again.

Folding forward at the waist, Maggie laid her torso against the kitchen island and gazed out at the apartment. Everything was cold. The matte metal of the lamps in the living room, the dark pitted granite in the kitchen. Maggie flipped over the phone in her hands and read the message from Rakib again. Even the illumination from her phone was cold and sterile. Nothing in the apartment burned warm like a flame.

What are you doing?

Nothing good, she texted back. *Care to join me?*

MAGGIE DECIDED SHE would give everyone an hour. She would give Rob an hour to send a smoke signal of reconciliation before getting fed up and leaving the apartment, and she would give Rakib an hour to respond before she'd cave and call him for whatever crumb of affection he was willing to part with. She spent the majority of the hour a jittery mess. She folded sweaters for the cold weather she wouldn't see again until next year. She returned to the kitchen and tied up the trash. She debated leaving it for Rob to take out but realized doing it herself would kill more time. She brought the bulging bag to the chute, then extended the errand, downstairs to their mailbox, where she retrieved what she knew would only be junk mail.

Back in the apartment, Maggie checked her phone. Three minutes had passed. Rakib still hadn't texted her, and, of course, no trace of Rob. Obviously, Maggie decided, there was something wrong with her for putting herself through this.

The hour elapsed, and Maggie had run out of tasks. She paced around the living room, looking for something to straighten or organize. Giving up, she returned to the bedroom and slowly removed the clothes she was wearing, to store them with her other obsolete winter items. She hadn't sweat much today, she told herself. She didn't need to wash anything before packing it. Something in her mind told her this was disgusting, but Maggie felt little power left within herself to actually be disgusted.

She slid the plastic storage box she had filled under the bed and took herself to the full-length mirror. Pale. *Like the belly of a fish,* she thought, eyeing her soft stomach. She tapped the flat mole by her belly button with her index finger, wishing it was something like a morphine drip. Something to slow her heart rate and turn her mind to slush. She brought her hands to her face and lengthened her fingers against both sides of her neck. It looked as if she were holding her head up, balancing it on her fingertips. She dropped her hands to see if her head would still stay up without them. It did, and she sighed. She was so long, had so many bones. Looking at them exhausted her.

A muffled buzz came from the bed, and Maggie was pulled toward her phone. She dove into the mussed sheets and turned it over in her hand. A message filled the screen:

Where can I meet you?

The sight of Rakib's name popped whatever had been ballooning inside her, and Maggie shriveled against the bed. She texted him her studio's address.

RAKIB CAME OUT of the deli next to the studio, unwrapping a fresh pack of cigarettes. Maggie was still a block away, but she knew it was him from his sturdy frame and the swoop of his black hair. Even how he stood seemed distinctively his own, how he pressed his weight into the earth through one foot and then, a second later, through the other. She was stuck at a crosswalk while Rakib hunched over, hands cupping his mouth to light up. When he inhaled, Maggie could see the red, singed edge of his cigarette.

The sight of Rakib sent a jolt of life through her, and Maggie's blood felt fizzy with the anticipation of being next to him. The waiting to be with him almost better than being with him itself.

"You beat me," she said, closing the gap between them. Rakib pulled the cigarette from his mouth, and a plume of smoke poured out of him.

"Would hate to keep you waiting." He grinned.

Maggie craned her neck to kiss him, and Rakib landed his lips squarely against hers for just a second before pulling away.

"I know you hate the smoke."

"Did I used to say that?"

"All the time."

Maggie couldn't conjure herself from back then. At least, not the same self that Rakib remembered. Maggie remembered wishing he would quit, especially their junior year when everything was happening with her dad, but she couldn't remember saying as much. Then her dad went into remission, so she figured what was the point in using her father as an example when he would end up being perfectly fine?

"I don't remember," she said, laying her head against his chest. He took her in with one arm and continued to smoke with the other.

"Something about your dad," he said. He stamped out the cigarette and kissed her again, this time holding her for longer.

"Let's go up." He patted Maggie's shoulders and squeezed. She reluctantly released him and started toward the studio.

Neither spoke as they spiraled up the stairs. Maggie hadn't returned to herself after Rakib's comment about her dad. So she *had* told him. Not that it did any good, but she had opened herself up to him. Revealed a shred of her life to show him what was really inside her. And yet she couldn't remember doing so.

Rakib stopped on the first landing and looked down at Maggie, behind him.

"This one?"

"One more."

They looped around and ascended to the third floor, where Maggie crossed in front of Rakib to unlock the door. She clicked on the lights, half of which she'd unscrewed, because they gave her a headache while she worked, and the room filled with the ethereal glow of her painting. Its burgundy background colored the light of the studio a dusty pink, and Maggie had forgotten that simple things in this world could be incredibly romantic.

Rakib stepped around her and took in her painting. Maggie stayed back and watched his evaluation.

He started far away from the piece, observing it from the corner where they had just entered the room. After panning his head from left to right, he began to move closer. The horde of women had grown so massive that it was hard to believe that she had started with only one. Twenty of them now peered out at the viewer. Rakib walked even closer to the painting before veering off to the left. He approached one of the younger women. She had long, dark hair, some of which concealed her oval face, dark circles under both eyes, and a small shadow on her nose, suggesting a nose piercing. She was thin—thinner than the women closest to her, but her youth made her seem robust.

"She looks like my sister," Rakib said, eyes still on the painting.

He stayed in front of her for a moment longer before pacing to another woman. This one, just off-center, was who Maggie thought looked most like her mother. Rakib peered at Maggie from over his shoulder.

"Obviously a favorite of yours," he said.

"And what makes you say that?"

"In a dark painting, you gave her the most light."

Maggie made no confirmation, and Rakib turned back toward the painting and moved on to the next woman.

His refusal to issue a verdict drained Maggie of all her energy. She kept waiting for him to make a sound, for his signature *hmm* to ring in her ears. She waited for one woman to strike him as so moving that the whole piece would click, and he would be flooded with warmth and understanding. He would know everything Maggie had ever suffered. He would see his sisters in a new light. He'd call his mother and make her happy by settling down with someone more Muslim than Maggie. Someone *actually* Muslim. Rakib would see all the truth in the painting and finally stop fucking around so much.

But instead, he was silent. Rakib stared at each woman—moving slowly, evaluating each individually, not ticking his head or cheating his shoulders one way or another. Steadily, he made his observations and gathered his thoughts.

Maggie couldn't watch him any longer. She sat on the edge of one of the empty tables crowding the studio in an attempt to draw him away from the painting. And, like she knew he would, Rakib abandoned the piece and moved toward her. He stood over Maggie and looked into her eyes. She was slouched toward him, fingers curled around the lip of the table, the heel of her hand pinned down and keeping her in place. She blinked and wondered what effect her eyes were having on him. Rakib reached for her chin with a finger, and Maggie let him tilt her head up. They stared at each other without blinking.

"What are you going to do to me?" she asked, leaving her mouth open a little.

But whatever it was Rakib was going to do, he'd already done it. He'd already torn at the seams of Maggie's life, and now he would split her in half.

RAKIB WAS ROUGH with her, pulling Maggie to the floor in a way that was more jarring than it was passionate. She reminded herself that this was Rakib and therefore somehow right. "Oh my god," Maggie said, trying to conjure a sense of pleasure, but nothing washed over her.

The beginning was Rakib's feigned interest in stimulating Maggie. A few seconds with his tongue, then a few with his fingers. But again, rough and clumsy. "Now," she said when she could no longer endure, and Rakib shifted eagerly between positions. His fingers dug into Maggie's hips. *Maybe actual sex will be better,* she thought. Rakib brought her up to meet him, and it became obvious how wrong she had been.

Maggie left her eyes open and stared at the lights she had unscrewed. That was a person who cared about her. Who said *My head does not deserve to ache,* and painstakingly moved the ladder around the room, carefully unscrewing lightbulbs that she would have to pay to replace if they broke. This person she was now, pinned underneath Rakib, letting him have sex with her even though it was terrible, did not care about her at all.

"Fuck," Rakib said suddenly. "Maggie."

His hands were pressed into the linoleum floor on either side of her head. "Mmm," she said as she continued to scan the ceiling. One of Rakib's hands traveled to her shoulder.

"I'm going to come," he announced.

Maggie waited for it to be over. She waited for the vain twinge of pride she felt any time a man finished to bubble up to the surface of her emotional body, but she felt nothing.

Rakib lay on top of her. He was heavy and out of breath. With their faces pressed together, Maggie could feel the start of Rakib's beard poking through his skin. He'd have to shave tomorrow. She rubbed his back with one hand and continued to stare up at the ceiling. *Oh my god,* she considered saying again, but she could force nothing from herself but deep, steady breath.

18

NEITHER OF THEM looked at each other. There had been a strained attempt at intimacy after sex. Rakib mussed Maggie's hair and kissed her forehead, but nothing sparked real connection. "You good?" he asked, and Maggie just nodded until Rakib rolled off. She sat up quickly and grabbed her coat to cover herself. Rakib stood to retrieve his pile of clothes.

Rakib focused intensely on the buttons of his shirt while Maggie hunched over to zip her boots.

"It's funny," she said, rising. "You've stopped calling me Müjde."

"What?"

"At Don's, at your place, just now." She shrugged. "You keep calling me Maggie."

Rakib finished the last button and smoothed his hand against his chest.

"Funny."

Rakib walked toward the painting while his dismissal settled around them. He stood tall, only waist-deep in its waters, while Maggie could feel it threatening to drown her. Rakib crossed his arms and stared ahead. Maggie was afraid to stand and wade nearer. She had lost faith that her closeness could soften him.

"You never told me what you think," she said from her chair.

He looked over his shoulder at her, then back at the painting. Nothing he did carried a sense of urgency.

"It's nice," he said finally.

"Nice?"

"What? What's wrong with 'nice'?"

"You've never said that about a painting in your life."

Rakib laughed. "Sure, I have," he said. "About the nice ones at least."

Maggie groaned, and a loud buzz sounded as someone rang the studio's doorbell. She forced herself out of her chair and dragged her feet to the intercom.

"Oh, c'mon, Ma—"

Maggie shot him a look, and Rakib closed his mouth. Static filled the room.

"Hello?" Maggie called into the intercom.

"It's me."

Rob's voice boomed into the studio.

Maggie's heart dropped. Her neck gave out, and her forehead fell against the wall.

"Is that...?"

Maggie nodded, her forehead massaged by the dimples in the drywall. Her finger found its way to the OPEN button and clicked. Maggie saw no other option but to let him in.

"OH."

Rob appeared in the doorway, holding a bouquet of orange flowers, most of which were tight bulbs that had yet to bloom.

"Hey," Maggie said. She flung an arm around Rob's neck and kissed him on the cheek. He winced as her lips made contact, and Maggie felt a coiling around her throat—the horror that he knew.

He could see the pink flush of her face, could smell the distinctly male sweat that had dripped down her neck. He knew Rakib had come inside her. Maggie was certain of it.

Maggie's hands fluttered around her face. She nervously touched her neck, ran her fingers through her hair, and drew her knuckles against her cheeks in an attempt to cool herself.

"You know Rakib," she said, twisting her torso toward him. She swung back to Rob, who stood still. "He was just giving me some notes before I have to meet with Lorrie next week."

"Didn't mean to interrupt," Rob said.

"Not at all." Rakib came toward them. "I'd actually better get going. It's later than I realized."

Rakib appeared beside Maggie and stuck his hand out to Rob. "Good to see you, man."

Maggie watched as Rob wrapped his hand around Rakib's, the smell of her still on Rakib's fingers now inevitably transferring to him.

"I'll shoot you an email with my thoughts, Müjde." Rakib pressed a hand into her back. "This seems like a really great start."

He slithered around Rob and Maggie to make his way out of the studio. When the last of his footsteps had petered out and they heard the front door click shut, Rob tossed the flowers onto an empty table. He crossed in front of Maggie and fully entered the studio.

"Only your parents call you Müjde," he said without looking at her.

"Other people call me that, too," she said. "It is my name after all."

She thought of Vin shouting her name over the phone and how all the butchers would say it in chorus the next time she came home.

From the opposite end of the studio, Rob turned to face her. "Don't talk to me like I'm stupid."

Rob looked at Maggie's painting. He assessed it carefully, his eyes filled with a certain earnestness that Rakib had resisted. It was the first time he had seen it this close to finished.

"Christ," he said eventually. "It's *dark*."

"I'd rather not talk about it."

"It's not a bad thing."

"Seriously, Rob. I don't want to talk about it."

"What do you want to talk about then, *Müjde*?"

Maggie pressed a long sigh through her teeth.

"Nothing," she said just before she was out of air. "I just want to go home."

Rob's eyes were cast down, his feet drilled into the ground where he stood.

"So you want to fuck other people and then come home to me?" He lifted his head slowly and looked directly at Maggie. "Is that supposed to be our new arrangement?"

"What?"

"Don't do that. Don't say 'What?'"

"Rakib was just— "

"There's a condom in the trash can, Maggie. And your skirt is on sideways."

Maggie looked down and saw that the zipper had traveled forward to her hip. She twisted the skirt around and smoothed her hands against her thighs.

"So he was giving you advice about Lorrie..." Rob nodded to himself. "About fucking her? Personally, I think you should be on top. She's getting a little old."

"You're such an asshole."

"I'm an asshole?" Rob's voice roiled like a wave climbing to crush her. "I'm an asshole?"

"Yes, Rob, you're an asshole. Fucking your way through all these 'late nights,' while I've been at home waiting for you! You think you're innocent in this?"

"Who exactly am I fucking, Maggie?"

"I don't know!" Maggie raged. "I hope it's your receptionist—what's her name? I know it's ridiculous, like some kind of cowgirl."

"Randy? Randy is twenty-two and thinks the moon landing was staged," Rob said. "*That's* who you think I'm sleeping with?"

"She's pretty," Maggie spat. "And if I'm going to be a stereotype, seems as good as anyone."

"I'm not fucking anyone, Maggie."

Rob shook his head, and she could see he was thinking of Randy, who Maggie had actually met at the holiday party last year. She chewed gum while drinking gin and tonics. The image of the shriveled blue wad traveling all around her mouth was unforgettable.

"How was the studio last night?" Rob asked.

"You don't care," Maggie said, waving him off.

"I do care," Rob said, starting to shout again. "I *especially* care because you weren't here."

Maggie was still.

"I came to apologize, but you weren't here. And I can't believe how stupid I was that I just figured you went to John's, or you were with someone from class or something. I should have known you were with him."

Rob started toward Maggie. She crossed her arms and screwed tightly into herself, bracing for him to stop in front of her, but he kept walking past. He stopped instead by the trash can and took a quick glance inside, as if to be sure he had seen what he saw. Maggie watched as a new look took over his face. No longer the climbing wave of rage, but something quiet. Something dying.

"I'm moving to London."

"What?"

"I'm moving to London," Rob said again calmly, unmoved by his announcement. All Maggie could do was blink.

"Dinner last night, had you come home with me to find out, was the last deal I had to make before being promoted. Tim, if he doesn't completely fuck it up, is taking over my role in the New York office. They're promoting me to head of the London office."

Promotion, Tim, dinner last night. It was all dizzying to Maggie. Last night felt like it was one hundred years ago.

"It never occurred to you that every night I spent at the office, every early morning meeting I took before you even woke up—that it was all building to something?"

Maggie looked at him blankly.

"You thought I was having that much sex? Are you fucking insane?"

"You never said anything." A pleading voice squeaked out of her. "You didn't tell me explicitly that you were getting promoted."

"I tried, Maggie. But you've been *here*. With *this*." Rob looked up at the painting and swung his arm toward it. His knuckles made a muffled scratching sound as they brushed against the canvas. "You haven't exactly been receptive to news outside of it."

Slowly, Maggie tried to piece together the reality of the past few months. Had she not been receptive? Had she not asked him every day how work was? Had she been listening when he answered or did his words pass through her like a sieve? Maggie could feel her legs weakening beneath her. She pulled a chair from one of the tables and flipped it over to sit.

"You're leaving?"

"I was going to tell you after dinner. I was going to take you out to explain and to celebrate, but you ran and found Rakib." Rob shook his head. "And I should have *known*."

Nothing in the room made noise except for the mild buzzing of the fluorescent lights. Maggie felt sick. Her head fell into her hands, and she brought her elbows to her knees. She had often happened upon her mother's mother in this position. Thinking and worrying, her lips rubbing together in anxious rhythm. Maggie's lips began to do the same. Her grandmother had been dead so many years now.

She looked up at Rob, her hands still holding the enormous weight of her head.

"Do you want to be with him?" Rob asked.

Maggie opened her mouth, but nothing came out.

"Right," he said, and began moving toward the door.

"Rob."

The sound of his name brought him to a standstill.

"I have to leave next week," he said. "They have a flat for us in Soho." He scoffed to himself, as if anything so stupid could matter.

"For us?"

"Well, I wasn't going to move without you. Obviously, you'd have to finish school. So I figured I'd go first while you were still in class, and then we could meet in Istanbul so I could propose."

"What?"

"Can and Serdar were helping me plan it. Serdar's getting the ring sized tomorrow."

Maggie's brain throbbed against her skull. She imagined Serdar at the same jeweler he'd used for Zeynep's ring, showing him pictures that Rob must have messaged him. Rob had done such a kind thing by including her family, making them feel useful. Running around the bazaar, no doubt, muttering "wedding," "marriage," and "bride" over and over. How wrong she'd been to ever doubt his goodness.

"And now I don't know," Rob said. He started again for the door.

Maggie returned to her grandmother's stance and spoke again without looking up. "I really fucked us, didn't I?"

Rob's footsteps were measured and hard against the floor. Maggie looked up to see him standing right in front of her.

"Yes," he said. "You did."

As Maggie watched him go, everything inside her began to rot. He didn't pause to look at her before passing through the doorway. He just left. She listened to his footsteps wind down the stairs, the same as she had with Rakib's. When she heard the door click, she lowered herself to the ground. With her eyes closed and her cheek laid against the cold linoleum, Maggie let out a wretched sound that she suspected had been living inside her for her entire life.

19

EVEN IN SWEATS, the Artist was a vision. Every article hanging from her frame was cream-colored and emitted a low vibrational frequency. She looked so soft that Maggie fought the urge to reach out and pet her.

"Maggie," she said, her voice light and cushiony. "Come in."

Maggie had texted John from the studio to see if he was home, but he was working a late shift at the hospital. *Artist is home,* he texted her back. Maggie figured being with anyone was better than being alone, so after boarding a bus she couldn't remember riding, she arrived outside John and the Artist's apartment.

Maggie trudged inside, aware of her feet hitting the hardwood while the Artist seemed to float. The comfort of the apartment flooded her senses. All the lights were on but dimmed, and the house was warm. *Like the womb,* Maggie thought.

She surveyed the walls, which were back to their former selves, boasting John and the Artist's collection of paintings. The first piece they passed was the triptych Maggie had made them, hanging prominently in the entryway.

"Whoa," Maggie surprised herself by saying. "You guys moved this."

The Artist glanced over her shoulder to see what Maggie was talking about. A blushing smile spread across her face.

"Oh yeah," she said. She waved her arms and gestured vaguely toward the other pieces around the apartment. "After the party, when we had to put everything back up, we realized nothing was in the right place." The Artist's voice drifted back to Maggie muffled, as she continued to face forward.

"Your piece has always been my favorite, so I wanted to move it up front." The Artist's head turned to Maggie as if guided by a breeze. "Everyone who comes into the apartment gets to see it now."

Maggie didn't say anything, but she was moved by the idea that something she'd made could be someone's favorite.

The Artist led them to the living room, where she had clearly been working before Maggie arrived. There were papers spread across the coffee table, and her open laptop, its screen black, sat atop a stack of books.

"I'm sorry if I'm interrupting your work," Maggie said, ashamed by how badly she needed to seek shelter.

"That's okay," the Artist said. "The work will always be there."

This approach seemed to fit in nicely with the Artist's whole persona—effortlessly breezy and somehow glamorous. *The work will always be there*. It wasn't something to rush toward or try to figure out. It would be there waiting for her to soar through it. To ascend to the next level of renown whenever she decided she was ready.

The Artist began opening kitchen cabinets.

"Tea?"

"Sure," Maggie said, collapsing onto the couch. She saw herself reflected in the blank screen of the Artist's computer and began prodding her face with the pads of her fingers. She could feel the clogged passageways of her sinuses as she pressed against her cheek bones. Maggie imagined sludge curving in on itself in loops beneath her skin. Everything about her felt convoluted and twisted like this. Like God had made her backward.

The kettle whistled, and Maggie rose to be nearer to it. She was drawn to anything that felt more alive than her and wished to be closer to whatever breathed, whatever made noise. The Artist lifted the teapot from the stove and poured steaming water into mugs. Maggie could already feel how it would warm her from the bottom up.

"Thank you," she said as the Artist handed her a mug.

They both stayed standing, their bodies propped up by the island as they leaned toward each other. The Artist blew air to cool down her tea. Maggie didn't bother. She sipped and sipped, and couldn't tell if she had burned her tongue or not. Her body had stopped sending signals to her brain.

"I slept with Rakib."

Maggie had contemplated how she would say this aloud, and in her mind her delivery had been much softer, not the awkward thing that came tumbling out of her mouth.

The Artist simply nodded.

Maggie thought about what to say next, but nothing arrived.

"And what does that mean to you?" the Artist asked. She set her cup down and looked at Maggie earnestly as she awaited an answer. She gently spun her mug around by pressing against the handle with her index finger. Everything about the Artist was slow and contemplative.

What does that mean to you? Maggie wanted to ask her. She wanted the Artist to interpret her life for her. It seemed to Maggie that was a task the Artist was better suited for than she was herself.

"I think it means I'm a bad person."

"I think you know it doesn't mean that."

Maggie sipped her tea and watched the Artist. Her way at home flowed so counter to the way Maggie had become accustomed to seeing her. While out in the world, the Artist could be histrionic, almost clownish. Bedazzled and hyperinflated. At home, she was stripped down. She was beige and easygoing.

"Rob caught us," Maggie said, to see if it would rattle her.

But in her attempt to test the Artist, Maggie ultimately struck something within herself. A stinging started in her nose, and her eyes welled up as she thought of Rob. The word *propose*.

The Artist reached out to touch Maggie's hand. She looked at Maggie and nodded sympathetically. "It's okay," she said.

Maggie's mouth quivered, and more tears welled. She shook her head. Everything was so far from okay. And with this look the Artist seemed to understand. She let go of Maggie and pushed herself from the island. Maggie pressed the heel of her hands into her eyes and felt them pulse.

"How about something stronger than tea," the Artist said.

WITH SHORT, FROSTED glasses, heavy with ice and brown liquor, they moved from the kitchen counter to the couch in the living room.

"Start from the beginning," the Artist instructed as Maggie took a sip. "Or start from wherever you want."

Maggie took a deep breath before what felt like a dive she might never surface from.

"Well," she sighed, "Rakib and I have had an amorphous relationship ever since I met him."

The Artist was already rapt. Maggie leaned her head against the couch as she thought of her days in undergrad. She told the Artist how charming Rakib had been at the beginning. And how even in his lower moments, flashes of his charm always shone through.

"He always found me," Maggie said. "I'd get myself in these stupid situations, or I'd be somewhere slightly dangerous, or I'd be just painfully lonely, and Rakib would come and find me."

"That's sweet," the Artist offered, smiling with her lips half tight.

"It *was* sweet." Maggie took another breath, to compose herself. "But then we got caught in this pattern. I'd be with him for a while, but then we'd split apart and I would date someone boring or, worse, mean. Rakib liked being free, and I think I thought I did, too. So we were never *together* together."

The Artist gave Maggie a look that seemed both sad and confused.

"What kept bringing you guys back to each other?" she asked.

"I think I felt safe," Maggie said. "Like he could see into my mind and read my thoughts. And he understood my family—constantly sending me food and calling me all the time, needing help with government forms, wailing at all the ways I wasn't what they expected as a daughter, whatever. I didn't have to explain any of that to him, and things between us were just easy."

Maggie saw something flash in the Artist's eyes, a flicker of remembering that John and Maggie weren't from here. At least, not in the way she was. The Artist's realization lasted only a split second. Her eyes dulled to their normal sheen, and she signaled for Maggie to continue.

"Well, one night I told him I wanted to make a go of it. I didn't want to split off and date anyone else. I only wanted to date him. And you would have thought I'd told him I was planning to drop a nuclear bomb. His face became hard and mean, and he just said, 'Why would we ever do that?' And it didn't seem so crazy to me! But he said he couldn't. And I just let him say that to me. I let him tell me he would never pick me, and essentially I said, 'That's okay. Because I'm always going to pick you.' He could kick me down the street every day for the rest of my life, and I really thought I'd still pick him."

The Artist gave Maggie a pained look from the other end of the couch. She reached out and placed a hand on Maggie's knee.

"Oh, Maggie. That's just awful."

Maggie shrugged. "I didn't realize it at the time, you know? I just thought that was how love was. Or maybe I thought it was what I deserved."

"After that, we didn't talk for a long time. And I was beginning to think we'd never talk again, like he was through with me. The year was spiraling toward graduation, and I tried to convince myself I didn't need him. Then, a week before we were supposed to walk across the stage and get our diplomas, Rob appeared. Just walked into a gallery opening and looked right at me. And he's handsome. I mean, when we first got together, he was *so* handsome," Maggie said, remembering his soft eyes and his smooth, even skin. His sculpted jaw and his youthful optimism. "He was just magnetic. Older than me, which I liked. And he made me feel special. He had this great job and this outlook that everything would be okay. Everything would work itself out. And he was so nice to me. After hearing Rakib say that to me—that he could never be with me—I couldn't believe that here was this gorgeous guy, and he was going to be nice to me."

Maggie had to stop, her voice shaking around memories of Rob. She hadn't thought of him and those early days in so long. They were getting to the worst part now. How Maggie had ruined everything.

"I'm sorry," Maggie said, looking at the papers spread across the table. There were piles of photographs and newspaper clippings and glue. "You're clearly here having a productive evening, and I just burst into your apartment, and I can't stop weeping. I'm behaving like a lunatic. I—I'm so sorry."

The Artist pushed herself up to scoot closer to Maggie. She planted herself so that their legs were touching, and she laid a hand against Maggie's bicep.

"This is what it is to be a person," she said simply. "This is life."

Maggie rubbed her forehead.

"Yeah, but you don't do this. You're not entering people's homes and unleashing tragedy on them."

"Well, not tonight, I'm not."

Maggie rolled her eyes at this attempt at levity. She could not imagine the Artist making herself vulnerable in a way that didn't involve an audience.

"You've never been like this," Maggie said, and caught the Artist's eyes widen. She took a quick sip of her drink. "And that's okay! I'm just saying you don't have to pretend."

"I think you know that's not being fair to me," the Artist said, not afraid to look directly into Maggie's eyes.

Maggie's mouth dropped open to defend herself, but nothing emerged. She thought of saying she had meant it as a compliment, that the Artist was so together that she didn't have to resort to acting like this. But Maggie knew she had meant to hurt the Artist. To deny her the capacity to be human.

"I'm sorry," Maggie said. "You're right, and I'm sorry."

"That's okay," the Artist said in way that sounded resolved. No lingering need to hear Maggie apologize again. "Sometimes I think people forget, because I can be so 'out there,'"—she said this with her eyes slightly crazed and her head moving back and forth—"but I'm a person, too. If you cut me, I bleed."

Maggie felt profoundly stupid and cruel. She'd walked around acting like the Artist was full of air or glitter instead of guts and sinew.

The Artist gave Maggie's arm a light squeeze. "So," she said. "Rob was nice to you, and..."

Her hand was heavy and warm. Maggie wished she would keep it there forever.

"You know Rob. He's lovely, and he takes care of me, and my mother loves him. He can be a saint. But every once in a while, I feel something tugging my sleeve telling me something's not right. He'll be looking at me sometimes, and I just know he doesn't really see me."

"And then lately, we just completely split apart. It was all these late nights, both his and mine. No one was ever home. I thought he was cheating on me, actually."

The Artist made an amused sound, and Maggie realized how preposterous this must seem to the world. The reality of Rob cheating had existed only for her. No one else could see it because she had made it up. Maggie sighed, thinking of how real it had seemed. How she could feel it in her body.

"And I ruined it," Maggie's voice cracked. "Rakib showed up—because he always knows when I'm at my weakest—and I fucked everything up."

The Artist took her hand back and rested it in her lap.

"What did Rob say when he caught you guys?"

"He said he hadn't been cheating. He's being promoted." Maggie looked at her lap. "He's moving to London."

Maggie's voice could not recover from shaking or cracking.

"He said he was going to propose."

"Oh, Maggie."

Maggie finally broke into a wave of tears, her head lolling toward her chest, snot flowing from her nose past her mouth. She wiped at the mucus with the back of her hand. It traveled in strings across her body and stuck to the fine hairs all along her arms. The Artist pulled Maggie into her chest and rubbed Maggie's back.

"Cry," she said over and over again. "Cry, cry, cry."

IT WAS EASY to stop the crying once Maggie caught her breath, but that had taken longer than she'd wished to be pressed against the Artist. She was relieved not to be alone, though, because alone she knew she wouldn't have bothered to stop herself. She would have stayed in the studio and let her tears fall freely and violently. Her mother had once commented on this when Maggie was in high school. "Müjde knows only to cry as though she's lost a child." Maggie overheard her saying this during a conversation in the living room. She didn't lower her voice to say it. She'd made the comment intentionally to shame Maggie, but it had the opposite effect. Maggie felt strangely proud at how profoundly and deeply she could feel. *I can mourn for everyone I've ever known,* she remembered thinking to herself. She was fifteen.

The Artist made no comment about how much or how hard Maggie could cry, which Maggie was grateful for. She just held Maggie and encouraged her to keep going. She kept saying it would be okay, which Maggie didn't believe. But when she looked into the Artist's face, she could see that *she* did. That felt motherly, Maggie thought—the certainty that life would turn out. Mothers always seemed to feel that way, because they had already lived through so much, and life had, for the most part, turned out for them.

After blowing her nose one final time, Maggie took a breath that was loud enough to be considered spoken.

"Jesus," she said. She was about to apologize again, but she knew that the Artist would push that away. That she would wave her hands and say something like "No need."

"It's so late," Maggie said instead, though she had no idea what time it was. "I should probably go home."

She clicked a button on her phone and saw that it was 11 p.m.

"Do you want to stay?" the Artist asked.

"Are you sure?" Maggie asked, ashamed she couldn't bring herself to politely refuse.

"Of course," the Artist said, getting up to go to the kitchen. "It might be nice to have some space to yourself for one night."

The Artist turned on the tap and began washing the mugs and glasses they had dirtied. The sound of rushing water was peaceful. Maggie was relieved that it replaced the need to talk or cry. She sat still on the couch for a moment before leaning over the coffee table and scanning what was spread across its surface.

There were towering stacks of glossy photographs and pages of text with scientific headings. Maggie skimmed some photographs from the top of one of the stacks. They were all of things on fire—churches, wooden logs in an outdoor fireplace, acres and acres of crisp, blackened trees.

She came across an image of a crib on fire. A white crib in a room with gnarled oatmeal-colored wall-to-wall carpeting. There was a rocking horse in the corner and those rainbow-colored plastic rings that stack around a white post. All you could see of the crib were its legs, as the rest had been engulfed in brownish-red flames.

Maggie balanced the photos back onto the tower she had pulled them from. Who had taken such a picture? Was it real? The house looked real. The carpeting looked real. So real that she could feel it beneath her feet just by imagining it. Maggie told herself that it couldn't have been, though. It must have been staged. She told herself that the crib was empty, but there was no way to be sure.

The Artist returned to her spot on the couch, which had become creased from her hours of listening to Maggie.

"What's all this?" Maggie asked, gesturing to the coffee table. She was surprised by how little alarm had infiltrated her tone.

"Oh, just some research." The Artist waved her hand over it like it was a nuisance.

"Your next project?"

"You could say that."

The Artist looked around the apartment, avoiding Maggie's gaze when it had been the least humiliating.

"Is it a photo exhibit?" Maggie asked.

"Oh *god*, no." She said this like photography was the most banal medium to ever exist. Almost like it had been a mistake to invent the camera.

The Artist broke down and began talking about self-portraits, the early Renaissance, and narcissism. Maggie was half listening, half looking at the burning crib, waiting for what the Artist was saying to align with what Maggie was seeing. She was rambling a bit, and as she slowed to a stop, the Artist said, shrugging, "I guess what I'm trying to say is, I'm making a kind of self-portrait."

Maggie's eyes flickered from the photo to the Artist.

"I'm going to set myself on fire."

THE ARTIST WAS apparently in the nascent stages of planning, gathering source material and plotting how she might set herself on fire. She fanned out a stack of images that horrified Maggie. They were from a pile that had been out of her initial reach. Surgical photographs of burn victims—charred flesh, gaping pink wounds, hair that had singed and clung to itself and became hard like plastic. Maggie tried not to gasp. The Artist was completely stoic, flitting through the photographs without producing a single reaction. The last one she fanned toward Maggie was the face of a burn victim, her eyes bandaged shut.

"Obviously, at first I looked into whether I could self-immolate without actually setting myself on fire," the Artist said, "but it didn't seem like I could do it without inflicting critical damage or even death."

Maggie stared at the Artist, trying to pinpoint how and when she had slipped from normalcy to insanity. Physically, it was imperceptible. She looked perfectly fine, pushing up her glasses to sit higher on the bridge of her nose. Her keratin treatment was growing out, revealing half an inch of coarse, curly roots. She picked at a hangnail on her thumb. Then she mentioned falling into a meditative trance while watching self-immolation videos online.

"Have you seen them?" she asked Maggie.

"No. I can't say that I have."

"I think everybody should see one. At least once."

Maggie felt sick to her stomach.

"Do you want to watch one?" the Artist asked.

The only self-immolation video Maggie knew of was of Mohamed Bouazizi and the Arab Spring. Her parents had watched it on the news, but Maggie couldn't bring herself to stay in the room. She had heard the broadcast from her bedroom—a woman enunciating every word with exacting precision. Curled up in her bed, Maggie had closed her eyes. She saw the screen in her mind: A blond woman with her big mouth moving, a clip of the flames in the upper right-hand corner, expanding to fill the screen. Bouazizi drenched in gasoline. The smell of burning flesh trapped behind the television. Screaming. Absolute terror. How anyone could watch something so gruesome was beyond her.

"I think I'm okay," Maggie said, trying to strike a tone that was devoid of judgment and horror.

"We'll just watch one," the Artist said, clicking a few keys on her laptop. A video must have already been pulled up, because it didn't take long for something to begin playing.

Maggie stood up suddenly and shut the laptop. The slap of metal against metal was louder than she meant for it to be.

"I think I need to go to sleep," she said.

The sentence she chose to speak seemed strange, even to Maggie, but what else could she have said? *I think there is something wrong with you. I don't want to watch someone who looks like half of my cousins set himself on fire. I don't understand how you can keep doing this.*

"Of course." The Artist shook her head. She looked like she was about to hit her forehead with an open hand, but instead she ran her fingers through her hair. "You've had a long day."

Sorry, Maggie felt the urge to say but didn't.

"Do you need anything?"

To be euthanized. Maggie shook her head.

"Well, there's extra toothbrushes in the guest bathroom. You know where everything is."

Maggie thanked the Artist and made her way down the hall to sleep.

THE ARTIST STAYED awake for a few more hours. Maggie could hear her rustling every so often and assumed she was waiting for John to come home. But at some point, the peachy light of the apartment went black, and the Artist went to bed. Maggie heard her humming as she washed her face.

Not meaning to, Maggie stayed awake long enough to hear John's key turn in the door, the clanging as he threaded the chain lock, and the dull thud as he kicked off his shoes. She listened to the water run for his shower, then the angry sounds of the water heater as it shut off. She thought of Rob in their apartment. How he must have done the same routine hours ago.

Maggie kept turning over in the bed, searching for cool, untouched corners to bring down her temperature. Her legs traveled diagonally across the mattress, where they'd usually collide with Rob. She kicked the empty space as if he were there, as if she could conjure a smile out of him. Maggie tried to imagine packing up their lives and moving to a new country, but it all came up blurry in her mind. She didn't know what the streets looked like in London, didn't know what it would be like to walk down them arm in arm with Rob. She looked at her hand and imagined a ring on her finger, then dragged that same hand across her face. Why did Rob have to tell her that he was going to propose? To punish her, she realized. And after fucking Rakib, she concluded that she deserved it. Maggie turned again, but nothing left in the bed was cool. Everything had been ruined with her touch.

20

JOHN WAS SITTING at the kitchen island reading the newspaper. Maggie watched him from the edge of the hallway before breaking his focus. It was like happening upon their father in their childhood home first thing in the morning, always on the couch with the lamp lit above him. His glasses near the tip of his nose and his head tilted toward the news. Except John had all his hair and kept his spine straight. He held the paper up in front of his face instead of lowered into his lap. Maggie imagined that he'd lower the paper when she entered the room, just as her father would have. "Kızım," her father would've greeted her. My girl.

"Morning," Maggie said, pulling a glass from one of the cabinets.

John flipped to the next page. The crumpling of the newspaper was loud like a gun.

Maggie's eyelids wouldn't fully open, thickened from crying all night. She imagined them scabbing over and never being able to see again. She thought of John Milton, who'd gone blind later in his life and narrated the entirety of *Paradise Lost* to his daughters. Of course to his daughters. Maggie wasn't sure if he'd even had sons, but the point still stood. Where there was slack, there were young women to pick it up.

The Romantics had painted him. Milton with his sight ravaged, sitting with his girls. Quills in their hands as they transcribed the fall of man. Who could Maggie dictate her work to if her eyes sealed shut? Would Mimmo be able to paint her women? Or John's girlfriend? Or rosy-cheeked, barely graduated Camille? Could Sofia do this for her? Set aside her equations and lab work to paint themselves standing together, holding each other up?

"Are you okay?" John asked, finally speaking.

Maggie looked up to realize she'd left the tap running with her glass beneath it. It had completely overflowed, and water was running down her hand. Maggie shut it off and left her glass in the sink to find a towel.

"Drawer," John said as Maggie scanned the countertop.

She eventually found the correct drawer and began drying her hands. Still holding on to the paper, John watched her.

"Do you need a ride home?" he asked.

"Is that all you're going to say to me?"

"What else do you want me to say, Müjde?"

Something kind, maybe. Something loving. The Artist had managed to do it. To say out loud that Maggie wasn't a bad person.

"How long did you know about the proposal?" she asked.

"Three months."

"And Mom and Dad?"

"They don't know," John said, setting down the paper. "They think the trip is a graduation gift."

Maggie looked at the couch where she and the Artist had spent the evening. She instantly wished for the Artist's palm to travel across her back again. Comfort pouring out of every surface of her being. Maggie glanced at the coffee table and saw that the photographs had been filed into long, rectangular gray boxes, lidded and labeled. Her laptop was gone. She must have left the apartment before Maggie had woken up.

"Did she know, too?" Maggie asked.

John shook his head.

"No," he said. "Just me and Serdar. Rob wanted it to be a surprise."

The rage Maggie felt bubble up inside her threatened to expel itself, like foam spewing from her mouth. What right did John have to say Rob's name to her? Like it wasn't the only word in the world that could kill her. Maggie turned to leave the kitchen and retreat into her room.

"Where are you going?" he asked.

"Home."

"Is that all you're going to say to me?"

Maggie gave him a look before disappearing to get dressed. "I'm not sure what else you want me to say, Can."

Her clothes from the night before were damp and sour with nervous sweat. Maggie masked as much of the scent as she could with a sugary perfume she found in the bathroom, but she had to stop spraying halfway through, because it was giving her a headache. She pulled the shirt away from her face as she passed John in the kitchen.

"I'll drive you," he said.

"I'll walk."

"Don't be a pain," he said. "Walking would take you two hours easily." He made this sound like two hours was the longest anything could be in the entire world.

"I'm not in a rush."

"It's cold," he said, trying once more.

Maggie wanted to lean in close to his ear, so close that the peach fuzz on his earlobe would graze her chapped lips, and scream. Instead, she planted her hand on his shoulder, hard, to show he hadn't crushed her even though he'd tried.

"I'll be fine," she said evenly.

John made eye contact with Maggie, his eyes punishing and steely.

"If you say so."

JOHN WAS RIGHT. It was cold. But walking on the sunny side helped, and eventually, when the sun hung straight above her, Maggie began to warm up. Her armpits sweat through the sickly-sweet scent of the Artists' perfume, through the oily scent of the night before, and generated a wholly new putrid smell. It smelled feral and wild, but it didn't repulse Maggie. This was her body. It excreted her disgusting pheromones perfectly, just as nature would have it.

Maggie considered whether this was the beginning of the end, or some kind of devastating chance at rebirth. Her plane had crashed and caught fire, and now was the time to either emerge from the rubble with a renewed sense of purpose or be pronounced dead at the scene. Dead on impact. Quick and painless.

No one seemed to mention how before deaths that are quick and painless, they are long and terrifying. Plummeting in a plane from thousands of feet in the air into the earth's crust is an endless amount of suffering, even if the death is not. There were the months of navigating the emotional gulf between her and Rob. There was the slow-motion fall of letting herself be drawn to Rakib. The crash—the look on Rob's face last night. And the explosion after the crash, when Maggie realized she had been the one steering the plane. All along she'd assumed it had been Rob.

Marriage had been where they were heading for the past year or so. And Maggie was proud they weren't the naïve couple who merely hinted at marriage in hopes the other would say yes. They'd made a point to be sensible. Maggie wanted to be done with school. She wanted to have a job. She was waiting for the moment to strike her when she felt *ready*. The conditions for feeling ready were ambiguous and always just out of reach, which frustrated Rob, but Maggie was sure the day would come. That one morning she would wake up and the feeling would have encased her in some way. "I'm ready," she'd whisper to him, still in bed.

Rob was different. He was dejected that they discussed marriage like it was a legal transaction. Which it *was*, Maggie kept explaining. He wanted it to be a surprise, to get down on one knee when Maggie least expected it. He wanted roses, romance. Maggie wanted it to be over with.

Her mother, unsurprisingly, had been the most excited when Maggie mentioned they were discussing marriage. Next most excited was Rob, then her father, her sister, and her brother, then Maggie. But now, Maggie doubted her reticence. *Propose* had sounded so serious and real coming out of Rob's mouth last night that it did something to Maggie. Was this it? The feeling she'd been waiting to befall her? Was this being ready?

So many things stood in their way. There was moving to London, which had never been a part of their plan. Would she go with him? Would she leave New York and start calling the elevator *the lift*? Her mother would die, Maggie thought. She already lamented, constantly, how far away Maggie had fled from home, that moving to another country seemed impossible. It's what her mother had done before Maggie and Sofia were born. Leaving her own mother in Turkey to go to another world, only to return a handful of times. Their grandmother had apparently refused to let go of baby Can the morning they left for the airport, wailing and wailing about what was to come, knowing she'd never really see them again—not every day, like she wanted to. Summers, maybe, but that could never be long enough. One night, through tears, Maggie's mother bemoaned that she had flown back to Turkey to be with her mother in death, but not in life. Maggie was heartbroken for both of them. Maggie swore to herself she would never commit the same kind of cruelty.

She turned the final corner and looked at her phone for the time. Her brother was right, again. She'd arrived in front of her building about two hours after leaving his.

Maggie stood in front of the door and waited for it to open, forgetting for a split second that it was a revolving door and she would have to push. Once inside, she remembered everything again—the button in the elevator, third floor, square key in the bottom lock. Home.

21

THE LIVING ROOM was filled with boxes that must have appeared overnight. They were still empty, for the most part, flat and leaned up against a wall, but Maggie could see that Rob was already going through their things. Plucking out his from hers, wrapping, stuffing, folding, and packing. She dropped her purse on the floor so he would hear her, but no one stirred.

Maggie approached a stack of boxes and reached for one. She pressed the sides until it opened like a mouth, folded the bottom, and taped it shut. Everything she lifted belonged to Rob. Miniature nesting bowls that were hammered copper, a lead-colored sculpture that Maggie always thought looked medieval but was made in the nineties, coffee-table books on neo-futurist architecture. There was a time when Maggie had tried to convince herself that she liked these things, that they had meaning and heft. But now, they just felt heavy and dark. There was something cathartic about nestling them into a box and taping it shut.

She thought about packing a few of her things, too. The candlesticks she'd bought online because they looked like the ones her aunt had when Maggie was growing up. What if she wrapped them in paper, gently laid them in with Rob's things, along with more of her belongings? She tried this, rolling the candlesticks in tissue paper and placing them in a way they wouldn't jostle around. They looked sad, pinned against the cardboard, calling to Maggie to reclaim them. She pulled them out and unrolled the tissue. They would stay with her, she decided.

The living room began to disappear as Maggie filled more and more boxes. Among their belongings, she found an old photo of her and Rob. It was from their last trip to Turkey. She had taken it during one of the up-late nights that preceded Serdar's wedding. The power in her uncle's house had gone out, and in the photo there were three white candles dripping wax onto a low antique table—something Maggie was eviscerated for the next day. The candles barely, but mightily, fought to illuminate Rob. In the photo, his face seemed in and out of darkness, his forehead and eyes mostly obscured, but his soft smiling mouth pink and glowy. His hands were perfectly articulated, as was Maggie's foot, being massaged between them.

Maggie could remember the day perfectly. They had gone on a long, curving walk through Istanbul. She'd told Rob that the really hot nights were the best for walking, because all the tourists stayed in their hotels and had dinner in over-air-conditioned lobby bars. Because of this, they'd had the emptied roads to themselves, and they'd walked for hours while the late-summer sun lingered.

"This is where I learned how to swim," Maggie said as they passed a crumbling pink building whose damp air reeked of chlorine. "I was the oldest kid there by so many years, and it was so humiliating. These four-year-olds kicking and turning their heads to breathe, and I'm seven and terrified, and everything is so loud." Maggie shook her hands by either side of her head. "If we ever have kids, we're teaching them how to swim when they're babies."

Rob emitted a low, gravelly hum. It was the same sound he made after sex, when Maggie would lay her head against his chest. The sound he made when he hugged her after a long absence. It used to be her favorite sound in the world. The rattle of pure, unending satisfaction.

When they arrived back at Mehmet's house, every room was hot and dark. The power was still out, and rather than stay awake and fumble around in the black, her family had gone to sleep. Rob positioned himself on the couch while Maggie rooted around until she found the three candles to light. His face appeared in an angelic beam at the strike of the first match. Like the birth of a star, Maggie remembered thinking.

"I love how you move here," he said as Maggie pursed her lips to blow out the match. She shook it by her side and dragged her hand through its trail of smoke.

"What do you mean?"

"You're so liquid here."

They sat on the couch facing each other, and Maggie draped her legs over Rob's.

"It's just different," he said. His hand lightly found its way to Maggie's shin, and he grazed his fingertips back and forth.

Maggie leaned her head against the couch, suddenly crushed beneath the weight of the heat and the length of their walk. She wiggled her feet, and Rob's hand traveled from her shin to her foot, taking it easily into his hands. His thumbs pushed into her sore arches, and Maggie closed her eyes.

"I love how every day is so hot," she mumbled.

"Yeah?"

"Long and hot. Not undulating, no break. You know what it's going to feel like all day, and you kind of get used to it. You get used to being hot and sort of agitated. You get accustomed to the sweat always gathering, even after you wipe it away."

Rob laughed. "I feel like I'm dying."

Maggie smiled with her eyes still closed. "Yabancı," she said sleepily. *Foreigner.*

Rob pressed circles into the balls of her feet, and Maggie peacefully succumbed to gratitude. She remembered producing a hum of her own, but nothing as sweet or as deep as the sound that could come from Rob.

Keys jangled at the apartment door, and the lock turned. Maggie, sitting on the floor of the living room, looked up to find Rob, his face obscured behind a teetering roll of Bubble Wrap, and a paper bag hanging from his wrist.

"Hey," Maggie said, extracting herself from the photograph. She set it on the floor next to her.

Rob placed everything on the kitchen island and observed Maggie from above. "You're home," he said, sounding surprised.

"I'm home," she said back.

He looked at how many boxes Maggie had already filled and shook his head. "You didn't have to do that."

Maggie shrugged. "I just wanted to help."

She unraveled herself and stepped around everything she had scattered on the floor. Maggie grabbed the Bubble Wrap from the counter and hugged it to herself. Rob watched her, and Maggie squeezed tighter.

"Where'd you stay last night?" he asked.

"John's."

Maggie looked at her bare feet and spread her toes. She looked back at Rob, who was waiting for more.

"His girlfriend is going to set herself on fire."

Rob smirked. "Good for her."

He stepped into the living room to survey what Maggie had packed. He turned from the unfinished box to the short stack of boxes she had sealed and labeled. He stepped over the scissors and ran a hand along an edge of cardboard. He waited to speak until the entire living room was between them.

"Well," he said, lifting his head.

Rob's pained anticipation shot through Maggie. This soft and tender person. He had already forgiven her. Maggie could see it in his limp body, barely murmuring signs of life. He had no interest in punishing her. *Let's move past this,* his limbs begged, nothing tense or taut enough to fight.

"Rob."

The sound of his own name struck him.

"You're not coming," he said.

"I'm not coming," she repeated, though it wasn't what she'd planned to say. Something had passed through Maggie that softened her own body like Rob's.

"I can't move to London, Rob. I can't get married and have a baby and paint in the spare room."

"We could rent a studio," he said, knowing that wasn't the point.

"And if my dad got sick again? How could I be that far away?" Maggie had taken a leave of absence from undergrad when her father was first diagnosed. John was just starting medical school and couldn't fly back and forth, so Maggie had flown out for every chemo treatment. If not for her father, then to help her mother or Sofia, who was still so young then—in high school, staying up all night memorizing biology, learning about what kind of cells were trying to kill their father.

Neither Rob nor Maggie seemed fully satisfied or convinced by her reasoning. Rob's whole life was here, too, after all. His father had died before he and Maggie had even met, but what if something happened to his mom?

"Is that all?" he asked.

A stone sank in Maggie's stomach. He would make her say it—the thing she had suspected for their entire relationship, which she'd taken painstaking measures to ignore. That they weren't right. That Rob's mother had called it up close, in their third month of dating. Maggie was exotic. Too strange and different. Too dark. Too mysterious.

"It feels like we don't work," Maggie said. "At least, not like we hoped we would."

"Not like we hoped we would," Rob repeated.

Phlegm coated his vocal cords, the threat of tears worse than tears themselves. The pain Maggie felt from not touching him, not rushing over to hold him in this moment, was something that could kill a person. *I love you,* she wanted to call out to him from across the living room, but saying so now felt unfair. Even if it was true.

"So you'll stay with him?" he asked.

At first, Maggie figured he meant John, but she watched the quiver of his throat as he swallowed and realized he'd meant Rakib.

"I'll stay with John."

Maggie hoped the sturdiness of her answer would mean something to him.

"I'll help set his girlfriend on fire."

She was relieved that Rob let this amuse him.

"You don't want to stay here?" he asked.

"I can't afford to stay here. You're too good for me, remember?"

"Maybe so," he said, looking down and shrugging. He peeked at Maggie. She smiled, unsure if he was joking.

"It's paid for through next month. You know you can just stay."

"Are you sure?" she asked. "I don't want to if you don't want me to."

"I want you to."

The tears had receded from Rob's eyes. After clearing his throat, he'd successfully recomposed himself. This brought Maggie in the other direction, close to dissolving.

"Okay," she said, tremors in her voice. "If you're sure."

"I'm sure."

Slowly dismounting from their conversation, Rob walked toward the open box and began casually gathering things to place inside. Maggie observed for a minute but then headed for the bedroom. She paused when she saw Rob pick up the photograph.

"See?" she said. "You are too good for me."

Rob's eyes flitted between her and the photograph. Maggie watched him shake his head until she had walked far enough that she couldn't see him anymore.

MAGGIE FELL ASLEEP while Rob continued packing. She woke up every twenty minutes, afraid she had slept through the whole afternoon, but fell back asleep quickly, figuring she had nothing better to do.

After almost three hours, Maggie got up and stammered through a chat with Rob in the hallway—Would they still have dinner together? Yes, they decided—and left for the studio.

The door to the studio was already cracked open, light peeking through to the stairwell. When Maggie stepped inside, she was surprised to find Wade's spindly frame stationed in front of her canvas. His arms were crossed, closed off to the universe.

"Wade?"

"Maggie," he said, startled. "I-I'm sorry."

Maggie approached a table and set down her bag.

"Nothing to be sorry about," she said. "I was just surprised."

Wade turned back to her painting, and Maggie made her way to stand beside him.

"Well," he said. "You certainly found a way to make them worse."

Maggie laughed.

"Oh gosh." Wade flung a hand to cover his face. "That's not what I meant. I just mean they look worse. Not worse, technically. Worse in agony." He looked at Maggie with pleading eyes. "You know what I'm trying to say, don't you?"

Maggie smiled.

"Yes," she said. "I do."

Wade gave a relieved nod, letting a puff of air through his lips. The two of them stared ahead.

Maggie saw the few things left to do. The tight black outline of all the figures, to make them sharp and defined. A foot she hated that she needed to shade more carefully. The bow on a small dog an outer woman was carrying in a basket.

"I'm sorry if I'm interrupting," Wade said. "I just wanted to come see it."

"Oh yeah?"

"I heard you may get nominated," he said, eyes still on the painting. "I was walking by Lorrie's office, and she was talking to someone on the panel. She didn't say your name, but it was easy to figure out when she started describing how big the piece was."

"It's just a maybe," Maggie said, nervous and nauseous. "She hasn't said anything official yet."

Wade turned to her again. "Look at it, Maggie."

Maggie tried to see her painting as Wade could, but it was, of course, impossible. She was too close, too deep in it, to know anything.

"I'll let you get to it," Wade said, already moving toward the door. "Congra—"

"Don't," Maggie said, harsher than she had meant to.

But Wade understood. As he left the studio, he swung his arm behind him, flashing a few fingers by way of goodbye.

IT WAS IMPOSSIBLE to reconcile Wade's premature congratulations with Rakib's "nice." Maggie sifted through each detail for what Rakib had meant, but the basis of his criticism evaded her. These women were not *nice*. They were harrowing and heavy and beautiful. Full and scary and dark. As she took them all in, not a single woman struck her as nice.

Peering into their faces, Maggie saw every woman she ever knew. Her great-aunt, who had outlived her two children and in her old age had now gone mute. The tragedy, so heavy, sat directly on her throat. Her mother. Her mother's mother. Little Sofia—who technically wasn't little anymore, but in Maggie's mind she was always so slight and shaking, desperately trying to tell the world that she was different but also looking for someone to cling to, someone she could belong with. Maggie saw her old neighbor in Ridgewood, who sat on her stoop in a purple robe and said "Good morning, baby" to every person who passed by. One morning, her neighbor's chair sat empty, and at its feet was a pile of bodega flowers. Then Lillian. She even saw Lillian in a pale, pained figure. How unimaginable it must be to wake up every day and know that your mother is gone. Maggie extended her gaze to see a woman on the far side of the painting who was so obviously Grace. Her tenacity, how she stuck it to everyone who stood in her path, emanated from her brow. Even though the woman's mouth was closed, Maggie could see Grace's gums flash in her smile. Then came a shorter woman with dark, beady eyes, and Maggie could see her second cousin Ayşe, who no one in the family liked, because she was a know-it-all. Poor Ayşe, who knew everyone disliked her but who didn't know how to stop being disliked. A tall, birdlike woman with a shock of dark hair pierced Maggie's memory of family and made her think of Lorrie. Her killer career and stinging fashion sense. Her kindness cloaked in sharp-tongued wit. No partner, no kids. *Like Cathy,* Maggie thought, *if she rid herself from Don.* Maggie shook her head when she realized her instinct had been to call her Kitty. *Cathy, Cathy, Cathy,* she repeated to herself. Her eyes traveled to the girl who had pulled Rakib toward her, the one he'd said looked like his sister. Maggie remembered seeing his three sisters at graduation. The youngest one had an eating disorder; Maggie could see her bones whispering beneath her skin. She was the sister studying to be an aerospace engineer, Rakib mentioned to Maggie once when she'd asked him about his family. She didn't give her much thought at the time, but lately Maggie had thought of that sister often. Her brittle bones floating in space. Holding all these women in Maggie's mind at once made her think of the Artist and all the ways she made John better, more expansive. Maggie thought about how her art was absurd but not stupid.

So many women, and they were all there on her canvas. They each had their pain, but standing together, side by side, they were like a steel dam. No matter what horror came for them, their sheer strength would keep them alive. It wasn't until now that Maggie realized what she had done. She had spent months and months trying to bring these women to death and what they proved to her was that she couldn't kill them, no matter how hard she had tried.

22

NAVIGATING THE APARTMENT with Rob was sticky at first. He was always heading into a new room, rummaging for things to pack, making an unreasonable amount of noise and mess as he gathered his belongings. Maggie felt the safest thing for her to do emotionally was to stay in the bedroom, sit perfectly still, and avoid any possibility of colliding with him. But then she had to shower, had to boil water for the one teacup Rob had left out for her, had to exist in motion. And so they started bumping into each other, exchanging "Sorry" and "My bad" ad nauseam.

The nights were easier. Everything went still at night. Rob spent most evenings reading on the couch. The lone light of the standing lamp would be the last to extinguish whenever he had finished reading. Then he'd convert the couch into a bed and fall asleep with his legs curled under him like an animal. If Rob was going out, he'd pop his head in and ask if she wanted anything. Maggie usually said no, but one night she agreed to takeout, paired with wine, which they drank straight from the bottle, since Rob had already packed the wineglasses. The movers had yet to come for their furniture, but Maggie and Rob sat on the floor anyway. They ate straight from the containers, like they had when they first moved in. Something about packing everything up lent itself to talking about their early days.

Rob reminisced about the party they'd thrown when Maggie got accepted to grad school. He'd asked everyone upon arrival to say their favorite thing about Maggie. And no repeats, he'd insisted. Maggie tried not to feel sad as she remembered along with him.

"And you wore that green dress," Rob said, bold after a swig of wine.

Maggie thought of the dress, printed with white daisies down one side.

"I was so much prettier back then."

"You're still pretty, Mags."

But she had aged in the few years that had brought them to now. Maggie remembered exactly how she had looked at that party, in that dress, which would probably be loose on her now. She had a wide-open look on her face, like life had yet to get to her. She looked like a little girl, trusting and sweet. Like bright and blushing Camille.

The passing years had made Maggie harsh. She'd been whittled down to her sharp bones, she no longer had the cushion of healthy fat that had made her radiant and rococo and youthful. She hated to admit this to herself, but she also scowled more and had a faint line between her brows to prove it. Maggie felt so far away from that glittering self that reaching back to touch her seemed impossible.

"You, on the other hand, have only gotten better-looking over the years," Maggie said. She grabbed the wine bottle and took a sip before adding, "Very annoying."

Rob laughed, and his gleaming smile proved her point. They could be kind like this, it seemed, only because it was the end.

"Maggie?"

She bristled at hearing Rob say her name in full. They were veering somewhere serious, and she wasn't sure she was strong enough to withstand whatever tender memory Rob was about to unearth.

"Robert?" she preemptively teased, hoping to discourage him from plunging them somewhere deep.

"I just wanted to tell you that I'm sorry."

Maggie twisted the napkin in her hand and tried to avoid Rob's eyes as he spoke.

"I know it's too late, but I'm sorry for all of it. For not telling you about London, for that horrible dinner, for letting us drift so far apart. I should have—" He stopped himself and waited until Maggie looked up at him again. "I'm just so sorry."

The muscles in Maggie's face quivered, and she gave Rob as much of a smile as she could muster. She reached out to hold his hand, both of them squeezing until Maggie let her hand go limp. She pulled her hand back and pushed her food around with her fork.

"I should probably get to bed," Maggie said. She began picking up the rest of the half-full containers from the floor. "I have my meeting with Lorrie tomorrow."

Rob helped her bring the food back into the kitchen.

"The big one, huh?" Rob said, more than asked.

"Yeah, the thirty-thousand-dollar one."

Maggie opened the fridge to put in their leftovers, and Rob appeared by her side. He laid his hand in between her shoulder blades, leaned into Maggie's ear, and whispered, "Bet you thirty grand she nominates you."

Rob kissed her cheek and left Maggie standing by the fridge as he went to run the water for a shower.

MAGGIE HELD HER breath as she watched Lorrie newly interrogate the painting. Unable to quell her anxiety and anticipation, Maggie had stayed up all night, and she now felt delirious. Like the fluid surrounding her brain was fizzy, everything threatening to pop. Was Lorrie being uncharacteristically careful and slow, pacing from one side of the canvas to the other? Or was she going at a normal speed? She seemed to pause at each woman, but she was also moving so much that it almost didn't seem to Maggie that she'd ever been still.

Either way, Lorrie was making her way from one figure to the next, occasionally asking Maggie questions.

"You sharpened her features?" she said, ticking her head toward one of the women.

"Mm-hmm," Maggie said, struggling to bring Lorrie's face into focus.

"Hmm," Lorrie said, and glided over to the next woman and then the next.

Maggie's body was filled with sand. Her legs were heavy and unmovable. She tried to wiggle her fingers, but they hardly stirred. Maggie was scared that if she opened her mouth, instead of words, ocher-colored granules would pour out of her like vomit.

She looked to her canvas and found the woman Rakib said she'd given the most light, her mother. *Mom,* she wanted to say aloud. Maggie wanted to conjure her into the room—to feel her arms around her, to be smothered into the folds of her neck. Then she thought again of the sand and kept her mouth closed.

Lorrie lapped the canvas once, then drew back to the center and stared at the painting in full. She tucked one strand of hair behind her ear, then moments later the other. Maggie let herself be hopeful, but then she thought of Rakib and his dreaded "nice." She knew if Lorrie herself said that word, the grant would slip from her grasp.

Lorrie leaned back from the painting and removed her glasses.

"So you did it," she said at last, and air poured out of Maggie, her body becoming her own again.

She bent her legs a little, then her arms, and was surprised by how readily she could move. Maggie felt her nostrils begin to sting. Her eyes filled up. She pressed her fingertips into her eyelids and took a deep, chilling breath to stop herself from crying.

Lorrie placed a hand on Maggie's shoulder and said it again, almost in disbelief herself. "You did it."

Maggie's tongue undulated in her mouth, unable to form a sentence.

"Now"—Lorrie squeezed Maggie's shoulder and retracted her hand—"you'll get an email when you get home saying that I've nominated you. The next email will be in a few weeks, and it will be good news or it will be bad news, but you've done all you can, so I don't want you to think about it anymore than that. It's just an email, and you will get thousands more in your lifetime."

This made Maggie laugh and puff out more of the tension in her face.

"Thank you," Maggie said. "Thank you so much."

"You don't need to thank me," Lorrie said, everything emitting from her very literal. "You did this, not me."

She patted Maggie's shoulder a second time, and they left the studio. Once on the sidewalk, just before they parted ways, Lorrie turned to Maggie and looked deep into her eyes. "I'm proud of you, Maggie."

Then Lorrie headed uptown, which was the real gift, so Maggie could finally shed her tears alone.

STANDING BENEATH THE doorframe of the building's entrance, Maggie took a deep breath and felt the air shifting toward spring, toward summer. She watched as people passed her: Students talking to each other, heads turned inward, not bothering to look forward, at oncoming traffic. Skinny guys with big headphones, bobbing slightly as they made their way to wherever they were going. Maggie joined the foot traffic and admired how the sidewalk absorbed her.

Snaking her way home, Maggie took a long, circuitous route, seeing in what ways she could extend her moment of relief. She stepped into her beloved bodega from undergrad. The thin Yemeni man who worked the register no longer recognized her, but he still smiled in her general direction when she walked in. Maggie bought herself one of the silver-wrapped Baci chocolates Rakib used to bring her, stepped back out on the street, and popped it in her mouth. She pretended it had been given to her, pretended she was eighteen, nineteen, twenty, and class had just let out.

Maggie tried not to get carried away by her news, but it was hard not to imagine the tantalization of winning. She tried to force down images of her standing in the middle of a gallery surrounded by all her best work. Resisted the pull to think about what she would wear, how glamorous she would look with a long-stemmed glass in her hand while she talked—smiling, all teeth showing—to a critic, to Valentina of *The New Yorker*. Not about Maggie's arms but about how wonderful the show had been, transitioning gracefully to how grateful she was to have won the grant. Maggie imagined Rob popping up by her side, then crumpled when realizing that, of course, he wouldn't.

Maggie flicked the silver foil wrapper into a trash can as she waited for a stoplight to change. She wished she had another chocolate. Something sweet she could fill her mouth with before descending into the subway and riding all the way home.

IT WAS THE first time Maggie had set foot in the apartment since it had been emptied. It felt like she shouldn't be there, like she had stumbled onto a movie set or had walked into a stranger's home. She felt the urge to close the door and leave. Try her key in another apartment, where the lock would turn and the door would open and all of their things would be inside.

Maggie stepped in farther and felt her spirit deflate as she observed what had been spared. They had left the carpet. Technically, it was hers and Rob's, since her parents had given it to them as a housewarming gift. Now, Maggie assumed, it belonged only to her.

The couch was gone, but the TV was still mounted. She wondered briefly where they had stashed the remote control, seeing as they had taken the end tables. She spotted it on the kitchen island, floating between a scented candle and a yellow receipt that she guessed was from the movers.

Though she knew it would do nothing other than make her sad, Maggie opened the kitchen cabinets. There were her pots and pans from Kmart, which she'd bought when she was in undergrad. The one teacup, whose pair had shattered many years earlier—which was a shame, because the cups had been her grandmother's. Maggie remembered bringing them back from Istanbul, wrapped in newspaper and hand-carried through the airport. She had told Rob that they were too delicate for the dishwasher, but he claimed she'd never said so. The lone teacup now sat next to a stack of paper plates and a sleeve of plastic cups that had newly appeared since Maggie last opened the cupboard. Rob must have bought them for her. Thoughtful but depressing.

"This feels like where people go to kill themselves," Maggie said aloud to what few objects remained.

She abandoned her tour of the kitchen and went into the bedroom, where the damage was split perfectly down the center. Everything on Maggie's side was still in its place, even though the furniture belonged to Rob. His side was bare.

Maggie shed her coat and crawled into her side of the bed—the side that still looked semialive. It was only the afternoon, but living had made her so tired lately that she fell asleep moments after closing her eyes.

SOMEONE WAS RUNNING the tap. It was night by the time Maggie woke up, and she ambled into the living room to find that things looked even worse in the dark. The faucet stopped, and Rob walked out of the bathroom with a towel between his hands. He tossed it onto the bathroom counter and moved toward Maggie.

"You're home," he said. "I didn't hear anything when I came in."

"I just got back," Maggie said, embarrassed suddenly, for always sleeping.

"Hmm," Rob said, and the room fell silent.

They had nothing to anchor them. Nowhere for one of them to sit and the other to stand. Nothing to open and look into. No food to eat. Maggie leaned her back against the kitchen island, and Rob stood opposite her with his arms crossed.

"Well?" Rob asked, raising his eyebrows.

"Well, I guess I owe you thirty grand... " Maggie cracked a smile. For the first time that day, she'd felt joy before she felt relief.

Rob uncrossed his arms and looked like he was about to take a step, but he stayed planted.

"We have to celebrate," he said, struggling with where to put his hands. "This is huge!"

Maggie shrugged. "It's just a nomination. It's not like I've won."

"Yet."

Rob had settled on casually tucking his hands in his pockets, sinking his weight into one hip and standing like an Italian statue. He hadn't stopped smiling at her.

"I see the movers were here," Maggie said, reaching for the crinkled receipt. She looked it over, and her mouth fell open. "And they robbed you! Jesus Christ!"

Rob laughed and took the receipt from Maggie.

"Turns out England is very far away."

"Who knew," she said, and quiet settled around them again.

Rob threw an arm toward the living room. "Well, they took my bed, so I just came here to grab some stuff from the bathroom." His arm made a dull thud as it swung back and hit his side. "I got a hotel for tonight. Figured that would be easiest."

"You're not staying?"

Maggie's brows pinned together involuntarily. Her body knew before her brain did that she could not stand to be without him in this place before she absolutely had to.

"I leave at some ungodly hour, Mags. And the couch is gone— "

"You can stay in the bed with me." She could feel her eyes widen. She didn't have an explanation for why she was pleading with him like this, but she couldn't stop herself. Rob looked at his feet and shifted his weight from one foot to the other, gently rocking himself forward and backward.

"Are you sure that's what you want?"

Maggie nodded, waiting for Rob to look up.

He lifted his head, and his eyes met hers, his face full of its usual softness.

"Okay," he said. "I'll stay."

IT FELT NORMAL, watching the light of the bathroom from her side of the bed while Rob washed his face and brushed his teeth. He always swiped on more deodorant before bed so when the wind from lifting the duvet and sliding beneath it wafted over to Maggie, she'd smell his clean smell.

Rob clicked the light off and walked into the bedroom unceremoniously. This was still his house, still where *they* lived. Maggie was surprised that his body gave no mind to the fact that it was all ending. Rob lifted the covers and slid into bed. The puff of air smelled like him, and Maggie wondered how long she would wait to wash the sheets after he left.

Everything was blue with the lights turned off. The white sheets looked like denim, and Rob was a grayish tone, like the subject of a black-and-white photo. Their bodies curled to face each other. Maggie kept one hand tucked beneath her cheek and reached out with the other to cup Rob's face.

"You're blue," she said, swooping her thumb along his orbital bone.

Rob's face was warm in her hand. He smiled but kept his eyes closed.

"So are you," he said without opening them.

Maggie's throat hardened into a tight black sphere, and she felt so dark blue that her bones became heavy and she sank deeper into the mattress. Every part of her ached.

I'm going to miss you when you go, she wanted to say. *Every day I'm going to wake up and miss you.* Instead, she pulled her hand back, and she watched how quickly sleep washed over Rob. His mouth parted slightly, and his breathing became un-self-conscious.

He wouldn't wake her up in the morning to say goodbye. She knew this about him. This would be her last look at him, and she was glad it was when he was like this. Not trying to be anything. Not telling her something or looking at her some way. Her last look at Rob would just be of him, and everything she thought of when she saw his face.

23

JOHN WAITED A week and a half before calling Maggie. She had texted him *Rob left,* and it took him three days from then to reach out.

You okay? he texted.

I don't know, she replied.

Again, days passed, but eventually he called. Maggie let the first call go to voicemail but was ultimately too sad and too tired to prove a point, so she answered when the second call came hours later.

"Müjde?" His voice, deep and concerned, sounded like their father's.

"I'm okay," Maggie said, trying to assure him, but she was immediately overcome. She could not stop crying long enough to catch her breath.

From then on, John alternated between calling, texting, and, if he had the day off, stopping by to bring over something edible: A sandwich from the bodega downstairs, orange juice boxes he'd swiped from the hospital cafeteria on his way out. One day, he drove to a Turkish bakery in Bay Ridge and brought Maggie fresh simits and whipped Bulgarian feta.

Maggie tore into a simit, pinching the bread with her fingertips, because it was too hot to hold in her hands.

"Do you remember the first time we went to Istanbul with Sofia?" Maggie asked. "These were all she ate."

She dragged a fingerful of simit through the feta and popped it into her mouth. John watched as she prepared mouthful after mouthful, each bite perfectly smothered in cheese. Maggie looked up at John, who had not yet taken a bite.

"What?" she asked. "Is there cheese on my face?"

John's voice was low. "You were hungry," he said.

Maggie put down her second simit, suddenly self-conscious. She rubbed her fingertips over her plate and listened to the patter of sesame seeds as they fell from her hands.

"I guess I was," she said, shrugging.

"When was the last time you ate?" he asked.

"I eat," Maggie said, now looking at her brother with her arms crossed in defense.

John walked around the kitchen island and opened the fridge, where he found only a jar of shriveled black olives.

"You cannot live on olives," he said, shutting the fridge.

Maggie licked feta off her thumb and forefinger. "Okay," she said, preparing another bite for herself.

John shot a huff of air out of his nose.

"Don't be annoyed," Maggie said while chewing. "It's annoying."

John sat next to Maggie as she ate. He looked around the apartment and broached the same subject he had every time he stopped by.

"Are you sure you don't want to stay with us?"

Living with the Artist sounded to Maggie like living with a science experiment—traces of her projects scattered throughout the apartment, the sound of self-immolation videos playing on a loop. She couldn't imagine an environment less conducive to heartbreak. Unlike Maggie's—and formerly Rob's—apartment, a barren living room and their ransacked bedroom suited her depression perfectly.

No need to fake her condition when what surrounded her was just as bad, if not worse.

"I'm okay, Can," she said. "I know I look terrible, but I have been single before, and if I remember correctly, it's not fatal."

Maggie brought the last pinch of dough to her mouth. Her wrist looked like it could snap.

"Mom called me," he said.

The way the earth stood still at such a declaration. Their mother never called John, out of fear that he was too busy. He worked so hard at the hospital, day in and day out, that she never wanted to bother him. Plus, he had the Artist. Obviously, as it was understood by their mother, John had to tend to her. He didn't have time to have a mother anymore. Didn't have time to be a son.

"And?" Maggie asked.

"She said you haven't been answering her calls."

"I've been busy," Maggie said.

John rolled his eyes. "Okay, but will you call her? When I leave?"

"Sure." Maggie shrugged.

"Müjde," John said. "Seriously."

"Yes, Can, I'll call Mom. You can relax."

Maggie stood and slowly made her way around the kitchen. She clasped the wet lid back onto the feta and slid it next to the olives sitting in the fridge. She ran her hands through some water in the sink to rid them of crumbs and seeds. She folded the paper bag from the bakery and stuck it under the sink. When there was nothing left to busy her, Maggie looked at John. He had taken one bite of his pastry, and she knew he had no interest in finishing it. She'd wrap it in foil when he left. Eat it with the rest of the feta and olives in a few hours and call it dinner.

John stayed a little while longer and chatted about nothing. Work was fine. Babies were being born every day. He talked about how the weather was getting better—warmer finally. Then he mentioned something vague that suggested an annoyance toward the Artist's latest antics.

"She's in a tizzy with the show coming up so soon."

Maggie tried to imagine having enough energy to be in a tizzy about anything. John must have seen how drained Maggie felt, because he began zipping up his coat.

"Speaking of which," he said, his voice becoming singsongy, "she'd really like you to come."

"Is that so?" Maggie asked, finding this hard to believe.

John pivoted from annoyance at the Artist to being protective. "She actually said you helped with her breakthrough..."

Maggie's head became heavy and tilted to one side as she considered how that could be possible.

"So will you come?" John asked. He was stiff, and Maggie realized he was holding his breath. She let him stay like this for a brief moment before answering.

"Of course I will," she said.

"Great," he said, sticking his hands in his pockets. "That's great."

Maggie gave him a weak smile and began walking him down the hallway. They stopped at the door, and John placed a hand lightly on Maggie's shoulder.

"Please eat something before going to bed, okay?"

Maggie gingerly lifted his hand and pressed his back toward the door. She promised him that she would try.

BY THE TIME Maggie had worked up the fortitude to call her mother, the sun had started to set. A mild orange hue soaked the apartment, lending a temporary beauty to its emptiness. As Maggie listened to the phone ring, she watched the light catch different reflections and flicker around the living room.

"Müjde!"

Maggie pulled her mother's booming voice away from her ear.

"I know, Mom. I know," Maggie said in Turkish.

Maggie kept the phone a few inches away from her cheek as her mother lamented how many times she had called. Something was wrong with Rob's phone, she kept saying, growing more and more frustrated as she described how it no longer rang but beeped and beeped, and then the line cut. She'd called him seven times. Maggie hung her head, wondering what Rob must have thought of her.

"Then I called Can," her mother said. "You made me so worried."

"I'm sorry, Mom."

She tried to explain herself in her stilted Turkish, but Maggie's problem was twofold. She didn't know the right words, and she didn't know which doors to open. First, she thought of saying she'd been busy with school. They were presenting final projects in class, so she'd been working late nights at the studio. That was true. At least, a while ago it had been true. Then, she could mention she'd lost her appetite from stress. That seemed to Maggie an acceptable amount of worry to lay on her mother. She was just stressed, nothing over the top. Her mother would chide her, say "Eat something," and maybe it would take a day or two, but Maggie would eat, and that would be the end of things. But Maggie fumbled over each explanation. She stuttered so much as she tried to configure the words in the right order that her mother finally interrupted her.

"You make so many mistakes," she said, not meaning it in any way other than as a statement of fact.

Maggie sighed. "I know, Mom."

"After school is finished, you can go live with Mehmet. You will speak perfectly in two months. Three months maybe."

They both knew she wouldn't go live with Mehmet, but they politely entertained the idea as if she might. Even if she did go, everyone in Turkey spoke to Maggie in English, waiting for her eyes to sparkle and for her to say "Your English is so good!" It was a phrase she gave away freely, as it was usually the only generosity people would let her extend to them. There, she was the guest, the receiver of things, so in an attempt to give something in return, Maggie complimented every stumbling tongue.

"Where are you?" her mother asked suddenly.

The question startled Maggie as it had emerged midway through their conversation, seemingly out of nowhere.

"I'm home," she said looking around the barren living room.

"It's so quiet." Her mother sounded amazed.

"Because it's just me here."

"Where is Rob?"

"He's on a business trip. In London."

Maggie heard her mother tsk.

"That is why he didn't answer. I knew something was wrong. Rob always answers when I am calling."

"Mm-hmm."

Maggie closed her eyes and considered how much truth her mother could withstand.

"I hope they are paying him more for traveling. He works so hard."

"They are, Mom," Maggie said. "He's getting promoted."

"Maşallah, canım— "

Maggie pulled the phone away from her face once more as her mother melted into a puddle of gratitude. Though it was muffled,

Maggie could hear her saying how Rob was such a hardworking and successful man and that Maggie was lucky she had found him. Maggie brought the phone back to her ear and interrupted.

"Did Sofia leave?"

"Did Sofia leave? She left one week ago! What, are you crazy?"

"I forgot." Maggie shrugged.

"You don't listen, and you don't call. If you answered the phone, you would know she was gone one week ago."

"Okay."

Maggie sank into the repetition of her mother's phrases. *One week ago*, the slightest *v* sound lingering beneath the *w*. The way she sometimes spoke in loops was like a song.

"What's wrong?" her mother asked.

"Nothing, Mom. I like hearing you talk."

Another tsk of the tongue, and what Maggie knew, but couldn't see, was her mother rolling her eyes.

"I'm making lamb tonight. Your father likes lamb."

Her mother's way of pivoting from somewhere tender to somewhere practical brought a smile to Maggie's face. This was familiar. She could live here.

"In the oven?" Maggie asked.

"Yes, but first on the stove." Her mother's voice sped up as she launched into methods and tactics.

"In Turkish," Maggie gently insisted.

"Tabii, canım," her mother said slowly, and indulged Maggie by going farther back in the story.

She started at the grocery store—where there had been no good parking, apparently. Carefully, so Maggie could follow along, her mother listed each ingredient she had picked up for dinner. Maggie knew most of the words, as food vocabulary was the easiest for her to remember. Then her mother got to the word for *butcher*, and her speech became hurried. Maggie heard Frank's name and then a slur of things she couldn't decipher.

"Yavaş, Mommy. Yavaş." *Slowly, Mom. Slowly.*

Her mother slowed down and began to use simpler words. She called Frank a cheat and said he always used a light hand when weighing her meat, but a heavy hand when charging her.

Maggie tried to defend Frank, but her mother spoke over her, talking again about the lamb and how to give it a good dark sear.

"How is Dad?" Maggie asked after dinner had thoroughly been described.

"The new doctor is an idiot," her mother began.

She'd switched over to English to talk about Maggie's father's health, because she knew medical words were difficult for Maggie, who could only really say "My head aches."

Her father had a checkup at the end of last week, and the doctor wouldn't let her mother into the exam room when discussing the x-ray. He spoke only to Maggie's father, and when they left, the doctor handed him a folded packet of papers that were stapled together and kept from Maggie's mother until her father had forgotten them on the table at home.

"Will you read them, canım? And tell me?" her mother asked, her voice soft and shy.

"Of course. Send them to me."

Maggie could hear mumbling as her mother photographed the pages, texting them to her one by one, sometimes upside down. They were filled with mostly medical jargon, which was hard to parse through, even for Maggie. She wished John had stayed over just a little longer.

She zoomed into a bolded section under a header titled RESULTS that seemed to suggest shrinkage, and that no new tumors had metastasized.

"It says there are no new cancers, Mom."

"Maşallah," her mother exhaled.

"Maşallah," Maggie repeated.

They talked more about the appointment, and Maggie could hear how her mother's descriptions of the new doctor had softened. Before knowing that the cancer hadn't spread, the doctor was too stupid and too young to know anything. Now, her mother appreciated his efficiency. The appointment had lasted only half an hour, and the receptionist had been nice. She'd remembered Maggie's mother from when she accompanied Maggie's dad to chemo and radiation therapy. This time, she had complimented her mother's haircut.

Maggie tried to let her father's good news seep into the apartment, but, looking around, it was still empty and still depressing. Getting nominated for the grant danced on the tip of Maggie's tongue as she peered out at her mostly sad state of existence. Speaking it aloud felt like inviting its death, though, so when her mother asked Maggie how she was, she said she was tired.

"I can hear it in your voice. You need to rest."

Maggie's mother was now a fountain of endearment, calling Maggie sugar, baby, and dear.

"I think I am going to rest, Mom."

"Yes, good idea," her mother said. Maggie heard the quiver in her voice, how it bordered on concern.

"I love you," Maggie said, hoping to dissolve her worry.

"I love you too, canım. Call me tomorrow."

Neither waited for each other's clicks that ended the call. Maggie eyed John's simit on the counter but abandoned it for her bedroom. Maybe she would be hungry in the morning.

24

THE DAYS WITHOUT Rob passed through Maggie in a slow-rolling fog. There was no distinction between morning and evening. There was only gray and sleep. In an attempt to give her life a vague shape, Maggie took up yoga. After waking up, she would spend twenty minutes lying on the floor in corpse pose. Maggie told herself, and anyone who asked how she was, that she was good. That she'd really gotten into yoga lately and that seemed to be helping.

"It is *so* good to move the body," the Artist had said to Maggie once, when she'd accompanied John on one of his wellness checks.

"So true," Maggie said in response.

Her mother's reaction to Maggie's newfound devotion to yoga was to ask if she was sick.

"No, Mom," she cooed to her mother from the hardwood floor of the living room. "This is making me healthier."

Her mother hmphed, and, after a pause, she changed the subject.

Most days, she thought of Rob, her back flush against the floor. She thought of London. How it must be raining—as everyone was always saying how rainy London was. Depending on the hour, Rob would be in his beige raincoat, battling the mist on his way to the office. Or was it the middle of the night? Could he fall asleep easily?

Had he been taking sleeping pills? She always thought of this as his secret vice, which used to make Rob self-conscious when Maggie teased him.

She, of course, had been having the opposite problem. Maggie could hardly stay awake long enough to complete a task. Toward the end of her yoga practice, she would flutter her eyes open, but her eyelids were so heavy they usually fell back to being closed.

Just a few more minutes, she would think. *Just a few more minutes, and then I'll be okay.*

A PEEK OF sunlight split through Maggie's world with an email from Lorrie. She sent a message berating Maggie for neglecting to file any of the paperwork required for the grant. *Deadline tmrw,* she wrote, *so be fast.*

Maggie scoured her computer for the necessary files—her artist's statement, her latest tax papers, proof of citizenship, and other excessive documentation to prove she was American and broke and that she would really like to win. There was something cathartic about the rush of chasing a deadline. It served as confirmation that just beneath the surface of her skin, in her blood and in her cells, Maggie was still very much alive.

She shut her laptop after submitting the last file and looked to the spot on the floor where she had spent every morning before this one. The stretch of wood called to her. It would be easy to get on all fours and crawl herself into that position. To lie down for just twenty minutes, just an hour.

But seeing it from where she sat in the kitchen made Maggie feel queasy. *Someone get that girl off the ground,* she thought, slowly realizing that it would have to be her, since she was the only one there.

Dismounting from her stool, Maggie walked past her spot on the floor and rounded the island to the refrigerator. The light clicked on to reveal her jar of olives, shriveled and black, shimmery with oil. Things had gotten out of hand. The drama of it all—the empty house, the inertia—it was getting to be ridiculous now. This was not who she had signed up to be. Someone who only ate olives.

Today she would go outside, reenter the world. Arriving at the mirror, her lips parted as she saw the deep bags set under her eyes, her hair going in every direction. This was how Maggie knew she was living alone. She would never let another person see her like this.

Maggie took great care in starting the day—the first good day, she kept calling it to herself—as she gently pressed her hands all over her face. She let the water run until it was scalding, then dialed it down to tepid and washed her face before lathering it in plumping serums and creams. Her under-eye bags were remedied, her cheeks rosy with blush. She brushed her hair and surprised herself by how much time it took for her hand to travel from the crown of her head to the ends. The back of her neck tingled as her arm stretched farther and farther away from her. It was disturbing how much her hair had grown, like the organism of her body had been carrying on without her.

Looking at her reflection now, Maggie couldn't believe how okay she looked. With a thin film of makeup and a hairbrush, she could fool the world into thinking she was like one of them—functioning and fine and real.

MAGGIE'S HANDS QUICKLY became wet with the mist spraying on the vegetables as she pulled more and more of them into her basket. Tomatoes, carrots, eggplants, lemons, limes, leafy greens, garlic, sweet onions, green onions. She squeezed the tomatoes, taking care to be gentle, and brought them to her nose. She investigated the eggplants for blemishes and subtly let one graze her face so she could feel something cool against her skin.

A plan for dinner was forming in her mind, and Maggie would soon abandon the produce for protein. She needed chicken thighs and wondered if it would be best to marinate them in yogurt or lemon juice. How did her mother do it for Sofia's high school graduation party? The chicken had been shredded into the finest shards, and yet juice still ran from each piece. Maggie felt her mind straining to remember the sauce—had it been yogurt or blended herbs? She would have to call her mother and ask.

As she turned to approach the butcher, Maggie stopped at a pyramid of yellow squash. With a squash in each hand, she tried to determine which was filled with water and which would be dry and woody. *It's not even squash season,* she thought. She was reaching back to the pyramid when she felt a hand on her shoulder.

"Maggie?"

Attached to the hand was Lillian, Tim's wife, in head-to-toe athleisure. She was like a tight black-spandexed arrow topped with a baseball cap with an iridescent trim—reflective, Maggie assumed, so something would sparkle off her in the dark. Her hair stuck through the back arch of the cap in a sleek ponytail. Maggie could not imagine anything that would look more out of place on her own head than a baseball cap.

"Lillian," Maggie said. "What are you doing here?"

"Oh, just picking up a few things," Lillian answered, unfazed by the suggestion that she shouldn't be somewhere. "What are *you* doing here?" she asked cheerfully. "Shouldn't you be in London by now?"

Maggie dropped a yellow squash, and it rolled away from them, its curved neck slowing itself down with each rotation.

"Oh," Maggie said, bending to retrieve the squash. "I'm not going to London."

Lillian cocked her head to the side, and her ponytail gently swooshed behind her. She looked at Maggie with unblinking eyes, not understanding.

"Rob and I broke up."

"I'm so sorry," Lillian said. She brought her hand to her chest as if Maggie had said Rob had died.

"That's all right."

"I just assumed."

Maggie placed both squashes back on the display. Lillian stayed by Maggie's side, a glazed look in her eyes. She swayed forward like she might take a step toward Maggie but floated back to being upright. Lillian's hand reached out and touched her again.

"How are you holding up?" she asked.

"Fine," Maggie said, her voice mostly air.

Maggie extracted herself from Lillian's concerned palm. She couldn't hear the inflection in her own voice, so she couldn't tell if she sounded zen or depressed, but she watched for a reaction in Lillian, who just nodded.

"That's a shame," Lillian said. "I always thought Rob was so good for someone like you."

"Someone like me?"

"You know, someone so . . . " Lillian's tongue pressed against the roof of her mouth. Her eyes rolled back as she sought the perfect word. "Unique."

Maggie blinked.

"Plus, you'd have gorgeous kids. Mixed babies are always so beautiful," she said. "So healthy and robust."

Dumbfounded now, Maggie simply fought to keep her mouth closed.

"Well, I have to run," Lillian said. She wiggled the bottle of almond milk she'd been holding while they spoke. "I was just picking this up between errands."

"Sure," Maggie said.

And as quickly as she'd appeared, Lillian disappeared, trotting toward the registers with her hair and hips swaying.

WITH A SHARP knife, Maggie sliced onions into ribbons. She blistered tomatoes in oil and added the onions, to wilt and become sumptuous and wavy. Eggplant, which she had cut into thin coins, went in with a splash of wine to deglaze the pan.

Nothing about herself struck Maggie as unique, almost to the point of frustration. Had she been unique, perhaps her career would have taken off already, like the Artist's. Or maybe she would have had more boyfriends leading up to Rob, making her more experienced and able to see their flaws sooner. Perhaps everything in her life would have been the slightest bit better, had she just been different.

Maggie picked a few mint leaves to fold into the eggplant and sprinkled everything with salt. Steam rose, and the kitchen filled with the scent of bubbling tomatoes. She wanted to spoon her creation onto a crusty piece of bread, eat it, and then fall into a coma.

She gently pushed everything around the pan with a long wooden spoon and considered whether Lillian had ever met an interesting person in her life. Like the student Maggie had watched swallow an egg whole, including the shell. That had been unique. Or the student who had covered himself in pigs' blood and took photos of himself naked like this, and photoshopped his dripping red body into mosques and synagogues. Other than Rob's nosebleed when he'd insisted they go skiing one Christmas, the only blood Maggie had ever confronted was her own. She ate her eggs cracked and cooked like every other person on the planet.

Unique fell into the same category as *exotic* or *mysterious*—words issued in an attempt to rightsize Maggie. She wasn't really interesting or smart; she was just *unique.* She wasn't beautiful, but exotic. Her otherness was a threat to be neutralized: *Don't worry—she's not special. She's just not from here.*

It was a thousand times worse for Rakib. Maggie remembered their years together full of teachers making unsubtle remarks about how "articulate" he was. How often people assumed they weren't together. And if they were corrected, how they figured Rakib was somehow corrupting her. People wondered aloud, casually, why he didn't wrap his head like the Sikhs, and if not like the Sikhs, then why not draped like the Saudis. They expected a thick accent, and practically short-circuited when he would mention he was from Texas. Indian, Bangladeshi, Pakistani—it didn't matter where they thought he was *actually* from. Once they heard his family was Muslim, they wanted to know where that infamous temper was. Waited for him to pledge some allegiance to jihad and bellow the greatness of Allah. People were constantly bewildered by the fact that Rakib was so mellow, so even-keeled. Taken aback that he was handsome. Disarmed by his charm.

A piece of eggplant was beginning to burn. Maggie scraped it free from the pan and flung it into the trash can. The pan hissed as she poured another splash of wine into the dark caramelized spot that had formed in its center. She raked her spoon against it until she could see the metal again. She took a long sip directly from the open bottle and let the wine warm her from the inside while the stove and all its lit burners roared in front of her.

Rakib had not attempted to reach Maggie since their horrible moment in the studio. She and Rob had pooled together in their final days, dissolved by one another's sweetness, longing to be close even though that made everything harder. After Rob left, Maggie had wondered where Rakib had disappeared to, but she didn't have the strength to seek him out. To see if he could really support her in the ways she'd always hoped he would.

Her hand traveled to her back pocket and produced her phone. Without her telling them to, her fingertips found Rakib and called him.

He answered by tsking his tongue.

"Maggie," he said. "What a surprise."

"A good surprise or a bad surprise?"

"I think you know the answer to that," he chided.

This was the Rakib Maggie had hoped he would be when she called. Not the one who had left her in the studio, circling his tongue around the word *nice*. He would be good to her tonight; she could hear it in his voice.

"Have you missed me?" she asked.

Maggie held her breath, and a year passed before Rakib answered.

"Terribly."

"Do you want to come over?" she asked, her voice softening without her meaning it to. "I'm cooking."

"Are you trying to tempt me?"

Maggie laughed.

"If there's anything I've learned over the years, it's that you're untemptable." She leaned her back against the lip of the stove, and the knobs pushed into the fleshiest parts of her. She took another sip from the bottle of wine. "You only do exactly what you want to do."

"Is that so?" Rakib asked.

"It is," Maggie said. "So the real question is, do you *want* to come over?"

Rakib made an idling sound as he considered his response.

"I'm not so sure your boyfriend would approve."

Maggie stared into the empty living room.

"He's not here," she said, distilling her reality to something simple and faceless.

"No?"

"Nope."

"Well, then," Rakib said evenly. "I guess I'll see you soon."

AFTER SHE HUNG up the phone, Maggie walked to the nearest mirror. The makeup she'd applied in the morning had endured, but it had thinned over the apples of her cheeks. She quickly remedied this with a swipe of something beige and then began the reassessment of her hair. With wet hands, she smoothed the top of her head and pulled the rest of her hair into a bun, perfectly in line with the height of her ears. Something an aunt had told her. This was the most flattering angle if you *had* to wear your hair up. Down was obviously superior in every way.

Maggie returned to the kitchen, pulled the chicken thighs early from their brine, and roasted them in the oven long enough to be shredded. After which she took the care to press them into a thin layer and shallow-fry them, so that half of each shred would shrivel up and brown and become crispy—something she remembered Rakib loving in a dish she had made years ago. Then she made rice—simple, with onions and pine nuts—and toasted some bread in the oven.

Maggie had the sense that something was missing, but she could hear Rakib already at the door.

"Hey, beautiful," he said, pressing his cheek against hers in greeting. "Smells amazing."

His skin had left her before Maggie could feel fully satiated by his touch. She thought of the term used for kids in overcrowded orphanages and the elderly in nursing homes who have no family to visit them: *touch-starved*. Maggie immediately regretted making the association, but she couldn't undo the thought.

Rakib strode past her to the end of the hall.

"Jesus Christ."

Maggie took her time before arriving beside him.

"It's like a bomb shelter," he said.

She felt stupid for inviting Rakib to see how she'd been languishing. Maggie had grown accustomed to the apartment's barren landscape and had forgotten that she, too, should be horrified by the gulf of the empty living room, the stupid carpet her parents had sent her floating in its center.

Rakib looked at Maggie and waited for an explanation—which she rushed through, alluding to the least amount of her own pain as possible.

"Did he leave because of . . . " Rakib drew a line from himself to Maggie with a waving finger.

"No, no," she said. "He'd been planning it for a while, I guess."

"And you weren't a part of that plan?"

"I was," Maggie said. "But now I'm not."

Maggie panned the room for something that could help her change the subject. The only two things there were her body and Rakib's.

She looked down at the carpet. *It's actually from Afghanistan,* she could say. *You can tell from the pattern.*

"I'm starving," Rakib said.

"Let's eat," she said, relieved her humiliation was finally over.

Maggie headed for the stove, and Rakib followed, the hard echo of his dress shoes clacking after her noiseless bare feet. He stood behind her and watched Maggie's process.

"What are we having?"

Rakib wrapped his hands around Maggie's waist, and she let herself lean back against him. His chest was so solid it felt like he should be flayed in front of medical students to show them the perfect human form—his hard chest cracked open to show all the muscles layered beneath, his blood being the most red, his lungs undoubtedly big and pink and healthy. Rakib's arms circled tighter around Maggie. She was grateful to feel encased like this, safely protected in his armor.

Maggie leaned harder against him and pointed to each pot.

"Eggplants with tomatoes and onions, rice, chicken, and yogurt."

"Mmm," he said before unraveling himself from her, leaving to rummage through a drawer.

"My god," he said. "Did he leave you anything?"

"What are you looking for?" she asked as he switched to the cabinets.

"Bottle opener."

Maggie pointed to the counter, where the corkscrew had last been tossed. Rakib retrieved it and began opening a bottle of wine while Maggie scooped rice from one pot into the high-walled pan of eggplant and tomatoes. She nestled chicken neatly between the rice and the saucy eggplant, as she couldn't bear to unstick two paper plates from each other and further highlight her destitute state. They would eat right from the pot like they had done in their early, broke days. When Rakib would buy forties from the bodega while Maggie rotated a series of cheap pans on his two-burner dorm stove.

As she arranged their meal, Maggie realized she would soon return to her broke days if nothing went according to plan. She'd be out of Rob's apartment and flung into the meager arms of a new roommate—or two, or three. Though she'd certainly had the time, Maggie hadn't considered the endless possibilities of her future.

She laid a checkered towel on the counter and rested the hot pan on top of it. In the middle of the pan, she dolloped a perfectly white mound of yogurt. Rakib filled two disposable cups with wine so dark it looked black. They clinked their plastic rims.

"To old friends," Rakib said.

"To old friends," Maggie repeated back to him.

The phrase felt so precious and tender to her. Like being an old friend was sacred. She let the idea be a comfort as they sipped the wine that would inevitably make her empty stomach sick.

Maggie spun the pot so the chicken was closer to Rakib. He could have it all, for all she cared. *Unique* had dissolved her appetite, and she would subsist on wine for the night.

Rakib pressed his fork into the side of the mound of rice and sent the perfectly flaky grains avalanching into the brick-red sauce beneath them. *Eat,* he said to her with his raised brow.

Maggie obliged, and her appetite found its way back to her more and more with each small bite.

They herded their favorites toward each other wordlessly. Maggie pushed shredded meat to Rakib, while he left piles of eggplant disks for her. *You have this, I'll have that.* It didn't take long for the food to dwindle down to meager flakes of rice. Rakib poured the last dregs of wine while Maggie dragged her fork through what remained in the pan. The only sound in the room was the scraping of metal against metal.

"Do you think we'll do this forever?" Maggie asked, still making spirals in the pan.

"What do you mean?"

"I mean, do you think we'll always be in each other's lives like this?"

"Like what?"

Rakib stood and lifted the pan from the counter. Maggie dropped her fork as he pulled it away from her and into the sink. He ran the hot water and filled the pan with soap. Maggie started to fidget with her cup of wine.

"Doing this." She shrugged. "Whatever it is we're doing."

"Having dinner?"

Maggie let go of her cup and looked at Rakib.

"Seriously?"

He broke into a smirk.

"I'm just working with what you're giving me, Maggie."

Rakib rolled up his sleeves and began scrubbing the pan. Maggie watched how the soap bubbles bobbed up and down his arms, how the water matted and swirled the hair against his forearms.

"You look good like that," Maggie said.

"Oh yeah?" Rakib was still smirking, thoroughly amused and handsome.

"There's something very sexy about you washing a dish."

He laid the pan in the bottom of the sink and grabbed the pot she'd made the rice in. He hovered it next to the streaming tap without filling it with water.

"Don't be a tease," she said.

Water crashed against the well of the pot and drowned out the sound of Rakib's laughter.

Maggie sipped the last of her wine as she watched him carefully turn the pot so that every surface steamed under the hot water. He was fastidious while still being relaxed, which somehow made him even more appealing. His expression remained satisfied and at ease even as he lathered the already-clean handles in soap and rinsed them until all the suds had trailed away.

"Don't do the rest," Maggie said. "Come be with me."

Rakib killed the tap and began drying the pot with a rag.

"It's getting late," he said.

Maggie looked to see the time on the oven. "It's not even nine."

Rakib set the pot on the counter and rounded the island back to Maggie. The silence of the apartment was deafening without the running water. Maggie couldn't believe she had forgotten this part.

"You're not staying," she said.

Rakib lifted his coat from the back of his stool. "Can't," he said. "I have a flight tomorrow." He spun his coat to feed an arm through. "Sinfully early, I might add."

Rakib looked like he was moving in slow motion, dragging his limbs through the thick air. It took ten minutes for him to tuck a hand into his pocket and adjust his stance.

"Where are you going?" Maggie asked.

"Milan," he said. "A friend has a show there. Then we're going to the coast to chat with a few galleries. She wants someone to help negotiate terms and conditions."

"I'm sure she does."

"Don't say it like that," Rakib said.

"Like what?" Maggie asked.

"Like I'm lying."

"I know you're not."

Maggie blinked at Rakib, who seemed to be waiting for her to say more.

"She's an old friend," he said.

"That's fine, Rakib." Maggie's extremities became numb as she realized Rakib's life was full of old friends.

He reached out and palmed the side of her face, his fingers burying themselves in her hair. He ran a thumb across her cheek.

"I'll call you when I'm back in the city."

Maggie could hardly hear him anymore.

"Aren't you going to walk me out?"

She rose from her stool, and they began making their way down the hallway. Rakib said something about how they might take the boat out for a spin if there was time between gallery meetings. "If there's time," he kept saying. Like the coast of Italy was riddled with galleries and they would be putting this woman's work in all of them.

They stopped at the door, and Rakib turned to face her.

"Hey," he said softly, trying to coax something out of her.

"Hey," she said back.

"I'll see you soon." Rakib leaned down and kissed her cheek. "Be good," he said.

Maggie opened the door for Rakib and watched his frame shrink as he floated away from her. As he got smaller and smaller, Maggie knew she would never do this to herself again.

25

MAGGIE HAD STRANGE dreams the night Rakib left, dreams that exhausted her. She was being chased, being trapped, being scared. Running, escaping, crying. She woke up often and was always sticky with sweat, too hot, and her mouth dry. From one dream, she woke herself up by screaming—something that hadn't happened to her since a bout of night terrors in early childhood. Eventually, Maggie drifted into a final dream, one that felt peaceful. And even though she was technically asleep, she could somehow feel the relief of this.

She was swimming laps in her grandmother's swimming pool in Turkey. It was a hot day, the sun beating down and forcing everyone into the shade, if not indoors. Her grandmother sat by the pool at a table with an umbrella. She was slicing green beans in half and counting Maggie's laps. "Come inside," her grandmother kept calling out to her, but Maggie could hardly hear with the water sloshing in her ears. It felt good to pull her toned arms through the thick water. She could feel how strong and young she was with each stroke. "You're going too far, canım, come home," her grandmother shouted. Maggie stopped swimming to tell her grandmother not to worry, that she'd come inside soon. But when Maggie turned her head, she realized she was in the middle of the ocean, so far from shore that she couldn't see her grandmother. She couldn't see anyone. The sun was no longer glaring, and it was the middle of the night. Floating in the pitch black, Maggie was alone. After another moment, she realized she was naked.

THE ARTIST'S EXHIBITION snuck up on Maggie. She didn't realize how much time had passed and that it was already upon them until John suggested meeting at her apartment and driving over together.

"It's at Washington Square Park," he said in a tone that implied this was his third or fourth time reminding her, though he had never mentioned it before.

"What time?"

"It starts at sunset, so I think tonight that's something like 7:43."

They decided to meet under the arch at 7:33, to have time to settle in before the show started.

"Okay," John said, sounding hesitant. "And you'll be there at 7:33?"

He had taken this tone with Maggie as she began resuming her life. Wondering if she was as ready as she claimed to be.

"I'll be there at seven and twiddle my thumbs for thirty-three minutes until you arrive."

"Sorry," he said. "I'm sorry."

"It's okay," she said. "I'll see you there."

They hung up the phone, and Maggie was privately grateful for the ways her brother worried and cared for her.

THOUGH SHE DID not arrive thirty-three minutes early, Maggie did get to the park significantly earlier than John. She wanted to be alone among the crowd before pairing with him. Even though lately, her days had exclusively consisted of being alone, she thought something new might happen to her this way. That alone, something might strike her, invigorate her somehow and pull her out of her malaise.

Washington Square Park was bursting with life in a way that was unimaginable in the freeze of winter. Everyone in the city had spilled out to greet the onset of warmth. College kids getting ready to graduate, pregnant women who Maggie assumed must be beyond every definition of tired and yet looked luminescent and at ease, and church groups with young front men singing songs about Christ were all out absorbing the vestiges of the day's sunlight. Everyone had shed their layers of puff and wool and looked like their innermost selves again, draped in chic ensembles and wearing heeled boots that would not be eaten by salt and snow. People were smiling, and Maggie turned her face to them in hopes that she could absorb the energy they were emanating.

As she approached the arch, Maggie searched for her brother's steady gait. It was 7:31, and rather than wait for him like she had promised she would, Maggie let herself be sucked toward the installation, like water toward a drain.

In the pit of the fountain, the Artist had strung up giant vertical banners—four around the edge of the fountain, like the cardinal directions on a compass, and one larger banner in the center. They were all photographs. The first banner Maggie saw was a photo of John. He was the east-facing image—tall and undulating slightly in the wind. It was like looking at a mirage, the ripples in the banner like waves of heat rising from desert sand.

The photo was sepia-toned, though Maggie had seen it before and was pretty sure it was John's photo from the hospital website. He was wearing his white coat and had a stethoscope around his neck.

The photo, in color, was perfect for a hospital pamphlet. John looked friendly and at ease. *Hi! I'm Dr. Arif, and I'll be delivering your baby today!* In hues of orangey brown, it looked like an image that would hang in their great-grandmother's house. Something she'd point to as if to prove that she had family in the US, and that hers was a family of *doctors*. It was almost ridiculous the Artist had done this to him.

Maggie slowly circled to the southern banner and as she waded through the crowd, a few familiar faces came into view. There was Maisha, standing with a tall man who resembled an MMA fighter—all sinew and muscle, with a shaved head that matched her own. She was laughing, trailing her hand down his arm. Far from the trembling creature Maggie remembered her as at the Artist's party. Nearby, gesturing toward a banner, was Valentina, in a fabulous burgundy-colored coat. She stood with one leg lengthened in front of the other, showing off the square toe of her boot peeking out from beneath the hem of her trousers. Maggie overheard Valentina discussing contrast with a colleague.

Then two disinterested teens caught Maggie's eye. They were on a bench, giggling, their fingers and legs completely interlaced. They were entirely oblivious to everything other than the energy between them, and Maggie felt relieved that no one's gravity was sucking her to their core like this. That the only gravity currently working on her was the one that kept her on earth.

Valentina said the word *contrast* yet again, and Maggie turned toward the banner to see what she was talking about. The image was a stunning photo of a woman who had to be the Artist's mother. She was beautiful in all the ways the Artist was beautiful. Delicate facial features, pale skin, wavy brown hair. She had soft, rounded shoulders and wore a heather-gray sweatshirt tucked into light-washed jeans. She looked like she could mother anyone, and Maggie felt a pang for her own mother, who did not have that same sense about her. Maggie's mother could have only mothered Maggie.

Scared to linger in front of the Artist's mother for too long, Maggie rounded her way to the next image, which was of the Artist and John's apartment building, *The Brain* front and center. Maggie could see everything from her prelapsarian life. The cold, sparkling *Brain*, the thick black wave of Rakib's hair. Rob just out of frame, perpetually on his way back to her. That entire life felt so far away from her now. She was left only with John, the Artist, and her women.

The north-facing image was one of the Artist's old paintings from before she became focused on her performance work. It was all cool blues and slate and oat. It was a piece that made the viewer feel weighed down with something—not quite sadness but something uncomfortable, like a dull pain. Maggie overheard audience members who had followed the Artist's work for years talk about its significance. She eavesdropped on a man who spoke without pausing to breathe. He mentioned the "*obvious* austere Scandinavian influence" on the piece, and Maggie had to roll her eyes. Why were men always saying things about women's art that was obvious?

Maggie backed away from the man and saw, in the center of it all, the Artist. Eighty feet tall, looking up Fifth Avenue, the Artist shot above the other banners, looking straight ahead, neither smiling nor frowning, in a long dress that both obscured her shape but revealed her general form. She looked strong, and unlike the image of her mother, she looked like she was made of steel.

Maggie backed up further, accidentally bumping into someone. A man draped his arm over her shoulder and pulled Maggie toward him.

"Hey! Watch where you're going."

John's voice filled her ear, and Maggie collapsed against him.

"Hardy har har," she groaned through a smile.

They stood together staring at the banner of the Artist.

"Have you seen all of them yet?" Maggie asked.

"Just this one so far."

They began circling the fountain. Maggie stayed close to John as they walked.

"So," he said. "How are you holding up?"

"Oh, you know. Bad, but fine."

"Not bad for losing the love of your life," he said.

"Rob wasn't the love of my life."

Maggie was dramatic and emotional and an intensely feeling person, but calling Rob the love of her life felt juvenile. Like she was a teenager pledging her love to the lead singer of a boy band. She had once, in fact, said that Ricky Martin was the love of her life. And even if Maggie had loved Rob more than she'd ever loved Ricky Martin, hers was not a loss deserving of such a title. She was sad. Not dying.

Her brother shrugged. "My mistake," he said.

John gave polite waves to the many people he recognized as they made their way around. Maggie smiled whenever he waved. They stopped when they arrived at his banner and backed up until his image appeared less warped and just huge.

"Does being seventy feet tall make me look fat?" he asked.

"Honestly, kind of," Maggie answered.

They both laughed, and Maggie could feel herself slowly inching toward lightness.

A voice came over a loudspeaker and urged guests to step away from the banners, as the show was about to start. A police barricade went up around the fountain, and the viewers were forced to keep a wide perimeter for what cops kept calling their "own safety."

Maggie looked at John to ask if he knew what the hell was going on, but John was staring ahead at himself, waiting for whatever was happening to begin.

The lights illuminating the banners suddenly went out. Not like the dimming just before a movie starts, but as if someone had blown out a candle. Something about being in the dark made everyone go quiet. Maggie looked around at the people in the audience, who seemed to understand that something extraordinary was coming, and they seemed smiling and eager—not unnerved by the dark or the hush. Maggie turned her focus back to the exhibit and waited like the rest of them.

A loud whoosh tore through the park, a bright light engulfed them, and a blast of heat came from the fountain. By the time Maggie could put it all together, the crowd had collectively realized that the banners were on fire.

Maggie and John were staring at a smiling seventy-foot John with flames licking up his legs toward his hands. The sepia film curled away from the banner and crumbled to the ground. Ash began collecting in piles at the base of the fountain, and black clouds of it swirled in the air. John's face quickly became threatened by the flames, his white coat and stethoscope already swallowed by orange. All that remained was his long, pale neck and his sweet face. Maggie shuddered. He looked just like her.

The smell of smoke wove through the crowd and awakened people from their previously stunned stupor. Some people ran away, as if the exhibit were a bomb or something, but most stayed still. The ones who had been prepared, knowing the Artist and expecting a spectacle, craned their necks in awe. Murmurs spread among them, and they began to mill about again, moving from one spot to the next to watch how everything burned.

A glass bottle was flung by somebody in the crowd. It soared in a perfect arc into the flames and exploded right by where John's torso had been. Glass shards flew into the crowd, and Maggie turned her face to the ground to shield herself. "Fuck you!" a man shouted, and it wasn't clear if he meant fuck whoever had thrown the bottle, or if he had thrown the bottle himself and he meant fuck the Artist for whatever it was she was doing.

Maggie looked to John to see if they should move, but he was back to staring at himself. As flames climbed toward his neck, he brought a hand up and rubbed the back of his own, as if expecting it to feel hot.

"Should we look at the others?" Maggie asked. The crowd had become so animated she almost had to yell.

"Right," John said. "Yeah."

They rounded the bend to see how much was left of the Artist's mother. Her face was surrounded by a halo of flames, turning her softness into something rancid. Maggie peered into the audience to look for the delicate woman she had only come to know briefly in the photograph. Was she here?

Maggie tried to keep them moving through the show at a decent pace, one in which they'd get a glimpse of everything before it burned, but John took slow strides between each photograph. His apartment building was nearly gone by the time they made it around. Only the rooftop remained. Maggie tried to think of their happy times on that roof so she could say something to break John out of his spell, but it was nearly impossible to remember the joy of something as you watched its destruction. Its last moments were ruined, and the memories would be split from then on. The memory was of the thing itself, but it was also of the thing's last breath. It was a memory of your grandmother, then immediately the memory of her death.

John and Maggie moved to the banner of the Artist's old painting, which was just a column of fire. All the blues had turned to black, and the flames raged upward with such force that it seemed like it would burn for hours.

The heat the exhibition gave off was incredible. Maggie had to swirl her hair up into a clip to keep it off her neck. She briefly patted herself to wick away sweat, but ultimately she enjoyed the warmth that blanketed them.

There was a gradual shift in energy among the crowd. Maggie stared at the fire for a long time before she saw it. The center banner—the Artist looming above them—had been spared by the flames. The Artist reigned over the scene as if destruction fueled her.

"This is fucking *wild*," Maggie said, filled with awe.

John said nothing as he tilted his head back to see the image of his girlfriend, solid and unmoved by all she had set on fire.

ONCE THE BANNERS had been completely engulfed, everyone except for John erupted into applause. Maggie hit her hands together with a wild force that was beyond her control. The piece evaded easy categorization, and certainly nothing about it struck Maggie as obvious. She was haunted by the image of the Artist's mother, her face swallowed by flames.

John was unresponsive for the remainder of the show.

When the fires had all been extinguished and the lights flickered back on in the fountain, he stood tall, a head above most of the crowd, and watched people disperse. Maggie wanted to talk to him, ask him if he was okay, but she was worried that addressing his mood would make it worse.

As more of the onlookers branched off in different directions, John turned toward Maggie. He looked through her.

"I'm going to go," he said plainly.

"Do you want company?" she asked him.

"I'm okay, thanks."

John finally met Maggie's eyes. "Just tell her I'll see her at home, okay?"

"Sure," Maggie said, but he was already walking away.

The air felt thin without the thrum of the crowd, and the heat from the fire was dissipating. Maggie circled the fountain again to search for the Artist and spotted her talking to someone with a clipboard who looked like he was a part of the takedown crew—strong, wearing all black, and giving out instructions to other strong men wearing all black. After Maggie had seen her towering over the park, the Artist seemed so small. Like herself but miniature.

She scribbled something on the clipboard and turned around to speak to a firefighter. He had his jumpsuit halfway on, the top part folded over behind him, like he was a fruit that had been peeled to expose the part you could eat. He patted a meaty pink hand on the Artist's shoulder, and they both laughed. The Artist thanked him, and the firefighter strode away, his strong body inured against his heavy boots and his crazy suit.

"Maggie!" she squealed.

The Artist wrapped her arms around Maggie, and Maggie reciprocated.

"Tell me," the Artist said as she pulled away. "What do you think?"

"I think—" Maggie tried to find any word that felt suitable for the moment, but nothing came to her. "I think, holy shit!"

"Oh, Maggie!" The Artist squeezed her again, thrilled with this assessment. "And John?" she asked. "Did he make it? I know he said he might have a delivery, but did you see him?" The Artist raised herself on tiptoe and lowered herself back down after a few seconds.

Peering into the Artist's glistening eyes, Maggie hated her brother for making her the messenger of his fragile ego.

"Yeah, he made it," she said.

Maggie's response punctured something in the Artist, and her eyes went from glassy to steeled.

"He said he'd see you at home."

The weight of the Artist's face crushed her lips into a thin pink line.

"Right," she said, looking away.

After only a few seconds, the Artist shook herself and returned to a version of chipper that was chillingly artificial. She gushed as she thanked Maggie, again, for coming to the show. "I need to finish a few more things here, but I'll see you soon!" she said, her eyes shooting all around the park. Sparkly and blue and still bouncy, they landed back on Maggie, and she said, "We'll do coffee!"

This was something the Artist had never said to her before, but Maggie agreed. They hugged again, the Artist significantly less spirited than in their first embrace, and Maggie began her journey home.

IT WAS A slow walk up the stairs to the apartment. Maggie had waited briefly for the elevator but then thought about how good it had felt to move. How walking loops around the fountain felt like it could extend her life. So she opted instead to take the stairs.

The cool grays of the living room flooded toward her as she pulled open the front door. Everything steeped in shades of navy, Maggie slid inside and felt the heaviness of the shadows as she crossed through them. Not even ten o'clock yet, and she felt like she could fall asleep standing up. Maggie passed the bathroom, kicked her shoes into a corner, and curled into herself on her side of the bed. She took a deep breath and realized her clothes stank of smoke.

The white light of her phone illuminated her face, and Maggie squinted to let as little of it pass through her eyes as possible. The internet was already bursting with praise for the Artist's show.

Social media posts were popping up by the dozen calling it a "triumph" and "aggressive, bold, and brilliant." A few others consisted of a bunch of questions, asking if anyone knew what was going on in Washington Square Park, when it would be over, and why it smelled so bad.

Lowering the brightness of her screen, Maggie scrolled through the think pieces—some of them were okay; more of them, though, were half baked and nascent. She copied the link to a piece with a dramatic black-and-white photograph of the Artist standing above the flames. Whoever had edited the photo had colorized the fire, making it redder than Maggie thought was possible.

She wanted to send the link to Rob, to show him how the Artist had really set herself on fire. She wrote about how beautiful it had been but deleted the email as quickly as she had drafted it. It was nearly 3 a.m. in London, and Rob wouldn't care about her life anymore. *He shouldn't,* Maggie told herself. That was the natural progression of these things.

Maggie flipped over to face the other side of the bed and debated texting John to see how he was holding up, but then she thought of the days she'd languished in Rob's absence before her brother had called. She thought of how she'd used the sheets to blow her nose so she wouldn't have to get up to get tissues from the bathroom. How, at first, when the pillowcases had snot or drool on them, she'd turned them inside out. But eventually they'd had snot and drool on both sides, so she gave up and slept on them just the same. John had waited days to call her. She didn't need to run to him now.

Also, she couldn't wrap her mind around his reaction. Wasn't storming off a bit dramatic? This was his girlfriend's art, her work. Maggie didn't want to go as far as saying it didn't mean anything, but did it have to mean everything?

Maggie stared at her phone and found, in one of the rare

occasions in her life, there was nothing for her to attend to. No unreturned calls from her mother or father, no autopay bills for her to double- or triple-check and see if there was enough money in her account for the payment to clear, no texts to send or to regret having sent. There was nothing. Until the phone buzzed in her hand with an email. She thought of ignoring it and just falling asleep without washing her face but saw that it was from the grant committee. Maggie clicked off her phone after reading the subject line, her head traveling back and crashing into a pillow. She saw the words one last time before falling asleep. *Congratulations, Müjde Arif...*

26

MAGGIE SLEPT LIKE she had been dead. No dreams but a deep, dark backdrop, which she emerged out of after ten long hours. Lorrie had forwarded her another version of the email she had already received, which announced the winners of the grant in each category.

Cheers are in order...

And Maggie felt the rush of elation and relief again.

Proceeding with her life felt strange. She had fallen asleep to and awoken to what she considered a fortune. She was afraid of how taxes worked and worried about how much of the money would really be hers. She didn't know who to tell or what to do. There were no instructions for her to follow.

She went down to her bodega and ordered an egg-and-cheese on a roll—something truly disgusting she usually allowed herself only when she was terribly hungover. Maggie sat on a bench, peeled back the paper, and nearly inhaled the sandwich, letting its grease coat her fingers and her lips. She had won.

A cabdriver was parked in front of her, sipping a coffee in his car with the windows rolled down. Maggie had accidentally made eye contact with him while the sandwich was in her mouth, and the two had politely nodded at each other. The cabdriver didn't say anything, and Maggie was relieved he had allowed her her peace.

Maggie licked her fingers and balled the paper and foil into a tight sphere. She let her arms rest by her sides while she leaned her head back and closed her eyes. She felt the sun's warmth spread across her face.

"It's a beautiful day," she heard from the cab.

Maggie opened her eyes to see he was looking at her.

"Yeah, it is," she said.

"It's my daughter's birthday," he said. "I'm going to take her to the skate park. She likes to skateboard. She's better than the boys."

"I bet she is." Maggie couldn't resist being touched by this. He was so proud.

"Doesn't cry when she falls."

"She's strong."

"Women are very strong," he said with a reverent intensity.

"Very," Maggie said.

"Very," he said back to her.

They both nodded, and Maggie stood to throw away her trash. The cabdriver put his coffee in the cup holder and started the car.

"Have a good day," Maggie said, waving. "Happy birthday to your daughter."

The cabdriver smiled and exposed his crooked teeth, gray from what Maggie assumed was a lifetime of smoking.

"Thank you," he said. He looked shy suddenly. "Sorry to bother you."

"No bother," Maggie smiled. They bowed their heads to each other, and Maggie made her way down the sidewalk as he pulled out of his parking spot.

The leaves on the trees were properly electric now, bursting with new life. As Maggie passed them, she occasionally swung an arm up to feel one between her fingers.

THE ARTIST AND Maggie kept their coffee date for that afternoon, and when Maggie arrived at the café, the Artist was already seated, peering down into her porcelain mug with a kind of focus innate only to masters of their craft. Like an astrophysicist in the middle of solving an equation or a concert pianist playing the same passage over and over. Maggie felt nervous to interrupt.

"Hey," she said softly, all the vowels elongated.

The Artist dizzily lifted her head.

"Hey," she said, and smiled in a way that reminded Maggie of people on drugs.

"Are you all right?"

The Artist closed her eyes and began swaying slightly, from side to side. Maggie could hear her emitting a low hum to herself. Then all of a sudden she stopped and opened her eyes.

"Yes," she said, sturdier now. "I'm fine." She laughed. "I'm fine."

Maggie sat down and took a sip of whatever the Artist had ordered for her. It was milky and sweet.

"Recovering from last night," the Artist said.

"From John or the show?"

"Both."

"The show was incredible," Maggie said, wishing for a well of words that could better describe what she meant. "It was perfect."

The Artist let a small smile curl up from her lips, but it didn't last.

"How do you feel?" Maggie asked.

The Artist took a moment to consider this thoughtfully. Aside from pulling her legs into her lap to sit cross-legged in her chair, she didn't move. She held her ankles and stared at the table. If Maggie caught her at the right angle, where she couldn't see her chair, it looked like the Artist was floating.

"I feel fucking crazy."

The Artist slowly peeled her eyes from the table.

"My manager called, and apparently there are galleries that want me to take the show on tour," she said. "In the US and abroad."

"Holy shit!" Maggie felt her tongue fumble to punctuate this with the Artist's name, so instead she repeated herself. "Holy shit."

"It would mean being in Europe until the end of the year." She pulled back her shoulders and took a breath. "But I think I'm going to do it."

"Of course you're going to do it! You have to!"

Then Maggie remembered her brother. "Oh."

"Yeah," the Artist said.

"What did he say?"

"He said, 'Do whatever you want.'"

"Christ."

They sipped their coffees. Maggie knew she should be the one to speak next, to somehow interpret or defend John. "He'll come around to it," she said. "Can is slow to change, but he can do it."

The Artist shrugged. "That's not all he said."

"Oh?"

"He asked me if I was going to leave him, and if I was, he said to just do it already and stop dragging him through this. He kept saying 'this,' but I don't know what *this* is." She began stammering. "*This?* Life? Relationship? I'm not dragging him through anything!"

"Why does he think you want to leave him?"

"Because I didn't tell him he was in the exhibit."

"Oh."

"Yeah."

"Okay," Maggie started. "Do you want to leave him?"

"Of course I don't," the Artist said. "But I don't think setting him on fire sent that message."

Maggie laughed, and the Artist smiled with her mug against her lips. She would be okay, Maggie could see this already. She and John would figure it out or they wouldn't, but she could see the Artist would survive.

The Artist sighed. "This is just volume one," she said. "We'll talk again, and that will be volume two. And eventually we'll get through however many volumes of this conversation there need to be, and we'll figure something out." She shook her hair out of her face. "I just wish he could be a little happy for me, too, you know? Or proud of me, or something. He saw how crazy this made me. It would just be nice if he could say something nice about it."

"He doesn't know how to," Maggie said, surprising herself that this truth lived inside her. John had mangled every reaction to any piece she had ever shown him. They were all so flummoxing to him that he could only say something factual in response. It drove her mad that he couldn't discern what made someone skilled.

"But he's proud of you," Maggie continued. "You know that."

"I guess so."

The Artist looked better now. Less cloudy in her eyes, her spirit tethered to her body instead of floating around it. She had returned to the present.

"Thank you," she said.

"You don't have to thank me," Maggie said. "I didn't do anything."

"You know that's not true."

Maggie just smiled and let there be something kind and understood between them.

"How are you holding up?"

Concern knit itself across the Artist's brow, and Maggie was confused, having briefly forgotten the conditions of her life.

"I heard Rakib left for Milan..." the Artist said.

"Oh, I'm fine," Maggie replied.

"Did you know he was leaving?"

"I think part of me always knows he's going to leave. Either for himself or for a burgeoning starlet in Milan."

The Artist rolled her eyes.

"I'd hardly call her a starlet."

"You know her?"

"I met her once at a gallery. She's an art school dropout who's obsessed with the integrity of 'the line.'"

This made Maggie laugh. She was probably obsessed with the integrity of the line, too, once. Now the line seemed beside the point.

"You seem good," the Artist said. "All things considered. You seem light."

"Actually," Maggie said, unable to stop a smile from spreading across her face. "I got some news last night."

"Oh?"

"I won this grant I had been nominated for."

"Maggie!"

Blood rushed from Maggie's brain into her face, then down into her whole body. She felt something warm bubbling in her center that made her skin flush. The Artist had shrieked so loud that a few tables turned to scowl at them.

"Tell me everything!"

As Maggie spoke, she felt every muscle melt into a position it hadn't occupied in years. Her body was at rest as she delved into the minutiae of her painting, and she felt genuine and pure joy coursing between herself and the Artist. She talked about how Lorrie hadn't nominated a student in years and how she had spent a few nights sleeping in the studio as she agonized over every detail in her painting. It had taken her so long, but now hearing the news of the grant made her feel like the painting was finally finished.

"Can I see it?" the Artist asked.

"Sure, we'll stop by the studio sometime," Maggie said, not giving it much thought.

"Can we go now?"

THEIR CAFFEINATED CHATTER subsided as they began the walk to Maggie's studio. Maggie retreated into herself, immediately doubting the merits of her painting. She had made such a big deal about the grant she wondered if maybe she had talked it up too much. Maybe the Artist would see the painting and simply say "Oh," as John had the first time he'd stopped by to see it. Maggie hadn't considered this part, that once her piece was out there anyone could go up to it and say something dismissive. Or misinterpret it or distort it into something she had never thought of. People could hate it. How could she have forgotten that?

Maggie stopped talking all together as they ascended the stairs to the studio. The door creaked open, and Maggie held it as the Artist stepped inside.

The lights flickered on, and the painting was illuminated.

"Oh, Maggie."

The amount of time the Artist spent evaluating each figure was not insignificant, but it wasn't dramatic, either. She simply took her time, and Maggie appreciated the care of her stroll from one edge of the canvas to the other.

"It's unbelievable," she said. "I mean on a technical level, Maggie. Everything is so exact and perfect." The Artist shook her head and flapped her mouth open and then closed. "It's fucking perfect."

Her long, thin arms found their way around Maggie, and before she pulled away, the Artist squeezed her again.

"I could never do this," she said.

Maggie thought about the Artist's work, and about how she could never be naked in front of a crowd or endanger her reproductive organs. She could never burn her mother.

Maggie mumbled through a defense—"Yes, you could; of course you could"—but the Artist insisted that this kind of talent was proprietary to her and to her alone. "It has Maggie written all over it," she said at one point, and Maggie began to feel delirious.

"You're the first person I've told," Maggie said. "No one knows that I won."

The Artist's hand pressed against her heart.

"I'm so happy for you, Maggie," she said. Then she said the thing that Maggie had yet to believe until she heard it from the Artist.

"You deserve it."

27

THE APARTMENT DIDN'T feel like an alien thing Maggie lived inside of anymore. There were crumpled up receipts on the counter and food in the fridge and clothes fed into a wicker laundry basket that she'd bought after deciding living among the piles had become unbearable. She had cleaned out her studio in preparation for graduation, so there were older pieces of hers propped up against one wall in the living room. It still wasn't beautiful or homey, but it at least showed signs of life. And with the grant money on the way, the clock ticking on the lease was not the death knell it once was. Things would fall into place, and now she could be sure of it.

Maggie sat against the wall on the floor in the living room and pulled her knees into her chest. With her phone balanced on one knee, she called her mom and put her on speakerphone.

"Hello!" her mother and father singsonged. They were in the car. That was the only explanation for both of their voices booming at once.

"Baba is driving me to the store," her mother shouted.

"Hello, kızım!" her father chimed in. Maggie could picture the rise of his cheeks as he called to her. Her father almost exclusively referred to Maggie and Sofia as *kızım*, as if there were something innately delightful to him that they were girls. That they were his daughters.

"Hi," Maggie said. "Hi, everybody. Hi."

The chaos of the car phone was overwhelming for all involved.

"Are you home?"

"Yes, Mom, I'm home. I just wanted to tell you something..."

Her mother began shushing her father, who hadn't been speaking.

"One second! One second!" she shouted into the speaker on the passenger side. Maggie saw it play out as if in front of her—trying to find the button that would disconnect her phone from the car so she could hold it to her ear to hear Maggie more clearly. Maggie's mother had done this with her own mother when she was still alive, insisting to Maggie, who was behind the wheel, that there was something wrong with the car phone, though there clearly was not.

"Okay, canım, now I hear you," she said.

"I won a prize," Maggie said, somehow unsure of how to explain what was happening. "It's a lot of money."

"Heh?" her mother said. The sound, depending on how it was uttered, meant "What?"

"It's for the piece I made. The painting for school."

Maggie tried to walk through the nomination process with her mother—how rare it had been for Lorrie to nominate a student, as she hadn't done so in years, how few students are nominated and even fewer awarded—but her mother interrupted her before she could finish.

Prayers spilled out of her mouth like water flowing from a faucet. Maggie could hardly keep up well enough to parse which prayers were in Arabic and which were in Turkish, but the sound of them lapping over her made Maggie sink her back further down the wall. She floated on the surface of her mother's theatrics and let them buoy her. Maggie allowed her mother this pride that bordered on garish, and it felt like something Maggie would never be able to articulate in words. It felt like a substance strong enough to sustain a life. It could be Maggie's every last meal until she died.

Finally, she heard her mother bless Maggie's hands for making something that could win so much acclaim. Something that could earn her money and allow her to support herself. "Maşallah, Maşallah, Maşallah."

"Thank you, Mom," she said. "Thank you."

"We are so proud of you," her mother said, beaming through the phone.

She then shushed Maggie so she could criticize her father's driving. Maggie could barely hear her father now that they had been disconnected from the car, but she heard him say to her mother in Turkish, "She is so talented, Maşallah."

Her father killed the engine, and the excitement in the car dropped to a normal volume.

"Okay, canım, we're here," her mother said. The sound of her voice had changed to the determined tone she took whenever a task was at hand. She would be on a mission in whatever store it was that her father had driven them to.

"Wait," Maggie spat out before her mother could hang up.

"Heh?" her mother said again.

"What's going on at home?" Maggie asked. "What are you getting at the store?"

Her mother made a series of noises suggesting that she had just about had it with everyone in the house. First, half the lights in the house had gone out, because Maggie's father had blown a fuse plugging in his coffee machine, which she had declared was too fancy as soon as he brought it into the kitchen. Now, in addition to being too fancy, it was good for nothing, stupid, and, according to her mother, posed a health risk to both her and her father. "What kind of coffee does a machine like this make?" she said. *Radioactive* had been the expected answer, but Maggie just let her mother imply without resisting her.

"So now we are going to the hardware store so your father can learn to be an electrician."

"And what about Sofia? What is she doing?"

Sofia was apparently busy wreaking havoc on her mother's mental well-being. She was newly obsessed with the idea of studying abroad and "expanding her horizons," so she was vying for her parents' support. She wanted to go to London, but neither parent could see what the point of going to England was when it was basically the same as the US. Sofia then had a meltdown arguing the differences, which did nothing to serve her case. Her father had suggested studying in Istanbul so she could live with Uncle Mehmet. Sofia apparently threw herself on the ground at this, so he suggested living with Serdar and Zeynep. But then her mother, of course, had some words about "the wife," as she called her—too conservative, and always sucking up to her for approval, which her mother would withhold until Zeynep's last breath. Then her mother repeated her critiques of their wedding, which had been four years ago now. The bad food, the heat, Zeynep's parents. Maggie had heard it all many times before, but she let her mother run through her list of grievances until she tired herself out.

A car door closed, and Maggie understood that her father had gone to the hardware store on his own, which may have been the smartest move a man in his position could make. With her mother distracted like this, he might be able to buy new lightbulbs in peace. And if he managed to rewire the house without electrocuting himself, Maggie's mother's memory could be short enough to allow him his fancy coffee maker.

"How is Rob?" her mother asked. "Are you going out tonight? Tell him somewhere *nice* nice."

"He's still in London," Maggie said. She didn't have the heart to crush her mother's spirit after revealing her only good news. *Another time,* Maggie swore to herself. *Next week.*

"Hmm," her mother said. She didn't prod further, and Maggie could tell she was already beginning to know this, too.

"Okay," they overlapped saying to each other. Maggie and her mother laughed. They exchanged "Goodbyes" and "I love yous" and one final "Maşallah" before hanging up. Then silence filled the apartment. Maggie had sunk all the way down the wall to the floor. She stared up at the ceiling in complete disbelief of all that God had willed.

ACKNOWLEDGMENTS

THE LIST OF people who deserve to be thanked for helping this book come to be could fill an entire book of its own. I'll try my best to limit it, however, to these few pages.

It begins with the biggest thank-you—the kind for which there are not enough words—to my agent, Audrey Crooks. For being there every step of the way, never waning in enthusiasm or support, and for always seeing the vision. My gratitude is endless, for you and the team at Trident.

To all those at Algonquin who had a hand in this project. Betsy Gleick, who acquired this book and saw what it could be. Nadxi Nieto, for her support and guidance. Jovanna Brinck, a true champion of this book and, frankly, my hero. Sally Kim, for guiding us across the finish line. June Park, for the most beautiful cover. And Brunson Hoole, Melissa Mathlin, and Elizabeth Johnson. Thank you all for making this book a book, something that I can hold in my hands. It is a gift beyond gifts.

To Saïd Sayrafiezadeh, who I have been thanking for a long time and will continue to thank eternally. I became a writer because you made me think I could.

To Sloan Harris, for taking a chance on me. Thank you for the years I got to be Radar, and for all your support since.

To my amazing professors and cohort at The New School. Thank you especially to Helen Schulman, Luis Jaramillo, Mira Jacob, Waverly Herbert, Jillian Eugenios, Asma Ladha, Sam Dilling, Maria Sakr, Justine Teu, Vanessa Freifeld, and Ruthie Weissman.

To Emma and Mike Fusco-Straub, for your kindness and generosity. To everyone at Books are Magic, for the same, and for giving me a home while I finished this book. And a special thank-you to the events team, Amali Gordon-Buxbaum and Bex Frankeberger, for all your love and support.

To anyone who has ever laid eyes on an unedited page of this book, I'm sorry and thank you—notably Waverly Herbert, Jillian Eugenios, Vanessa Freifeld, Natasha Bluth, Beau Dealy, Andrianna deLone, Megan Woodruff, and Isabella Barbuto.

To Cat Shook, there's not enough thanks in the world! I couldn't have done it without you. Thank you and I love you.

To Julia Huse, for everything. And for being my goob. I love you to the moon and back.

To Brynn Gallahue, for crying every time I share my good news. I love you.

To Eliza Gilbert, for many years of eggs, and what you do to my heart. And for making me a godmama.

To Isabella Barbuto, for all the love and the best voicemail I've ever received.

To Asma Ladha, for seeing me and knowing me.

To Maria and Elie, can you believe I wrote this book twice? Thank you for your love.

To Allie Smith, Megan Woodruff, and Caleb Hausman, for being the best support system a person could ask for. I love you all.

To Adina Rosenberg and Hillary Good, your support and belief in me has buoyed me more than you could know.

To Han Dewan, for being by my side in the artist's life. I love you.

To Chukwukpee Nzegwu, for all your support and letters and love. Your friendship is so precious to me.

To Ruchi Roy, for all the early support. Thank you for believing in me, wildly and perhaps baselessly. I hope you know I carry your love always.

To Nicolas Vivas Nikonorow, for the days on Knickerbocker, where we started talking about the earliest seeds of this book. Thank you for your support then and now and beyond.

To the teachers who opened my mind and exposed me to books and art and the world, most especially Robert Mulgrew and Gary Hendrickson.

To Sharyn, all the thanks I have for you cannot fit in this book, or in any others to come, so I will just say thank you for everything.

To Ayda and Jay Weiss, for all your love and support along the way.

To my exceptional brother, Lucas Brahme. The best artist and person I know.

And finally, to my parents, Sevil and Johan Brahme. I couldn't have made this, or anything, without you. I love you more than I could ever say. Thank you for the life you've given me.

RAISING READERS

Books Build Bright Futures

Thank you for reading this book and for being a reader of books in general. We are so grateful to share being part of a community of readers with you, and we hope you will join us in passing our love of books on to the next generation of readers.

Did you know that reading for enjoyment is the single biggest predictor of a child's future happiness and success?

More than family circumstances, parents' educational background, or income, reading impacts a child's future academic performance, emotional well-being, communication skills, economic security, ambition, and happiness.

Studies show that kids reading for enjoyment in the US is in rapid decline:

- In 2012, 53% of 9-year-olds read almost every day. Just 10 years later, in 2022, the number had fallen to 39%.
- In 2012, 27% of 13-year-olds read for fun daily. By 2023, that number was just 14%.

Together, we can commit to **Raising Readers** and change this trend. How?

- Read to children in your life daily.
- Model reading as a fun activity.
- Reduce screen time.
- Start a family, school, or community book club.
- Visit bookstores and libraries regularly.
- Listen to audiobooks.
- Read the book before you see the movie.
- Encourage your child to read aloud to a pet or stuffed animal.
- Give books as gifts.
- Donate books to families and communities in need.

BOB1217

Books build bright futures, and **Raising Readers** is our shared responsibility.

For more information, visit **JoinRaisingReaders.com**

Sources: National Endowment for the Arts, National Assessment of Educational Progress, WorldBookDay.com, Nielsen BookData's 2023 "Understanding the Children's Book Consumer"